I0827650

The Unseelie Queen

Tallie Rose

-CHAPTER-
-ONE-

GRIT DUG INTO Fia's knees. To the naked eye the floor beneath her was clean, but a thousand years of dust and a thousand other knees had made the floor uneven, dirty in a way that could never be truly clean.

The other girls didn't seem to notice—women, really—except none of them looked much like women, but instead perfect dolls, unblemished skin, smooth hair, and little pouty mouths. The kind of women that belonged here, if anyone belonged here on their knees, waiting for the doors to open. But, she hoped, they had chosen this. They had heard of the Joining their whole life, their bodies had hummed with joy when they had realized they would be the right age, they'd signed the letters and told all their friends. They were happy.

Not Fia. Sure, she'd been to the borderlands a few times, partied among the fae, told stories to her rich friends and laughed at their strange customs, but she had no interest in leaving her human life behind. Her human life was great, she loved her fancy apartment, her nice clothes, her tiny car.

Sure, all that fun came at a price, and that price was her father and his seemingly endless bank account. He'd never been proud of her, often told her as much, yet still he bankrolled her life. So, what was she supposed to do when he asked her to present herself to the fae prince? She'd said no at first, but he'd wanted the exposure, a nice story to pop up if anyone searched their name. Something had felt off to Fia, but her father's eyes had lost their shine, his pleasant demeanor turning sour and she had not dared argue any further.

So here she was, kneeling on the stupid, dirty floor at the edge of the human lands waiting for the faerie prince to show up. She couldn't wait to go home. He wouldn't pick her, she was older than all these girls by at least half a decade and had none of their saccharine charms.

One of them would be the next human bride of the faerie prince, joining the human lands to the Seelie kingdom for another few decades, and allowing fae magic to be harnessed in small amounts so the humans could power their medical marvels and scientific discoveries.

She looked around at the girls, wondering which one of them he would pick? Would whoever he picked cry? A girl with blonde hair caught Fia's eye and smiled. Fia smiled back, it was the polite thing to do.

She considered saying something, though she had no idea what, but all these beautiful women would certainly need comforting when the Prince didn't choose them. And who better than Fia? She smiled to herself, casting her eyes back to the floor.

The doors opened with a creak. All around her the women made little noises of approval at the appearance of Callum, the Seelie Prince. He *was* quite a specimen, with his golden blonde hair and piercing blue eyes. Muscles rippled underneath his half-buttoned shirt, and his cheekbones were so sharp that shadows pooled beneath them. If one was going to enter into an arranged marriage to serve their people, they could do worse than Callum, assuming he was not a complete monster. She hoped, for the sake of whomever he chose he was kind, if a spoiled prince could be such a thing.

Fia looked up at him, her knees starting to hurt from kneeling so long. She had no idea what she was supposed to do and was growing agitated with the whole thing. She'd made her appearance, she'd done a little tv interview about the Joining, and posted selfie after selfie on social media. The reality though was sore knees, irritation, and a headache forming behind her eyes.

Two other fae stood behind Callum, some kind of guards if she had to guess, though they wore no weapons. Why would they though? They'd hardly need them against a dozen waifish human women.

"Rise," Callum said, gesturing for the women to stand and Fia was the first up, grimacing when her joints audibly popped.

He walked in front of the row of women like a customer at a butcher shop, eyeing them all, but not speaking. Fia clasped her hands behind her back and looked towards the floor again to keep from rolling her eyes. Not a single question? The ten page questionnaire they had filled out must have been enough for him, now he just needed to match appearance with answers.

Seriously? Could she leave? The room was cold and she was bored.

The prince cleared his throat and Fia looked up to find him looking back at her.

She blinked, waiting for him to keep moving but he didn't.

Shit.

"What is your name?" he asked.

Fuck. Fuck. Double fuck. This could not be happening. She was going to strangle her father. "Fia."

"Walk with me, Fia." Callum offered his hand, sparkling with golden rings. Around her the other women made noises of disappointment, with one red haired girl breaking into sobs.

Well, better to not stay here and get eaten alive. Or maybe she could run. She glanced toward the door. No, that wouldn't do. He cleared his throat again and she felt herself flush.

Maybe she could explain herself when they were alone. Whoever he eventually picked might have some resentment at not being his first choice, but she'd get over it. Fia took his hand and let him lead her out of the room and into the chamber beyond, which unlike the room she'd been in for the last half hour had floor to ceiling windows. Outside a smattering of trees swayed in the breeze, casting shade on a field of wildflowers, and beyond the flowers was mist that separated the human lands from the fae. The end of the borderlands and the start of the highly guarded fae territory.

She stared out at the swirling, sunset colored mist for a moment, trying to wrap her head around what was going on, but she couldn't manage it. She'd never really considered what would happen if Callum picked her, and even now, standing in the sunshine, listening to the other girls leave, she still couldn't. They had to come back. He wasn't done picking yet. One of them had to be the princess.

"Fia," Callum said, grabbing her attention and she turned towards him. He was so handsome, golden and glowing, like the sun favored him. "I assumed your father had spoken to you, but your face is telling me he did not. For that you have my sincerest apologies. I know what it is like to be a pawn."

"You're right. He didn't. But Callum, or...your highness?" Not only had her father not told her, he'd said she wouldn't be chosen. That it was just for the show of it. And so, she'd done none of the training, learned none of their customs. Panic threatened to grip her.

"Callum is fine for now."

"You want to marry me? Out of all those girls? I mean did you see those girls?" She tried to make a joke of it, keep everything light, funny. Would he be angry if she didn't want him? Was he dangerous?

He chuckled. "A fine-looking group, yes. But you are beautiful, as well." He took a deep breath. "I did not consider I might be agreeing to something my future wife had not. If you will not go through with it, please tell me now, before the girls leave. It will save us all so much embarrassment."

Could she? Could she not go through with it? Would it be as simple as that? "Can I think? I mean...what exactly is the deal?"

"I do not know the extent of the deal, but your father has been here many times for meeting. I was just told that in exchange..." Callum looked at the ground.

"In exchange for me. Go on. I get it."

He sighed and glittery golden magic sparkled around him for a moment. Fia struggled not to recoil "Yes, well, in exchange for choosing my own wife, I would get one a little more lively, and my father and yours would continue their business dealings, combining our families for both their benefit. But if you do not want it, it will not be forced. Perhaps your father meant it as a joyful surprise."

Fia scoffed, trying and failing not to pace the room. "You know I grew up hearing about how the Joining was coming, about how lucky the human girl who would grow up to marry the third born faerie prince would be. But those girls grew up preparing for it. I didn't prepare for this, Callum. I barely know anything about the fae, besides the clubs you keep on the Borderlands. I…I need to think."

"Your choice. I will certainly not kidnap a wife." He gestured to the door in a clear dismissal, but behind his haughty look there was something else. Apprehension.

"I'm sorry, Callum. I really am." She tried to think of more to say, but no words came to her mind, and she needed to leave. If she stayed, she was certain she would vomit, so she ran away, back through the undecorated room she had knelt in, and out to where her father's car waited, the window rolled down.

"I thought you might come." His face was unreadable except for the glimmering hint of violence that always lived in his eyes.

She pulled open the door and sat down, her brain a mess, her breathing fast. "What the fuck?"

She waited for him to put the car in drive, but he didn't move. He was always so stoic. She'd once thought it was a virtue. "Are you unhappy I bought you a crown, Fia?"

She wanted to lunge at him, to jump across the gear shift and wrap her hands around his neck. She wanted to bury her face in his chest and sob, but he'd never been that kind of father. No one had ever been that for Fia, not since her mother, and that memory was faded like a photograph left in the sun. "You lied to me. You *sold* me. How could you do this to me?"

"Do what? Make my daughter a princess? Double her lifespan? Let her be the most famous girl in the world?" He pinned her with a stare. "You will go back in there. You'll stick around in royal estate for a few weeks until the wedding and then you'll go live a happy, rich life in a country town surrounded by beautiful fae who will attend to your every whim. As for lying? Did I lie, Fia, or do you only hear what you want to hear?"

"I don't want to do it."

He turned to face her fully. "I won't force you to marry that man, Fia, I can't—modern times and all—but there is more to this than you can understand, business deals years in the making."

"Don't I mean more to you than your business?" She'd never asked it before. She'd always known the answer. Every move he made was to climb another rung of the ladder and Fia meant nothing in comparison to his money, his power. She'd told herself it was a blessing. His business was rarely legitimate, so she'd pretended he was keeping her safe, but the lie she'd clung to her entire life was crumbling.

"Of course, I care about you. I've provided for you for nearly thirty years. You will never want..." He checked his phone and then sat it back down on the dash. "Unless you do not go. If you do not go to the faerie lands then it is time for you to make your own way, my darling daughter. I will no longer pay for your things, your apartment, your car, your vacations, your life. Not a single day more."

"It's the end of the month. I wouldn't have time to figure out somewhere else to live before rent is due." She would not cry in front of him, he'd hate her for it, so she pinched the side of her thigh to keep the tears from falling.

He shrugged. "You have friends, and you're like a cat. You always land on your feet. Now go back inside that building and I will see you for the wedding."

Tears clouded her eyes and her chest tightened. What was she going to do? She didn't have a single cent of her own. What a fool she'd been, and he'd encouraged it, bound her to him, never let her stray. Hatred for her father flared hot in her chest. "No wonder mom would rather be dead than around you."

His cold eyes turned colder. "Get the fuck out of my car, you ungrateful brat."

"Gladly. I'm going to make you regret this. Think of all the power you're putting in my hands."

“A glorified housewife? I don’t think so.” He reached across her and pushed the door open.

- CHAPTER-
-TWO -

AS HER FATHER'S car pulled away, the adrenaline drained from Fia's body, and the reality of her situation slammed into her chest. She didn't want to go back into that room, didn't want to take another step closer to the mist. But the other way was the thin strip of land separating human lands from faerie, the small border outpost where she knew no one, then nothing for miles.

Would they let her call someone? Like he'd said, she had friends. But did she? Women she went out with, called when the sun went down, sure. But someone who would take her in when she had nothing? Someone who would care enough to give up a room and feed her? Not just buy a pizza when she lost her credit card, but feed her when she couldn't pay them back a single cent, when she would need a job?

And what job would she even get? She had no skills, no career history to speak of. She'd assumed she'd either marry someone in a few years or ask her father what she could do for the business. He already paid for everything, she didn't think he'd mind giving her a padded paycheck.

Apparently, he had minded the whole time. And what had she expected? She was twenty-nine and had never tried anything. But she didn't know how. Had no idea where to start. Who would hire Zachary Gray's daughter? No one had proof but everyone knew he was dangerous, that his real estate business wasn't where his real success came from.

Even more depressing was that she knew all those reasons were lies. She'd never tried. She'd never had to. She'd been his perfect little princess when she was too small to make problems, and she'd let that become her whole personality. Why get a job? Why struggle or wake up to an alarm clock when she could turn a blind eye to her father's business dealings and reap all the rewards?

She should have seen this coming. He'd always wanted a son but after her mother had died, he'd never dated seriously enough to get one he would acknowledge, though she wouldn't be surprised to find out she had a whole slew of siblings out in the world.

She'd never be the child he wanted, simply because he wouldn't treat a daughter the same way he would have a son. He had never seen her as an equal, but in the last few years he'd brought her to so-called business meetings, never letting her hear enough to testify against him, but he'd paraded her in front of men, made it clear that his daughter was a prize that could be won. Of course, eventually, he'd sell her off to the highest bidder in the type of macabre, old-school way he loved. All suits and cigars and women who kept quiet and still and beautiful.

And she'd been too stupid, too eager to please to see it coming.

There was nowhere to go except inside the building. Back to the fae waiting to take her through the mist and into a life where she would be expected to be that quiet, still, beautiful woman for the next two hundred years.

The starkness of the building exterior seemed to mock her as she forced her feet to move, one after the other, until she was inside. It was miles to any human civilization, and she didn't know how to cross into the faerie realm except at the designated ports. She'd always been warned against walking through the mist alone. She hadn't been allowed to bring her phone with her. She couldn't call someone even if there was someone to call.

Her options were to walk miles and miles and still have nowhere to go, to sleep in some parking lot and walk again the next day until she made it the forty miles back to her apartment or go inside. At least inside she'd hopefully find a bed for the night. She could make a plan after she'd had some sleep, something to eat.

She pushed the heavy wooden door open. The room she had knelt in was empty, but she could hear the faerie prince in the next room so she followed his voice. Locking eyes with Fia, he dismissed the men he was with.

"I am sorry it is like this. It would not be my choice." Callum's refined voice was even, not quite cold but not warm either.

Fia shrugged and blew a loose strand of black hair out of her eyes. "I'm the unwanted daughter and you're the third son. I don't think either of us gets our way this time."

"Perhaps we can find some common ground, or at least you might come with me without screaming and give it a chance. There are worse fates than being my wife. I am not a cruel man, which may be more than your father can say, though please don't tell mine I said that."

A smile pulled at Fia's mouth, despite her unease. "No, I don't think I'll do any screaming. And I am sorry you did not get one of those women from before, who would be crying and falling into your arms."

Now Callum shrugged. "I never wanted those women."

"Is that why you didn't call them back when I left? Because you didn't want them? Did you want this at all? The Joining?"

"I did not call them back because I have met your father before. I rightly believed he would not care about your desires. It seemed cruel to keep another girl here just to send her away again, and as I said, I'm not a cruel man. As for your other question, no one has ever asked me that before, Fia. Do I want the Joining? I want to be useful, to do the things all the third sons before me have done. Despite my quips, I am honored to serve my father, and I have always been fascinated with the human world. I never found a faerie girl I loved enough to refuse. So, do I want it? I suppose, in a way, not deeply. I did not dream of this day, but I am not full of dread, even now with a future wife who would rather be in her own bed."

The obedient son. She nodded because she did not know him enough to prod him any further. "What do we do now?"

“Well, normally you’d take a few days at home to get your things together, but since your father left you can come with me back to the fae realm if you’d like and I can send for your things.”

“Okay, sure.” Agreeing to give up control of her life made tears well in Fia’s eyes again, but she bit the inside of her cheek and willed them not to fall. Crying was not allowed in the Gray household. Her father called it manipulation.

“Forgive me for saying, but I don’t think I like your father much. If we were to have children, I would not abandon them in this way.”

If they had children? A wife? Was she really going to walk through the mist into the faerie realm and become some housewife? A mother? No, worse than that, a princess—a figurehead. She swallowed hard, her stomach twisting.

Of course, her father had gotten exactly what he wanted, he always did. She wondered what the deal with the faerie king had been. What were they getting out of this? Certainly, a match that would bring much more media attention than it usually did, and it was usually a circus, but everyone knew what her father was, even if he’d never been charged with anything, even if he had several supposedly legitimate businesses that he filed taxes on. What would he be saying to the media? Was the appeal of the marriage simply that it would be much harder to prosecute the father of a beloved human daughter, the faerie princess?

Because whoever was chosen was always loved. They'd studied past wives in history class, their gowns were in museums, their life stories written again and again. Girls pretended to be them when they were little. When they made appearances in the human world, fashions would change, women emulating their outfits.

But really, she couldn't begin to imagine what her father would get out of this deal. Even if she'd agreed, gone back to his car, and thrown her arms around his shoulders in gratitude, he would never have told her why he did what he did, never would have confided in her. To him she would always be disposable, a tool, and the carpenter does not explain his plans to the tools.

She nodded to Callum and moved closer to him. For a moment he moved like he might take her hand, then thought better of it. Instead, he pushed open a wide door with a golden handle on the far side of the room. The guards were waiting on the other side in a wide hallway lined with more elaborate doors and large hanging lights that lit the whole place as if it were closer to the sun than the rest of the world.

She followed all of them to an outside door, feeling like she was headed to the gallows but trying to find something good in this. This life might be simpler, no more worrying that all her belongings might be seized, that her life might fall apart around her. Maybe Callum would be a good man, maybe they would find some common ground. Maybe she would love the fae and her country home and being special. Maybe.

Maybe she would escape. Though to what end she could, at that moment, not begin to imagine.

As she walked towards the mist, her feelings swung from anger to fear to numbness. She clung to the numbness, the only feeling she could muster that didn't make her feel like she was drowning, the only feeling that didn't make her stomach turn and her eyes sting.

The mist was upon them, swirling, completely unlike the fog that sometimes descended on the city. This mist was sunset hued and lightly sparkling, though the dawn-dappled light did not extend from the mist, only gave the impression that if you stepped inside it you would glow to, glow like Callum and his sun-kissed skin and his gilded hair. It was solid yet not, impossible to see through, yet she knew there was so much on the other side.

Callum put out his hand, giving her a small smile that she returned briefly before letting him close her fingers in his own.

Hand in hand, they passed through the mist and it danced along Fia's skin for a moment like a lover's fingers before they were on the other side. More guards, or whatever they were, waited on either side of a long road paved with pale, smooth stones that stretched and wound towards a city she could just make out on the horizon.

Fia took a moment to take in the faerie world, the strange ting of magic that she could sometimes feel on the borderlands was stronger here, alerting her senses. This was nothing like the in-between place where the faerie clubs were kept, this was the true world of the fae.

The sky seemed brighter, a more brilliant blue, the grass thicker, the trees stout with wide trunks and dense canopies, but all in all there wasn't much to see at the moment, just several fae men, thicker than most humans, with gorgeous hair and eyes that shined too bright waiting for them to take the long road to the city beyond.

"Sir," one of the men said, gesturing Callum to walk with him and leaving Fia with the rest of the guards they had crossed the mist with. One stepped closer, he had dark hair, bright green eyes, and the slightly pointed ears of the fae poking through his mass of curls.

"I'm Fermir," he said. "You'll see me a lot."

"Fia," she said, starting to stick out her hand then thinking better of it. She didn't know if it would be right for a future princess to shake anyone's hand. Hopefully it wasn't rude if she didn't. "You like working for Callum?" She inwardly cringed at the question, but Fermir laughed.

"Yeah. I've known Callum since we were boys. He's a good man. I know you—never mind." Another small laugh made his curls fall into his eyes.

"What?"

He shook his head slightly and glanced ahead, where Callum was looking at them. He started to walk towards them, the easy smile he'd worn earlier was gone, replaced with a serious expression that made Fia curious, but before he could take more than two steps a noise from up the road drew their attention.

A strange vehicle was coming towards them. It looked to be powered by steam, or coal, or something—some unknown power that made it quieter than any human car. The only sound was the wooden, carriage-like wheels moving along the stones. She knew things were different here, certain human things didn't work around so much magic, but she'd rarely seen fae objects in person before.

Nothing pulled the vehicle, there didn't seem to be any space for an engine, in fact it looked almost exactly like the carriages she'd seen in period movies and old pictures, but only the carriage, no horses, no driver, seemingly nothing moving it forward, and yet it did. Magic, most likely, yet the sight was still jarring.

No one seemed concerned, though Fermir put his hand gently on Fia's back to move her off the road as the vehicle came to a stop in front of them.

Fermir pulled the door open and a gorgeous woman with the same shining, golden hair and big eyes as Callum stepped out, grinning. "Is this my future sister?" She swooped in, kissing Fia on both cheeks before Fia had time to react. "Callum, Father sent me to fetch your bride to be."

Fia glanced at the carriage. They wouldn't all fit unless there was some serious fae magic going on.

"Thank you, Aurora," Callum said. "I suppose you have heard the news as well."

"Of course. I hear everything." The fae woman—Aurora—was still smiling, her voice candy-sweet. "Come on." She put an arm around Fia's shoulder like they were old friends and leaned in close, whispering too low for anyone to hear. "Believe me, you'll have a better time with me."

And for some reason, Fia believed her, even if it was just to get away from Callum and everything he represented for a moment. She was also desperate to get a look inside the carriage. How did it work? Not the most pressing issue, but a curiosity all the same.

"I will see you tonight or tomorrow, Fia. I apologize for abandoning you so quickly, I'm sure my sister will give some explanation." He walked between the guards and took Fia's hand, kissing it gently and whispered to her, "Don't forget to breathe. Today will pass."

"Thank you." Tomorrow would come, and hopefully she would feel a little less overwhelmed with each passing day. At least she would no longer have to worry the feds would show up at her door at any moment, or she'd turn on the TV to see her father arrested. Here she might be safe, free of the fear being Zachary Gray's daughter brought to every day.

At another urging from Aurora, she followed her into the carriage and was surprised to see a serious lack of a steering wheel, yet it was more luxurious than any car she'd ever been in. The seats were wide and cushioned in the softest dark, floral fabric. The ceiling was tall, she did not even need to bend when she stood and there was plenty of room to stretch both their legs.

Something smelled good, woodsy and lush, though she couldn't name the scent, and the air was the perfect temperature. The windows were wide and bright, so clear it was like they weren't even there.

"First time in a carriage?" Aurora asked then laughed to herself. "Of course it is. I remember my first time in a car. I prefer this."

Well, she'd been right about what it reminded her of. Without anything seeming to make it move, the carriage started moving and with no chance to brace herself, Fia nearly tumbled off her seat and that was enough to make the tears she had been holding back start to flow. "Sorry." She wiped at her eyes. "This is the most shit day, which I know I'm not supposed to say, but my father sold me, and I'm sure your brother is lovely, but I wasn't ready. I'm coming to terms with the fact that my father doesn't care about me, I mean, I know he's not a good man, I'm not an idiot, but he's my dad. I thought some part of him loved me." The words tumbled out and she couldn't stop their flow.

"Oh, honey," Aurora said, reaching out and squeezing Fia's knee. "He didn't tell you? Bastard. That's so fucked. He's been here half a dozen times working this deal out. I know I'm probably not supposed to say that, but you obviously need a friend, so we'll be friends."

"He didn't just not tell me, he lied, said Callum wouldn't choose me. And I was stupid enough to believe him. Again." She took a deep, shaky breath. "Do you know why he did it?" Fia knew that was pushing the limits of their supposed friendship, but she'd already said too much, what was the point in stopping?

Aurora shrugged. "I'm a daughter too. They don't tell me anything. I know your father is... not a good man, so he probably gets a lot of favor in your world from being the father of the chosen girl and he strengthens his connection with my father and my father gets whatever it was he wanted in the human world your father can provide. If I had to guess."

She'd been sold, but what was her dowry? What exactly had been promised? She had guesses, but did it really matter? "So, what did Callum think you'd explain to me?"

"Oh that." She frowned for a moment, chewing on her perfectly formed bottom lip. "Just some fae political nonsense. We're having some troubles with the Unseelies and one of them, the so-called queen just arrived. She was invited to the wedding by protocol, but she's shown up early to discuss things with my father. It shouldn't be a problem for you, but my father always wants Callum to deal with things. It should be our older brothers, Helio or Cyrus, but alas, Callum is reliable, unlike the other two."

"The Unseelie?" The word tickled the back of Fia's mind, she'd heard it before, but she couldn't draw the definition from the recesses of her brain. Regret at studying none of the notes sent to her ate away at her insides. If she married Callum she would be seen as a fool, unable to participate in even the most basic conversations.

"We don't spread much information about ourselves to the human worlds, but there are two kinds of fae. My kind is the Seelie, more human like, generally more powerful in many ways, certainly in influence. The Unseelie are the wilder fae, they have more..." Aurora cleared her throat. "Animal characteristics. You'll see. They have different principles than we do, different values that drive them. But like I said, it really isn't something to worry yourself about. We aren't at war or anything, just some disagreements over land."

"Oh." But wasn't that always how it started? A disagreement that grew and grew? But she did as Aurora said and let the thoughts drift away, she had more immediate concerns, and a curiosity she couldn't contain, driving her to ask, "Why are you all being so nice to me?" Outside the window a city came fully into view, large buildings rising as they crested a small hill. Streets teemed with people and more carriages, but also horse drawn carts, and hand pulled wagons.

Aurora shifted in her seat, a twinkle in her shining blue-green eyes. "Why would we be mean to you? You're marrying my brother. Today has to be overwhelming for you, even if you had known what was going to happen. What would be gained by being unkind?"

Some of the tension Fia had been carrying since she had knelt on the floor left her. No one had ever been particularly kind to her in the human world, not her father, not even her friends, really. Everyone was nice enough to her, friendly once they realized her father had money and she probably did too, but not kind. "Maybe we can be friends then."

"I hope so. Now look, this is your first glimpse of the real faerie lands, none of that borderland nonsense. A few more minutes and we'll be at my father's estate. And if you think this is nice, just wait until you see where Callum lives. There are a few perks to not being the heir or the spare and his house is one of them."

- CHAPTER- -THREE -

THE CITY THEY drove through was nothing like Fia had been expecting, though if she was honest, she wasn't sure exactly what she had been expecting. Something ancient, like out of a storybook.

And it was, in a way. Many of the buildings were obviously older than anything Fia had ever seen before, but it wasn't all old, there were cute little houses and tall buildings that she suspected were apartments, with shops underneath them. More of the carriages rumbled about, though not nearly as many as there would be in even a small human town, but the streets were thick with fae, tall, lanky, magical fae. She could practically taste the magic, could see the shimmer in the air when the wind blew.

And plants, so many plants the buildings seemed to spring out of the ground, some of them were nearly covered with hanging vines thick with enormous flowers and wide, waxy leaves.

It was beautiful and entirely its own, full of faerie culture and beauty. "What's this city called?"

"Soleil. It's my ancestral home, the biggest city in the Southern Kingdom, my father's domain. Our magic is more powerful in the sun, unlike some others, though it's hard to explain if you don't feel it. Everyone's magic works in its own unique way. It's not like I don't have magic at night or on rainy days." Aurora smiled. "Sorry, I'm totally rambling. I'm a bit nervous. I really want us to get along and..."

"And I had a little meltdown." Fia laughed, finding it hard to pull her eyes away from the scene outside the carriage. She didn't voice the thought, but she hoped that Aurora was telling the truth, a friend would be more than she could have hoped for an hour ago. And for that friend to be her fiancé's sister, well that couldn't be bad. Aurora might be the thing that got her through all of this.

Or not. The thought chilled her, all the ways it would hurt if all of her kindness was fake, if they were going to be horrible to her and this was just some game. What did she really know of the fae? Of how they treated the few humans they allowed in their lands?

And yet this place was beautiful, and Aurora had been kind. Even Callum, who perhaps would not be the most attentive husband, had not been cruel, not when she was rejecting him, nor when she crawled back from the parking lot. Would that be enough? Could she flee? Where would she go? Would they track her down or let her leave? Would the humans hate her?

"Busy in that head?" Aurora asked as they turned a corner onto a less populated street. "We're almost to the Estate. It's kind of obnoxious, but it's nice."

"Just nervous," Fia said as an enormous iron gate, just as thick with vines and blooms as the rest of the city came into view, and then it was all she could view. The wall around the estate stretched so far she couldn't see where it ended.

Two large gates swung open at the carriage's approach. Once again, nothing was as she expected. Fia had heard words like king and princess and expected a castle, but this was something modern, warm wood and huge windows that let the sun in, surrounded by beautiful gardens full of more plants she couldn't identify and... "Wow," Fia said as a large flock of birds that looked like stretched, crimson peacocks came into view. "You grew up here?"

"Do not be modest. I've seen pictures of your home. There was plenty of opulence in your childhood as well."

No, her home had not been small or lacking aesthetically, but it wasn't this either, though her father had also called it an estate. "We didn't have birds," she said as the carriage came to a halt in front of expansive doors of carved wood and inlaid colored glass.

Aurora pushed open the carriage door, exited and extended her hand to Fia. The door closed behind them and the carriage moved on its own to park behind a line of carriages at the end of the driveway. Fia didn't think she'd ever get used to things moving on their own.

"I'll show you where you'll stay until the wedding and—" Aurora said more but her words were drowned out by the front doors opening and several faerie men—and this time Fia was sure they were guards—rushing out.

"Princess, come inside with us. Your father has been looking for you. He did not know you went to fetch Lady Fia."

Shock kept Fia from fully appreciating the entrance to the estate, but even with a strange man's hand on her back, urging her quickly forward, her breathe caught in her throat at the size of the doorway, the intricate details, the glittering stained glass sun and hand carved knocker.

"Is there trouble?" Aurora asked, her eyes darting from guard to guard, though there was no real fear in her voice. "If you are so worried about the Unseelie, perhaps Fia should stay in my room tonight. I can make sure no harm comes to her."

The guard who had spoken before glanced towards Fia. Her heart pounded in her chest, though it was not really fear of the Unseelie filling her body with adrenaline. She did not know enough about any of this to be afraid. Instead, she felt ignorant, like a small child trying to make sense of words they cannot yet understand.

"She knows." Aurora said, kicking off her shoes and bending down to pick them up, and Fia wondered if it was habit or a show of power, of how unbothered she was. "*What*? Is Elara storming the castle? Shall we run to the cellar?" The question was clearly meant to be a joke but none of the guards laughed.

"There is no cause for immediate alarm, however she brought a larger contingent than we anticipated and, as I said, your father was looking for you."

The shoes swung from Aurora's lithe fingertips. "Why? Because I had lunch with her once? Is he worried I will abscond with all my jewels and join the Unseelie ranks?"

"Aurora!" A deep voice boomed, and Fia came face to face with King Ellio. There could be no doubt of who he was, though he wore no crown and barely looked older than Callum, there was something royal him— power and strong magic tinged the air, making the hairs on the back of her neck bristle.

"Hi, daddy." She kissed his cheek. "Meet your daughter-in-law."

He looked Fia over and nodded. "It is lovely to meet you, Ms. Grey, and I apologize for the manner in which you have arrived. My son will be back very soon, and I know he looks forward to spending time with you before the wedding. Please, do not let my daughter's antics alarm you. We are only taking precaution due to the early arrival of some less than pleasant guests, but we would never let that spoil your time in Soleil or your engagement."

What a speech, right off the cuff like that. Was she supposed to bow? "Oh, well, yeah, no alarm. Just...a long day." *Great job, Fia. Great initial words to the king.*

"Of course." He smiled briefly. "You and I will talk later. I am sure we will have much to say to each other once you have rested, and I have some things I'd like to explain." He turned towards the guards. "I have spoken to the Unseelie woman. All seems well for now. A message was sent regarding her early arrival, but the note was apparently lost."

"Fia can stay with me if you're worried, daddy. I'm surrounded by brothers. I would not mind a sister."

"No, I think she will stay in her own room. She has had a long day," Ellio said, his preternaturally blue eyes boring into his daughter. "She is not a plaything."

"I never believed she was." The playfulness left Aurora's voice.

"I must go and meet Callum and Helio. You will join me for dinner, Fia."

"That sounds lovely," Fia said, unwilling to anger the king just yet. She had many, many questions for him about her father, about the deal they had struck, and the way she had been kept in the dark, but this was a powerful man, and she was used to dealing with powerful men. Better to start off sweetly, to get his guard down, make him see her as innocent and naive. "I look forward to it, sir."

"I can take you to your room." A guard reached for her again, but Aurora stepped between them.

"I'll show her, Hector." Aurora led her up a wide, wooden staircase with flowers carved into the railing, their petals inlaid with colored glass.

Everything here was so beautiful, detailed, and full of magic. This was a different land, no incandescent light but the soft twinkling of faerie orbs, the tang of power in the air, the castle full of pointed eared fae. Her entire world had changed in a matter of hours, and she had been too stupid to see the signs, to know it was coming.

As the reverberation of the king's footsteps grew dim, something lying coiled inside Fia snapped, overwhelming her. She couldn't breathe, couldn't make sense of this unending day and her new life. She wanted to cry, wanted to scream, wanted to run back through the mist and go home, have her phone and her clothes and her fair-weather friends. But she didn't, instead she bit in the inside of her cheek until the warm, metallic flow of blood filled her mouth. She wasn't some meek little flower, she wasn't the woman who cried in front of strangers. And she hadn't thought she was a woman who got traded like cattle or falling stocks.

She didn't want to become that person, to shrink and shrink in the faerie lands until she looked in the mirror and no longer recognized the woman she saw. And yeah, there were a lot of qualities about her no one would call virtues, but they were hers. She'd earned each of those bad qualities through tears and trauma, and she'd be damned if she was going to let them go and become something even worse—invisible.

But no matter what platitudes she told herself, she didn't know how to stop it, the words to say or the things to do. She didn't know the customs, or if the royals were truly kind people. Would they turn on her in an instant? Would they ship her away or lock her in a tower if she rebelled? Would Callum be kind, or would he leave her bruised and battered and full of children she did not want, half-faerie children who would be just beginning their lives as hers ended, short and brutal in the faerie world.

"Here you go," Aurora said, pushing open a door to reveal a spacious, pastel and pink room with wide, clear glass windows overlooking a vast garden, several outbuildings, and the edge of the property, where a grove of some kind of enormous trees grew, their branches spilling down to brush the ground, trimmed only where they met the fence that surrounded the estate.

And despite her desire to be strong, to find something inside herself to hold onto, Fia had to fight back tears as she took in the beautiful room. She wanted to go home, and yet her home had never been hers. Everything she'd ever owned had been provided by her father and now she had nothing, and she *was* a woman traded like fallen stocks.

"It's going to be okay," Aurora said, placing a hand on her shoulder. "As I said, we will be friends, and I'll stay with you. I'll get you through."

Desperately, she wanted to believe her, but she could not, because as kind as Aurora had been, Fia did not know her. But Aurora was all she had, so Fia nodded. "I think I need a minute."

"Of course." Aurora withdrew her hand. "We will have dinner soon, my brother, Prince Helio, should be there as well, and you can properly meet my father. You'll feel better after you eat. Our food is very good."

"I have heard that," Fia said, still looking out the window, where the breeze rustled the leaves and she pictured her body falling, pitching through the window, and crashing towards the earth.

Aurora headed to the door but before she could turn the latch there was a knock. Aurora pulled the door open. Outside was a guard Fia recognized from early though she could not remember if she had heard his name. “The Unseelie Queen will be joining us for dinner. Please make sure you and Lady Fia are dressed appropriately.”

“Oh.” Aurora glanced back at Fia. “What a surprise.”

“Indeed,” the guard said. “So many surprises as of late. Shall I send a maid?”

Again, Aurora glanced at Fia. “I can help if you’d like, but you can have a maid if you prefer.”

Did she want a maid? She’d had one who cleaned her house, but she’d always dressed herself, however she didn’t know the customs here, had no idea what dress to pick or how to do her hair to not look as utterly out of place as she felt. She was also taking far too long to answer the question, she could see it on both their faces, so she made up her mind. She’d continue to dress herself. “I require no maid, but I would not spurn your help, Aurora.”

“You heard her. We will be down for dinner and well dressed,” Aurora said, closing the door. “I’m sorry. I know you needed a moment.”

Fia shrugged. “I’ll survive.” And she decided it was true. She would survive and eventually she would do more, she would find a way to thrive. And this time the words didn’t ring hollow. She *could* do this. She would find a way. She would not let her father ruin her life and would find something beautiful here. Though it was not the way she would have chosen, she was finally free of her father, the apron-strings she had always been too scared to let go of had been cut and this life could be one of her own making. As long as Callum was not cruel, and he did not seem to be, she would find things to occupy her time, find friends and hobbies and a way to live.

"So," Aurora said, pulling her out of her thoughts. "Let's just put your mental breakdown to the side, schedule it for tomorrow, and we can get you dressed." There was a glint in her eyes that Fia was sure meant trouble, but it made Fia like her more.

It also calmed her. Aurora was the daughter of a powerful man, and she was clearly up to something. Maybe they could be friends, maybe in all the shit the universe was throwing her way it had also thrown Aurora at her, maybe she really would help Fia get through it. "You look... mischievous."

Aurora let out a bark of laughter. "A few hours together and you already know me better than my father. He never knowns I'm up to something until it's too late. I shouldn't say more though."

"Come on." Fia sat on the bed. "Let me in on the secret. As you said, I'm putting off a mental breakdown. That requires distraction."

Again, Aurora laughed. "It's nothing really. It's just my father...well, he's a father, you know." She gave Fia a pointed look. "I do love getting under his skin, and his first dinner with you also including Elara, The Unseelie Queen, is going to piss him off. He hates her, and I know she's supposed to be my enemy and everything, but I think she's alright. So, I guess I'm not up to something, I'm just incredibly amused."

She really was going to like Aurora and nothing could have given her relief like the prospect of friendship. "Okay, so I don't get your clothes at all. What am I supposed to wear?"

"Oh yeah, good call on the maid. I'll dress you much better than she will."

-CHAPTER-
-FOUR-

HALF AN HOUR later, Fia still didn't understand faerie fashion, but she didn't hate it either. All the materials she'd tried on had been light and airy, brushing her skin like soft fingers, though the outcome was that she felt almost naked on the way to dinner in a long, linen dress. She'd never worn anything like it, the skirt was long and floral patterned against a light green background, tailored tight at the waist with a white top cut to resemble petals forming an asymmetrical neckline that brushed her collarbone on one side.

Walking down the stairs, the fabric kissing her skin when it caught in the breeze blowing through the open windows, she really did feel like a princess. She'd had plenty of designer clothes back home, but none of them even came close to this dress, though she wasn't sure if the incredible quality of the clothes was a faerie thing or a daughter-in-law of the king thing. Whatever the reason, she loved it. Somehow the clothes made the world around her seem more solid, more real, and yet more magical in the best way, because no human would go to a possibly politically charged dinner dressed in a beautiful, flower-inspired dress, and wasn't that a shame? Not to mention, she'd seen a few pairs of pants tucked into the closet maybe of the same soft linen-y material and she was dying to put them on. They were only pants, but they were something to look forward to.

After half an hour of getting ready, gushing over her own dress and the pretty pink, lacey dress Aurora had chosen for herself, Fia had nearly forgotten why she was there, thinking only of the fun she and Aurora might have tomorrow and the days to follow, until she saw Callum, glowing and golden, waiting in the hall for her. A lump formed in her throat, and she swallowed hard.

"You look beautiful," he said, offering her his arm.

She took it, letting him press himself close, wishing desperately she felt something. He was handsome, a literal prince, and more importantly he was the man she was going to marry, but despite the kindness in his voice or the perfect symmetry of his face, nothing stirred inside her. She would be able to marry him, she might even find happiness, but Fia did not know if she would ever come to love the faerie leading her gently into the next room.

One step inside the doorway, she lifted her eyes to the table, and all the breath left her body. She nearly stumbled, focused not on walking but on showing no reaction and praying it was working. The fae were not like humans. With their perfect skin, long limbs, and pointed ears she'd always thought of them as something other, but at the sight of the Unseelie woman across the room, she realized just how humanlike the Seelie fae were.

The woman had to be Unseelie, had to be the queen that had upset everyone since her arrival, because she was unlike any of the other fae sitting around the long, intricately carved table. She was unlike anyone or anything Fia had ever seen.

Tight, curled horns sat on either side of the woman's head, nearly like a ram's horns, except the surface of them looked more like iridescent ivory. And twisted and curled around those horns, her long, silvery-purple hair hung loose, falling to her shoulders. Her face was nearly like a human's, and yet it was not at all, her eyes were too big, her features too sharp, as though they had been carved not from bone and flesh but marble, and yet she was beautiful. All of it should have been off-putting but it was not, it was enthralling.

The woman stared at Fia, just as she was staring at her. Dark eyes of endless depth. She blinked and the light caught in those eyes, not just dark, they were rimmed with silver, the smallest thread of molten metal separating the iris from the white.

The king moved, but the woman was faster, pushing herself up from her seat, she rounded the table. At Fia's side, Callum stiffened, his grip on her arm tightening, but if the woman noticed the change in his demeanor nothing in her face reflected it.

"You must be the new Princess."

"She is not yet," the king said gruffly. "As you well know."

"Of course. I forget how important titles are to the Seelie. Lady Fia, then? I am Elara, of the Unseelies to the North, and I offer my sincerest apologies for encroaching on your arrival with my own visit. I did not mean to make your first day so fraught."

Again, Fia was left without words and again it did not sit right with her. She wanted to say something, not stand there like a simpering idiot, but all she could say was, "Oh, that's fine. No need to apologize."

“She is a kind girl,” the king said, making his way to Fia’s side. “And I am pleased that soon I will have her as my daughter-in-law. She will clearly excel at her duties. Let me show you to your seat, Fia.”

Callum let her go and King Ellio led her to her chair, close to his own and right across from Elara. A beautiful faerie woman who must be his wife, judging by the crown on her head, smiled serenely at Fia when she sat.

Her suspicions were confirmed as she took her seat and Ellio introduced the woman as his wife, Calliope, then the man two down from her as Cyrus, his second son. The rest of the group was made up of Aurora and the king’s eldest, Helio, the future king and nearly his father’s twin.

Fia had been to some awkward family dinners, but this one really took the cake, and yet Elara sat across the table, leaned back in her chair and smiling, despite the air being thick with tension and unease, all of it aimed at her.

“I can’t wait to get to know you, Fia. I’ve never been to the human world, and I am so very curious,” Calliope said. “Ellio said he would take me when we got married but that was a decade ago and we haven’t gone yet.”

A decade. So not the mother of any of his children. Fia tucked that information away.

"I do apologize, sweetling," Ellio said. "Things have been busy, but you are correct, a promise is a promise."

"I have never been either," Elara said, her eyes still on Fia. "Though of course my kind is banned from the human world so that is no surprise."

"You are?" Fia said before she could stop herself.

"Father," the heir to the crown, Helio said then paused, obviously choosing his words. "This is a most unusual dinner."

As if on cue, servants appeared from the doorways, carrying trays of soup, the mouthwatering smell making Fia realize just how hungry she was.

"We will speak later," Ellio said, a sternness to his voice that made all his sons sit straighter in their chairs. "I am sure Elara has much to discuss if she has come all this way and been amenable enough to have dinner without any council, but for now we will have a nice dinner with Lady Fia. She is soon to be your sister, certainly you have questions for her."

"Of course, Father." But Helio did not so much as glance her way, and if his eyes did stray from his plate, they were drawn like a magnet to Elara.

"I for one am excited to have Fia as a sister-in-law," Aurora said, dipping her spoon into the brothy soup. "We've already decided we're going to be best friends, so I was thinking of joining her and Callum in the countryside after they are settled. I believe the fresh air would do me good. I grow weary of the city."

"Seriously?" Callum said, leaning back to make room for the servant to deposit his soup. "Where would you even live?"

"Oh, you wouldn't want me to live with you?" Aurora teased. "I'm sure I could find a little cottage."

Ellio laughed. "I can't imagine you in a cottage, dearest daughter."

Her brothers laughed, continuing to tease her, and for the first time since her arrival, Fia felt truly at ease without having to convince herself she was okay.

The bed in her room, in addition to being ridiculously huge, was the most comfortable bed Fia had ever slept in. Before getting in, she had been sure she would toss and turn, trying to make sense of her day, but instead she fell asleep quickly, exhausted and full after a ridiculously delicious five-course meal.

Her sleep was sound and dreamless until she awoke to voices in her room.

"Don't make a sound," a familiar voice said close beside her.

Fia opened her eyes, but it took several moments for her to make sense of the scene in her room. The Unseelie Queen, Elara, was inches from her face, her hands braced on both sides of Fia, trapping her to the bed. Beyond her was Aurora, throwing things from Fia's dresser into a bag.

"I..."

"Don't make a sound," Elara repeated., moonlight shining off her horns. "Don't alert anyone. Don't scream. Just cooperate. Do not make it hard on yourself and know I can hurt you faster than anyone can get here."

Hurt her? Fia did want to scream, she wanted to push Elara and run from the room, but something in her strange, silver-rimmed brown eyes told Fia she could hurt her, she *would* hurt her, if she did not listen. So Fia nodded.

"Good," Elara said. "I am going to stand, and you will do the same. Then you will follow Aurora and I out of the castle quietly. I am sure you have questions, assume I will answer them later once we are gone from this place. Do not think you can run. Do not think you can escape."

"You will be fine, Fia," Aurora said, slinging the bag over her shoulder.

Nothing was going to be fine, Fia was sure of that, not until she was free of this place and back in the human world where she belonged. She had been a fool to trust Aurora, a fool to trust the king. Always a fool.

As she stood from her bed, she vowed to herself, she would be a fool no longer. She did not know if she would stay here or find a way out of this place and back across the mist, but wherever she landed she would trust no one until they earned it, and she would make something of herself, make herself into more than a pawn, more than an idiot, dragged from her bed.

This was not the magical place little girls were promised when they were raised to be brides. It was a misogynistic hellscape on the brink of war and her father had knowingly sold her into it for reasons she still didn't understand.

"Go," Elara said, shoving her towards a hole in the floor that had been concealed beneath a thick rug.

Fia took a step closer and fear wound its icy fingers around her heart. There may be no home for her, no escape from this place, only descent into a cold dark hole. She was going to be Elara's hostage, betrayed by Aurora who she'd actually believed might be her friend. She had not made it even a day.

“Careful on the ladder,” Aurora said, lowering herself into the dark space, the bag of Fia’s things still slung across her shoulder. “We’ll be out of here in a minute.”

Fia followed, unsure of what else to do. Everything in her body told her not to go, to turn around and run, but she believed Elara when she said she could hurt her faster than anyone could get there and she had no hope of getting away from two faeries.

The dark hole led to a musty passage, barely illuminated until Aurora produced a ball of light in the palm of her hand. Fia watched Elara climb down, her horns terrifying in the dim light, her depthless eyes nothing but silver specks, and the dread in her chest grew.

She tore her gaze away from the queen and looked back to Aurora, and the faerie must have been able to read the question she was too afraid to ask. “I have not betrayed you. You will understand soon. For now, only follow,” she said, before turning down the passage.

Fia inhaled sharply, willing her body to move, but it stood stiffly, her legs like stones. Elara moved beside her, and movement returned, her whole body shrinking away, unwilling to let the Unseelie get too close to her, though there was little space in the passage. “Please,” Fia breathed.

Elara chuckled. "No need to beg, Princess. I do not intend to harm you, though I can if I must. Must I?"

Fia shook her head, her throat going dry. "No."

Elara leaned close to Fia, she smelled of something that Fia knew but could not place. "Good. I would so hate to mar your perfect skin."

Fia inhaled sharply against the tightening in her throat. "You don't need to do this."

"You have no idea what I need to do." Elara's voice was a low whisper, drawing goosebumps across Fia's arms.

"Shh," Aurora said glancing back at them and disappearing around a bend in the passage.

There was light ahead, more than what Aurora had conjured, and Elara shoved Fia back as voices reached them, pushing her into the wall. The stones scraped her flesh through her thin nightgown "Stay," she commanded and Fia did as she was told, flattening herself further against the stone wall, her head banging into the rocks as Elara once again braced her hands on either side of her.

"Princess Aurora?" a male voice said, full of curiosity and confusion.

"Evening," Aurora said. "Just out for a walk."

"A walk? Through the tunnels?"

Elara locked eyes with Fia, a silent command, though Fia wasn't sure she would have been able to move even if she wanted to. The queen leaned in close, her nose brushing the length of Fia's neck, her horns scraping against the stone, before pushing herself off the wall, one hand reaching into the pocket of her jacket as she too disappeared around the bend.

Fia's heart pounded, and she wrapped her arms around herself as noises reached her. People moving quickly. A shout that quickly turned into something worse. The wet sound of something wounded. Then a hard thud.

Against her better judgment Fia moved from the wall, following the curve of the tunnel round the corner. She came to a halt, bracing herself on the wall to stop herself from stepping into a growing pool of blood flowing from the slit throat of a guard laying on the ground, his eyes open and staring sightless at the ceiling.

"Keep moving," Aurora grabbed Fia's hand and pulled. The three women rushed down the passage, no longer speaking, only the sound of their footsteps to break the silence. No one else intercepted them and Fia didn't know if she wanted them to or not. The sight of the fae man on the ground was burned on the back of her eyelids, the only thing she could see each time she blinked.

They came to another ladder and Aurora dropped Fia's hand. "This time, *wait*," she hissed at Elara.

"Not if we are compromised," Elara hissed back, stepping close to Fia, trapping her once again against the wall with her body.

Aurora leveled a look at Elara and then climbed the metal rungs of the ladder, pushing open a door at the top. Moonlight streamed into the passage. This was it, after this was outside, through the fence that Fia was sure Aurora would know every break and hole in, then they were gone from the estate, out in the city with no one to stop them.

A guard's voice reached them, and she drew in a sharp breath without thinking. Elara's hand clamped over Fia's mouth and she shuddered. Her skin was inhuman, her fingers too long, entirely encompassing Fia's jaw.

"My father was looking for you," Aurora said from above. "Can you meet him."

There was a pause and Fia could hear each beat of her own heart pounding in her ears. "He was looking for me?" The guard sounded unsure. He didn't believe her. Maybe he would stop them. Maybe he would die too. Her palms turned clammy, her stomach turned.

"Someone is ill or something. I don't know." Aurora's voice had a breathless, schoolgirl quality that Fia had not heard her use before and she giggled. "Don't mention that I met you here, maybe."

"And why *are* you here?" The guard remained unconvinced. How long until Elara removed her hand and ended this? But the Queen didn't move, only stood, clearly listening to the conversation but looking at Fia. Her thumb brushed against her jaw where it still covered Fia's mouth.

"Because I am." The breathlessness was out of Aurora's voice, now she commanded, back to a princess. "And you are not paid to ask questions, only protect. Do I look as if I am in danger? Go. My father asked for you."

Another pause, a second too long, and Elara's fingers slipped from Fia's face.

The man answered, his voice tight. "Yes, your highness."

Fia nearly collapsed with relief. She did not want to go with them, but neither did she want another man turned into a body tonight. Not when the blood felt like it was hot on her hands.

Aurora's face appeared in the opening above them and Elara pushed Fia forward roughly. The air outside was cool and the stars overhead were the brightest she had ever seen, but she had no time to take them in before Aurora was dragging her into a shadowy corner of the estate courtyard and pulling something out of her bag.

The faerie held up a garment Fia didn't recognize and couldn't immediately make sense of. "Wear this," Aurora said, shoving it at her.

The fabric was thicker than what she had worn earlier, though buttery soft and after a few fumbles—her fingers didn't seem to work anymore—Fia was able to pull it over her head. It was something like a poncho, but too short, only coming to her ribcage, with a wide hood which Elara pulled over her head.

"Do not speak to anyone," Elara said, her dark eyes boring into Fia. "Again, I do not intend to hurt you, nor anyone else. However, if you speak to someone I may be forced to act. Understood?"

Fia nodded, stomach roiling, and Elara pulled up the hood of her own strange shawl. Fia wondered if all of them being hooded would make them more conspicuous but didn't voice her concerns. Instead, she obediently followed Aurora as she headed for a piece of fence mostly obscured by vines and pushed the leaves back to reveal an opening.

The gate was not far, all the guard needed to do was look to his left. But he didn't.

The three women slipped through, onto the streets of the city of Soleil. The first street was empty, but the second was a thoroughfare, crowded with pedestrians, carriages, and even a few fae on horseback. Within minutes they were out of sight of the estate.

They turned onto another street, then another, again and again until Fia had no sense of direction. The crowds thinned, the chatter of hundreds fading, easily muffled by the heavy foliage, but several faeries still walked under the canopy of the plants, city sounds replaced by nocturnal birds and skittering, small animals. Despite the heavy fear in her gut, Fia could not ignore the beauty of this place. But there was hardly time, Aurora and Elara moved as quickly as possible without drawing attention and Fia was not brave enough to attempt escape.

Where were the people Elara had brought with her? Fia had heard mention of them but had not seen them. Wasn't that unusual? She knew little of royalty, but they seemed to always be surrounded by people. With every step she expected more Unseelie to appear, but no one did and if anyone noticed the Princess among them, they did not react.

They took another turn onto a deserted residential street. The foliage was even heavier here, not only from the vines that grew up the buildings, but from tall trees, their branches stretching across space above the road and making the already dark night darker.

Several of the strange, horseless, motorless carriages were parked along the street, waiting outside dimly lit houses. Elara stopped in front of one and pulled the door open, her gaze falling on Fia. Was this it? No Unseelie had joined them. She thought she had longer. But she had done nothing to come up with a plan and now there was no time left.

Behind her somewhere was the estate, but Fia was not sure she wanted to go back there, though she did not want to get in the carriage either. If she tried to run, where would she go? She was alone in a strange city, the only human this side of the mist. It seemed so unlikely she would make it more than a foot or two before Aurora or Elara stopped her and even if she did, even if her blood did not join the pooling shadows of night, how would she make it through the mist? Where would she go if she did?

As though in answer, Elara came closer. "Get inside."

And Fia did, leaving the city of Soleil behind without knowing if anyone had yet noticed she was missing.

-CHAPTER-
-FIVE-

SINCE SHE HAD not anticipated being chosen by the Prince, Fia had never learned much about Daonith, the faerie lands. She had gone to the borderlands to party occasionally when she was younger, but she had not studied, had not learned their customs, or even the names of their cities and kingdoms. She had occasionally wondered about the lands beyond the mist, as she was sure all humans did, the same way she wondered if there was life on other planets or what was going on beneath the ocean, but it had never called to her the way it seemed to call to some people. The fae had intrigued her father and perhaps that was why she hadn't bothered to wonder, knowing deep in her soul that the things that interested Zachary Gray were not meant for her.

Her father's lifelong interest in Daonith and the fae should have been her first clue, she now realized. She had been foolish and naive to think he'd send her there for no reason, that a man who had made a career of lies would not lie to his own daughter.

None of that really mattered now, as she rolled through the woods in a strange carriage, along backroads and over wooden bridges, unable to make out much of anything but the trunks of trees in the darkness. She thought the faerie worlds would have more people, but once they left the outskirts of the city she saw no sign of them. Then again, it was dark and she was with two women who knew the lands. They wouldn't roll their hostage through cities and towns.

The three women sat in silence for a long time, tension thick, only the occasional bump of the wheels on uneven to terrain to break the monotony, until Fia couldn't stand it anymore. "How does this thing work, anyway?" she blurted out. "No one is steering it."

"Magic," Aurora said, picking her head up from where it had been leaning back against the carriage.

"No shit, but how? It doesn't look like you're using magic," Fia said, and both the women looked at her like she was some curious creature. She was surprised when their eyes on her didn't draw adrenaline into her veins, but it seemed her body had used up all its fear. There was a low murmur of it low in her stomach, but no one was hurting her, no one was threatening her and she was tired of silence and uncertainty. "I mean, if you're going to kidnap me after what was already the worst day of my life, you could at least answer my questions. Or gag me, I guess."

The shadow of a smile played on Elara's face. "What do you know about faerie magic?"

"Not much." Fia shrugged as the carriage made a turn down a path that couldn't be called a road. Branches scratched against the windows and the wheels crunched rocks with every turn.

"Each of us gives off magic, in the same way all living creatures give off heat. It isn't something we think of doing, or try to do, it is just how we are. There is a current of magic running through our bodies and with each breath we lose some to the air around us. We've found a way to harness that magic to make things like this carriage work, as we do not have electricity here."

"Is that why electrical things don't work? Because of your magic?" Outside the soft glow of the morning sun was beginning to light the horizon.

"Clever human. Yes, though one of our scientists could explain it better than I can. But something in our magic screws up electrical devices. Years ago, a boy from my village brought home a television. He'd smuggled it from the human world and was so excited. I knew it wouldn't work but I was curious. I gathered in his living room with everyone else. We had nothing for the cord to attach to, so for a moment we all stood around, unsure of the next move. He held the cord in his hands, his eyes closed tight and for a moment the thing flickered then it let out an awful noise, followed by the boy's scream as he dropped the cord, but not before the television started to smoke. No electricity, just our magic and the thing was fried."

"We can sometimes get battery powered objects to work if they are simple," Aurora said, moving closer. "And other things, like light bulbs have been modified to work with our magic instead of your electricity. If we had more cooperation between our races, I'm sure we could manage even more."

Elara shot a look at Aurora. It certainly meant something, but Fia could not figure out what. She did not know the women well enough to read their emotions and Elara was like a painting of a person, none of her features quite right, which made her even harder to read, but Fia did not want to go back to silence.

"So where are we going?" she asked for something else to say, hardly expecting an answer.

"The same village I mentioned," Elara said, with a smile, though even that looked mildly terrifying on her. Several of her teeth came to sharp points. "I believe you will like it."

"Won't that be the first place they look?" Fia asked, though she immediately regretted it. Why was she helping them kidnap her more efficiently?

"The king does not know where I grew up," Elara said. "He hardly knows anything about me, and my primary residence is no longer in the village. You have many questions."

"I'm bored," Fia said, stretching her hands above her head.

Aurora chuckled. "Could be worse emotions for a hostage, yeah?"

"Maybe she could threaten me with more violence," Fia said. Now that she had started talking, she seemed unable to stop, and though she knew Elara was easily capable of violence, she didn't seem very threatening at the moment, with her long legs stretched across the carriage and stray pieces of her silvery-purple hair caught in her horns. Fia's eyes caught on the horns, a flash of moonlight on them, and she thought of the flash of a knife, the sheen of blood spreading across the tunnel floor. Yes, Elara was certainly capable of violence, and yet Fia was not as fearful as she knew she should be.

Elara simply shrugged. “No, ask your questions. You should understand the place you will live, though I find it strange you did not learn about even the Seelie before you offered yourself to their prince.”

“I didn’t mean to,” Fia said. “My father said—”

“Your father decided who you would marry? I thought those practices were mostly lost in the human world and you do not look so young.” Elara sat up straighter in the spacious carriage, looking down at Fia as though she was some strange specimen in a lab.

“Her father is very powerful,” Aurora said before Fia could answer. “I believe I have explained this to you.”

“Still,” Elara said. “She should have learned about your people if she was showing up at all. What if the prince had simply liked you? You’re very beautiful, you must know that. It was foolish not to learn anything about the fae, in fact, I think it’s foolish humans seem to teach their young nothing about us. We share a world.”

Fia hated the way they were speaking about her, making her feel so small and stupid, but even worse she hated how she could say little in her own defense. "I should have learned, you are correct. But as for the rest, my father is not a man you can easily say no to, even harder if you are his daughter."

"Did he hit you?" Elara was still staring at her, seeming to see more than just Fia's face. "I hear many human men hit the woman."

"Not often." Fia crossed her arms across her chest. She didn't want to talk about this, not with the woman who had been threatening her so recently.

"I will teach you self-defense. The next time he hits you, you can hit him harder."

Fia doubted that. "You just kidnapped me. Now you want to teach me to fight?"

Elara waved a dismissive hand. "You won't be stronger than me, no matter how long you train. And while I do not want you to lose a healthy fear of me, I am opposed to violence unless it is necessary."

"Do you often find it necessary?"

"More and more as the years go on." Elara spread herself across the seat once more, crossing one leg over the other. "Any more questions?"

"Do all Unseelie have horns?"

"No. We are varied, as are the Seelie, though less in appearance and more in abilities. Most Seelie look much like the humans."

"How are the Seelie varied?"

"In magic." Elara said, rolling her neck. "Some have more, some have less, for example the Western Court has spell magic."

"Elara..." Aurora said her name like a warning. *Interesting.* Fia tucked the knowledge of the Western Court away.

Again, Elara waved her hand dismissively. "She will learn soon enough, why not answer her questions as best I can."

"You know why," Aurora said, though there was little bite to her voice. The two women were obviously friends. "The situation is precarious."

"What situation?" Fia asked.

"I think you will like my people, Fia," Elara said, ignoring her question.

"You said that already."

"No, I said you will like the village, but I also think you will like the Unseelie people. Perhaps your kidnapping will not be too much of a burden."

"Yeah, I'm sure it'll be a real blast." Another branch hit the outside of the carriage and Fia returned her attention to the window, watching the forest roll past them while the other women lapsed back into silence.

She was not sure how much time passed, but as the carriage rolled on snow appeared on the ground, small white patches tucked into shadows, untouched by the sun and unable to melt. After some time, they crossed a bridge and the trees gave way to shrubs and low greenery, the snow once again disappearing in the open space, though the windows of the carriage were cold to the touch.

They crested a hill, and a village opened before them. Small cottages with puffs of smoke rising from their chimneys lined the narrow streets and large mountains, green at the bottom but bare rock covered in snow further up, stretched towards the sky behind the homes, like eternal protectors over the people who lived there.

The village did not appear to take up more than a mile or two in any direction. Though she could not see the entirety of it from her window, she had the feeling she could walk through the entire place in a morning. Unlike in Soleil where everything was jammed together, the houses here sprawled out, large overgrown gardens spilling from one house to the next.

As Fia craned her neck to see more, the carriage slowed to a stop and both faeries turned to look at her and, with the feeling of ice rolling down her spine, she remembered where she was. For all their easy charm while they traveled, these women had kidnapped her, they'd murdered a man and whisked her away, and she had no idea what they wanted.

How quickly she had forgotten seeing a man die as she'd watched this new world pass outside her window. He was not the first dead man she'd seen, nor the third or the fourth. Her father had killed men and he'd had men killed, and though he usually kept that part of his life away from Fia she had not always been so lucky.

But this was the first time the death had felt like it might be her fault. When her father killed those deaths felt like something she had to endure, a burden she had not asked for and an act she could not stop. This was the first time she wondered if she could have stopped it. Should she have screamed? Fought? She had been borne to her father, but she had chosen to trust Aurora.

And she had forgotten in only hours. Part of her wished she hadn't, that she felt guilty, more upset than she was no, but there was something even more strange eating away at her. Fia knew she should be afraid, some part of her was, each second like a ticking bomb she was waiting to explode, but she was also curious. She wanted to see this world, wanted to know why Elara had taken her, wanted to see more of the Unseelie, wanted, wanted, wanted.

For her entire life, Fia's father had gone on great adventures and she had tagged along for many, but each vacation, each plane ride, or catamaran on clear blue waters had been safe. She'd never been allowed to explore on her own. Safe Fia, tucked away like the family china, waiting waiting, waiting. And finally, she had been pulled off the shelf, finally she had been set free, and though she was terrified, she was also ready for her own adventure.

Or at least she hoped she was.

-CHAPTER-

-SIX-

ELARA PUSHED THE carriage door open and exited. The cold mountain air filled her lungs, bringing with it scents of pine and smoke. Elara stretched her arms above her head before turning to offer her hand to Fia. "Careful. The ground gets slippery here sometimes. Muddy. Or ice."

Fia looked down before she took a step and considered refusing Elara's help, but the ground was muddy, and she'd been sitting in the carriage for hours, her muscles stiff, so she took the offered hand.

She was glad she had. The ground seemed to move beneath her feet for a moment before she found her balance. Aurora put

a hand on her back steading her. “You never realize how much those things are swaying until you’re still again.”

They’d come to another cottage, small and modest with ivy growing up its side, and a wild yard that looked like it might grow enough vegetables to feed the entire street if anyone bothered to tend it.

“Will you take our stuff inside, Aurora? I have something to talk to Fia about,” Elara said.

“Are we really staying here?” Fia asked. Did the king really know so little about The Unseelie Queen that he did not know where she was born? And did Elara truly have nowhere better to hide than a tiny cottage in a sleepy village? What did ‘Queen’ mean to the Unseelie?

“Yes, we are,” Elara said as Aurora made her way up the front path, a bag under each arm. The so-called Queen watched her as she made her way through the creaky front door and then turned back to Fia, reached down into her boot, and pulled out a knife in one quick motion.

Fia jumped back, slipping in the mud and landing on her ass with a wet squelch, visions of the dead man once again dancing across her mind. Oh, she had been a fool not to be scared. This bitch was going to kill her in this stupid, overgrown, podunk village.

She tried to scramble back until Elara's expression registered in her mind. Her eyebrows were scrunched, her head tilted slightly, and she certainly wasn't making any murderous moves towards Fia. Except the *knife*.

"Are you okay?" Elara asked, putting out her knife free hand and offering it to Fia.

"No!" Fia nearly yelled, but Elara grabbed her by the wrist and pulled her to her feet. Once she was steady, she tried to step back, but Elara kept her grip firm.

"Don't be scared," she said, frightening Fia even further. "It's just a pinch."

Fia's heart rose into her throat. She could feel each beat tumble through her as Elara pulled at her hand. The faerie slid her thumb down Fia's palm until her hand was splayed in Elara's. She whispered something and the mud disappeared. Fia let out a little sound she didn't think she'd ever made before.

Elara brought the knife to Fia's finger, pricking it. A drop of blood welled and Fia had no idea what to expect, no idea what was happening, only that she felt something, some strange pull, a low thrumming heat behind her navel worming its way up her chest.

Elara brought Fia's hand to her mouth, shutting her eyes as her lips closed around the pad of Fia's finger, and Fia had no idea what to do except watch. Her body went rigid, she could barely breathe, couldn't swallow, the pounding of her heart grew frantic and the pull in her stomach turned into a fist, gripping her.

When Elara lowered her hand, opening her eyes once more, the silver rings around her irises were ablaze. She blinked and took a step closer, until Fia was breathing the same air as Elara, until her scent filled her nose, a scent she still could not place, was not sure she had ever smelled before, a smell that was simply Elara, dark and twisting, like a bonfire, a bright night, fear and anticipation and things that should not smell but somehow did. And Fia shook because the dagger was in Elara's other hand and she was so close and so frightening, her teeth sharp though her lips had been soft. Her eyes too bright, her features like a predator, something that would bite and tear and shred.

"You will not leave. I know you can feel that we are bound. If you run, I will find you. So, do not run, Fia. Stay."

What choice did she have? She *could* feel it. She nodded, forcing her head to move. "I won't run."

"Of course not. You will enjoy your freedom," Elara reached up, tucking a strand of Fia's dark hair behind her ear. "You will shop and eat and laugh, but you will not run. You will not leave. And you know I *will* hurt you. I do not want to, but I will. I have people to protect and one day I hope to count you among them, but I don't, not yet, and I will protect them." She brought Fia's hand to her mouth once more and kissed her knuckles gently. "Let us not talk like this again. Let's get you to your room where you can take a shower. Then we can get you some new clothes."

Fia nodded, feeling returning to her body as Elara dropped her hand, though she was not sure her heart would ever stop pounding. "You grew up here." She did not know why she said it, except she could not imagine such a formidable force of a woman existing in this place.

"Yes. There is more, Fia, so much I wish to tell you. I did not lie when I said I hope to one day count you among my people. But I need to know I can trust you."

Fia almost opened her mouth, almost said she could trust her. But they would both know she was lying. Was Elara lying? Did she truly want to trust Fia, or did she just think she would be easier to manage if she was on Elara's side? She didn't know. Elara was a mystery, a pendulum swinging from kind to terrifying and Fia never knew what to expect, what each moment would bring.

How could someone trust a person like that? Someone so capricious, so easily led to violence. And yet, still Fia was curious. Why were they at this house? What was the plan? Why had they kidnapped her?

Without another word, Elara walked towards the house and Fia followed her up the cobbled path. When they entered, Aurora was bent over the fireplace, stoking a crackling fire. The house was cozy, and if Fia had guessed at any point where she was going, she never would have imagined this cottage. Did Elara live like this? Did the sharp tongued, sharp featured fae curl beneath crocheted blankets at night? Did she garden, her horns dirt-smudged, her silvery purple hair in a messy bun between them?

"I can show you to your room," Aurora said. "if you would like to rest. Or we can head into the village. You will need clothes."

Fia thought of all the clothes hanging in her apartment. The rows of shoes and dozens of purses. She thought of her phone and her laptop and wondered if her father knew she had been kidnapped. Did the world? Was she trending across social media?

She had never loved her life. She was the daughter of a horrible man who longed for a son. She did not think she had a single friend she could truly count on. But she missed her life. How peaceful it would be to go back to everything she knew. Instead, she would sleep in a strange bed and wear strange clothes while a voice in the back of her mind replayed Elara's words that she could never run.

"Yeah, I guess I will," Fia said, swallowing the lump in her throat. She would not cry. She was good at not crying. "I don't need to sleep."

"Are you sure?" Elara asked, looking at her curiously.

"I don't think I could." The blood in her veins had to be half adrenaline at this point. She balled her hands into fists to keep from wrapping her arms around herself. Their surface level kindness was almost harder to endure than cruelty. At least she would know how to react to cruelty, at least the eventual blow would not come as a shock.

This was like living at home again, never knowing when she returned from school what mood her father would be in. Would he laugh and order dinner? Would he yell and hit her for the slightest misstep?

"I will take her to the village, I know it best," Elara said. "Perhaps you could find out a timeline for our visitors?"

Aurora nodded. “I will do my best.”

“If there is no word yet, I would not be overly surprised. I suspect he enjoys keeping me waiting.” Elara returned her attention to Fia. “Are you hungry?”

She was, though she wasn’t sure if her stomach would hold food. “A bit.”

“Good. We’ll grab something to eat then visit the shops. Would you like me to bring you anything, Aurora?”

She shook her head. “I’ll find something on my own.”

“Alright.” Elara smiled. “Let me show you to your room and you can wash up before we go.”

-CHAPTER-
-SEVEN-

THE VILLAGE OF FROST was one of the most beautiful places Fia had ever seen, nestled between mountain ranges with snowy peaks. Despite the chill in the air the landscape was lush and green. A creek ran beside the road Elara led her down and she could see bright colored fish swimming beneath the surface.

But despite the beauty, signs of hardship dotted the village, the people they passed were thin, many of the homes needed repairs, and Fia realized the sprawling gardens were not just a hobby in this place, but a necessity for many of the people.

"This seems like a beautiful place to be a child," Fia said as the heart of the village came into view and the road diverged from the river, because Fia knew the whole world was full of hardships, that even a full belly and a perfect home did not guarantee happiness, and this place was full of beauty. If someone had loved Elara when she was a child then even though there might have been lean times, she guessed there was a lot of happiness as well.

Elara looked over at her. This was the first time Fia had seen her in the daylight and her horns had a slight shimmer in the sunlight. She was horrifyingly beautiful and Fia could not deny that despite her fear, she was drawn to the woman.

"I did not appreciate just how lovely it was a child, but yes, I climbed the mountains and swam in the stream and had plenty of playmates. But do not grow too attached. We may not be here long."

Fia shoved her hands into her pockets trying to decide on her words. She did not know if she should keep her thoughts to herself, protect all she could from this strange woman, or if she should endear herself to her. "I know you won't give me details, but there is a plan for me, right? You didn't just do this to be cruel to the king?"

"Correct."

Before she could ask another question, Fia was distracted by the inhabitants of the Village of Frost. They had passed four Unseelie on the road, all strange in their own way, one had been palest blue, another had hair like straw, but no features as shocking as Elara's horns. She had wondered if Elara was an outlier, or if Queens were different from the rest. She thought maybe most of the Unseelie were only a bit different, pink or purple or something of that sort. She had misjudged.

A woman with skin like tree bark and hair like candy floss was cleaning the sidewalk outside of a storefront. Another man, even taller than Elara, might have passed for human at first glance but he had eyes like a cat and a chin that came to a sharp point. One child ran by and Fia was nearly certain she saw the tips of *wings* protruding from the back of her jacket.

Another woman did look like Elara, with the same ram horns, though the hair flowing down her back and was pitch black. She smiled as they passed, nodding once to Elara, her eyes narrowing at Fia, but she continued without saying a word.

Oh, how little Fia knew. How little all the humans knew of this strange land where trade was fiercely guarded, and all goods went through the Seelie king's lands at the border. What other mysteries would she find?

"Do you like lamb?" Elara asked. "I believe Rachelle also has chicken." She gestured in the direction of a small stand where a faerie with dark skin and antlers was cooking over a grill, or something like it.

"Uh, yeah. Lamb is fine."

"Stay here," Elara said with alarming gravitas and a withering look that left Fia feeling chided. She was gone only a few minutes and Fia waited on the side of the road, trying not to notice all the Unseelie double taking when they noticed her.

Elara handed her a sandwich wrapped in paper and she peeled it back slowly, enjoying the warmth of it in her hands. Her stomach growled. How many hours had passed since dinner. She took a bite, the meat was perfectly spiced, the cheese sharp, and the bread soft. It was delicious. "Wow."

Elara smiled. One of her cuspids was slightly longer than the other. "I was hoping Rachelle would be selling today." She sat on the curb and Fia did the same. What a strange queen Elara was, buying food from stalls and sitting on the side of the road, travelling unaccompanied.

When they were done, Elara helped her up once more. At the touch of her hand the magic that bound them perked up, alarming Fia for a moment. How did one get used to magic being inside them after a lifetime without it?

"What clothes do you prefer? Dresses, pants? A little of both?" Elara asked.

“I don’t know what faeries wear,” Fia admitted. She’d had one day in Daonith, a day where she’d been forced into evening wear and then kidnapped.

“Well, you aren’t a faerie, so what do you *like* to wear?”

“I know, but your clothes are different. I mean...I don’t know. What do you like?”

Irritation pulled at Elara’s features, then she laughed, but did not respond, only looked at Fia as though she were a child behaving erratically.

There was a lot Fia could put up with, but she hated being patronized. “So, if I just up and dragged you to the human world and you had no idea what the temperature was going to be like, or what activities you’d be partaking in, you’d just be able to walk into the mall and pick out a whole wardrobe?”

Another moment passed before Elara responded. “I suppose not. I think pants will be best. And the temperature should remain much the same for a few more weeks. If you are here longer, we can buy you clothes for winter.”

“Thank you.”

Elara led Fia into the shop of a woman with bark-like skin. She looked up at their arrival and her eyes went wide. “Oh!” Her hands flew to cover her mouth. “Elara! How unexpected.”

Then her eyes caught on Fia, and several emotions vied for control of her face.

"It is good to see you again, Trillia. As I indicated in my letters, please use discretion. Fia will need a full wardrobe for the season, and you can take it out of my account."

Though it should have hit her sooner, Fia realized that Elara planned to keep her for a while. And she wanted discretion. She wasn't being ransomed, and the king's daughter was in on the plot. So why was she here? Would she ever leave? And though she was afraid, though she longed for her freedom, she had not been with the prince long enough to long for him. She had never wanted him. Part of her wondered if this might be a small reprieve. At least she would not be married off like a frightened debutant.

Looking around the shop, filled with both beautiful and practical clothes, Fia was filled with wonder and apprehension. What did she want? Did it even matter?

Trillia walked towards Fia. "Why don't you pick a few pieces that speak to you. Once I see what moves you, I can grab a few more."

"Okay," Fia nodded, feeling Elara's eyes on her as she took a step towards the rack of clothes, but before she could reach them the door opened again, making a small bell ring.

Aurora stood in the doorway, looking a bit out of breath. "Elara, the word you were waiting for just arrived. May I speak to you for a moment...possibly longer." She glanced over at Fia. "Those are lovely pants. I own a few pairs."

"Fia, can you make it home on your own after this? Do you remember the way?"

Home on her own? Elara had kidnapped her the day before and she was leaving her alone to go shopping? Again, Fia was thrown off balance, unable to understand her situation or how she was supposed to behave. Prisoner or guest?

"I believe I can make it," Fia said. What else was there to say? She certainly wasn't going to argue for more confinement.

"Will you help if she needs pointing in the right direction?" Elara asked Trillia, though it was clear it was no real question.

"Of course. She is in good hands."

Elara fixed Fia with a stare, the silver rings of her eyes seeming to flame. "You will not leave." She took a step closer, then another. Her breath brushed across Fia's face. "Understood."

Fia gulped. She could smell her again, the scent that seemed so familiar, warm yet sharp, but she still could not place. For a moment she thought Elara would put her hand on her and she almost pulled away, picturing that hand with a knife, that hand on her skin. "I will not leave."

"Good." She turned, her long hair swaying behind her and Aurora followed, sparing only a moment to smile, in what she must have thought was a reassuring way, at Fia.

An hour later, Fia stood in the street, wearing new clothes, a small parcel tucked under her arm, wondering if she should have insisted on taking all her bags with her, but Trillia had promised she would send them first thing in the morning. Would Elara be angry when she showed up nearly empty-handed?

Aurora had been right, the pants were great, soft and fitted at the waist, loose at the bottom, and just the right length, brushing against the top of her shoe without hitting the ground. They'd been a bit long but Trillia had altered them with a needle, about thirty seconds of pinning and a pop of greenish, smoky magic.

A breeze blew through the village, rustling the ample leaves and whistling across the roofs of the shops. The Village of Frost was not as overrun with greenery as Soleil but still had more than any human town Fia had ever been in. Moss and low foliage grew atop the roofs of houses, branches hung low at the edges of the streets, some of them heavy with climbing children, and vines seemed to creep up every surface.

Fia had the strongest urge to wander, to see more of the town, but she was so worn down from the last day and a half. Exhausted and confused and the sun would set soon. A very human part of her did not want to be alone in this strange world after dark.

Was it really only yesterday she had been promised to the prince? She'd woken up in her bed at the crack of dawn, driven for hours with her father, and everything had changed.

And then it had changed again, with another early wakeup. Fia started walking in the direction of Elara's house. No wonder she was not as frightened as she knew she should be. She'd hardly had time to make sense of anything. Each moment had been full. She'd gotten maybe four hours of sleep the night before and not much more than that the previous night.

Perhaps tomorrow she would wake up and be downright terrified. Maybe she would scream and throw things and see exactly what would happen if she ran.

But she would not. Of course she would not. She had watched Elara kill a man and she believed her when she said she would turn that violence on Fia. And besides where would she go?

Back to the prince? Unlikely she would make it. She turned onto the road she was pretty sure was the correct one and shifted the package under her arm. Was the prince even a better option than Elara and Aurora? He had seemed kind, but she didn't know him. He was handsome, sure, but Fia did not want him, not in any real way, not the way the other girls kneeling on the floor had.

In a way, Elara had saved her from a life that seemed perverse. Though she did not agree with the entire premise of the Joining, Callum had not had any more choice than she did. Without the scheming of their fathers, he could have had a wife who wanted him, who would be excited to marry him.

Fia stayed lost in her thoughts, thinking more than she had in so long—in the human world there were so many ways to fill one's mind to prevent unnecessary thinking—until the cottage came into view.

Just in time. The sun had disappeared behind the mountains and whatever issues she had with her kidnapping, she'd prefer to sleep in a bed tonight. Sleep and hopefully not be awoken at knife point. In fact, if Callum was planning a rescue, she hoped he at least waited until the sun was back up.

Candlelight danced in the windows of the small cottage and Fia hesitated. Should she knock? That seemed strange, so she pushed the door open, shutting it softly behind her, but the cottage was quiet. She called Elara's name, then Aurora's, but there was no answer.

So, she headed up to her bedroom to find a note stuck on the door. She pulled it off and read it. "Urgent Business. Will be home soon. Get some rest."

Her room was as peaceful as the rest of the house, golden in the dancing light of a small fire in the hearth. The quilt atop her bed was pulled back, the mattress soft and inviting. She was so tired. She stripped off her clothes and crawled into the impossibly soft sheets.

The room was nothing like her own, in fact it looked like someone's grandma had decorated it several decades ago, but it was warm and cozy and despite all the thoughts that had kept her company on the walk back, it was not long at all before Fia fell asleep.

-CHAPTER-
-EIGHT-

THE NEXT MORNING, Fia awoke to the sounds of cooking and the smell of sausage frying. She stretched her hands above her head and for a moment tried to make sense of the previous two days. But there was no making sense of it, and as far as she could tell, no escaping, at least not until she understood the faerie world better. So, she would get on with the morning, learn what she needed to learn, and then, when she knew more, she would decide what to do.

She pulled on a robe someone had left hanging on the back of the door, the fabric butter soft over her body, and made her way to the kitchen. Elara stood in front of a stove that Fia suspected ran mostly on magic, and from the smell, gas. Her body swayed, dancing to some silent music in her own mind, one bare foot keeping time on the wooden floor.

It was odd, King Ellio had called Elara a queen, but she didn't seem like one, at least not any queen Fia had heard of. Here she was in a tiny cottage, in a small village, cooking her own food. She had no servants, wore no crown. Again, nothing made sense.

"Morning," Fia said to announce her presence and Elara turned. Her horns shone in the early morning sun streaming through the window, her hair was slightly mussed, and despite her sharp, inhuman features there was something very human about her in the moment, a frying pan in her hand, sleep still at the corners of her eyes.

"Morning. I trust you slept well," she said, moving sausage from the pan to plates. "I apologize for leaving you alone yesterday."

Fia stopped herself from snorting, but there was something amusing about her kidnapper apologizing for leaving her alone. "It's fine," she said instead. "Can I?" She motioned to the carafe of what she believed to be coffee on the counter.

"Of course. Help yourself. Sorry, I don't have any hot. I prefer it cold, though at this point I'm not sure if it's a true preference or just the remainder of my childish desire to upset my uncle." She smiled at some memory. "Do you want food?"

How strange. Of all the things she would have expected to find in Daonith iced coffee had not been among them. "Please," Fia said, and the queen pushed a glass off ice across the counter at her. She poured the coffee and slid into one of the seats at the table, where the so-called queen served her a breakfast of sausage, eggs and toast, before sitting beside her.

"The woman at the shop said she would send my things."

"Yes, they arrived this morning. I left them near the door. We will be having visitors soon and there are some things I must explain to you."

Fia made a noncommittal noise, waiting for Elara to continue but she didn't. Whatever she intended to explain she clearly did not mean to explain it at that moment. There were so many questions in Fia's head begging for release, but she pushed them away for one she thought unlikely to upset Elara, who clearly took great pride in the small Village of Frost. "Will the visitor arrive today? I was hoping for another walk. It is so beautiful here and I'd like to see more." Plan her escape, yes, but in truth she did want to see more. She wanted to climb the mountains, and follow the stream that ran beside the road, explore every shop, and meet every strange Unseelie, all of whom had been nothing but pleasant since she had arrived.

"No, not today. They should arrive in three days," Elara said, skewering a sausage with her fork. She chewed slowly, looking Fia over. She opened her mouth, as if to say something, but at that moment Aurora made her way into the kitchen.

Her golden hair was pulled back from her face, and she rubbed at her red-rimmed eyes. "I slept like shit."

"Good morning, Aurora," Elara said. "I was informing Fia that we will have guests arriving soon."

"Where will they stay?" Fia asked before she could stop herself.

"There is an inn," Aurora said, pouring her own cup of iced coffee. "Hopefully Ezriel finds it to his standards." She sat at the small table with them, regarding Fia over her cup. "Do you really think she won't run?"

Elara shot her a look. "No, I do not believe she will. Will you, Fia?"

Fia took a sip of coffee to buy herself time. "I wouldn't even know the way." She kept her voice low and even, though she wanted to scream. But screaming would get her nowhere except possibly in a worse position than she was in now. What she wanted was answers. Desperately she wanted to understand the situation she was in. There could be no plan until she understood exactly what was going on. No point in running if she would only run to something worse.

"I believe I will take her up to the pass today, perhaps a bit higher," Elara said. "Out of earshot." She took another bite of her breakfast. "If you would not mind handling everything else."

Aurora looked between the two of them, clearly thinking things through. "If you think that wise."

Irritation flashed across Elara's face. "Obviously I do. Have you thought of something better since last night?"

Aurora put her fork down, royal indignation running across her features, and Fia wondered how the two of them came to work together. What had driven Aurora to turn against her father and help the Unseelie Queen when it appeared the two of them could barely get along? Another curiosity to add to her list. But then the princess's features softened and Fia wondered if any of her judgements were correct. "Elara...I do not mean..."

"No, I know," Elara said. "But I ask that you trust me."

"I do," Aurora said, picking her fork back up and the tension in the room broke. "You know I do. But trust is not understanding."

Fia shoveled eggs into her mouth, hoping the two women would forget she was there, though, of course, they would not.

"You will understand in time." Elara glanced towards Fia before turning her attention back to Aurora. It was clear from her visage that she had more she wanted to say. A moment passed, the only sound a rooster crowing somewhere nearby. "The secret I keep is not one of importance to you, Aurora, though it impresses me how quickly you knew I kept it."

"I have always understood you, Elara. If I did not, I would not have given up so much to be here." Aurora sighed, stifling the yawn it turned into.

"We understand each other, but you will drop this. I do not wish to hear of it again," Elara said, standing from the table and taking only her cup of coffee with her. "Your sacrifices are appreciated, but I am the Queen of these people, and you have pledged your allegiance to me."

Aurora's fingers tightened around her fork, her knuckles turning white. "There is no need—"

Elara cut her off. "Fia, we will take a walk later, a hike really. Dress appropriately and meet me at the front door in an hour." She looked down at Aurora. "Everything will go well."

Aurora's voice was clipped. "Of course."

Once Elara had left, Aurora loosened her grip and her fork clattered to the plate. She dropped her head to her hands, tugging at the roots of her hair then looked up, her face weary. "My intention was never to put you in danger, Fia."

What was there to say? What response could fit such a stupid statement? What words could possibly pass Fia's lips that would not anger the fae nor sound so hollow they might as well not be uttered at all? So, she nodded.

"This is a better place," Aurora continued. "Better than the one we left."

"You said your brother was a good man," Fia said, because she could not help herself.

"I believe he is. But a good third son does not fix a broken kingdom. You are good, are you not? And yet your father is still a danger. An arms dealer, I believe, among other things the humans would call him. Few of them kind, I dare say."

The words were blunt. Fia didn't think anyone had ever said them to her before. Certainly not when she was small and everyone pretended he was something he was not, that she was a normal girl, with a normal life. Certainly no one had dared speak ill of her father after her mother had killed herself and all she had left was that dangerous man. "Am I good?" Fia muttered.

Aurora chuckled. "I lay in bed and ask myself that same question. I hope you find your answers sooner than I do."

Fia regarded the faerie in a new light. Had she meant all the words of friendship she had uttered? Was Aurora her best chance of returning to the human world, of freeing herself from a brewing faerie war she did not understand yet found herself in the middle of?

An hour and a half later, and Fia was out of the village, making her way up an inclined dirt path that wound its way up one of the many snowcapped mountains that surrounded the Village of Frost.

Elara had said little, though she kept glancing at Fia, and Fia had found it hard to pull her eyes away from Elara either. She could not read the strange Unseelie woman, but she wanted to.

Desperately she wanted to understand her motivations, to know why she had been kidnapped her, what she had argued so elusively with Aurora about, to understand her mind. She did not quite know why—for all the obvious reasons, of course—but there was something else, some need to know that she did not dare peel back and find the reason for.

A tree had fallen over the path, recently judging by its still green leaves, and Elara's brow furrowed as they came to it. Again, she looked at Fia, contemplating something, then with a sweep of her hand the tree—the entire tree—flew off the path and crashed into the forest beyond.

Fia's heart skipped a beat. Her throat grew too dry to swallow the lump that had emerged. Faerie magic. She knew of it, of course she knew of it, but she had not seen it, the power of it. She dug her fingers into her palms, reality breaking through the lies she had been telling herself since she had been taken. She would never escape.

"You are pale," Elara said, continuing on their hike.

"You're strong," Fia said. There was no reason to deny it. She knew the truth was written on her face.

Elara smirked. "You would do well to remember."

"So you said." Fia's legs were already beginning to protest but she would not allow Elara to know. She would make it to the top of this hike if it killed her. She had to know why she was here.

“So, dearest human, what do you know of the faerie king?” Elara asked. There was a knife strapped to her leg and Fia wondered why it was there. If she could throw a tree with a wave of her hand what use would a knife be?

“Little,” Fia said, hating to admit it, hating how foolish it made her sound. The idiot human who had knelt on that stupid stone floor without a thought given to the bargain she was agreeing to. “My father promised, or at least insinuated, that it would not be me. I was stupid enough to believe him.”

“There is hardly stupidity in believing your own father would not trade you away,” Elara said, her voice full of sympathy, so foreign to Fia she wanted to shy away from it.

“You clearly don’t know my father.”

“No, I think it best I don’t.” All of the sympathy left her voice, now sharp and biting. “Do you know any details of the deal he made with the king?”

“The deal for me? I guess I know now.” The path narrowed, trees closing around them, blocking the sun and throwing them into shadows. It seemed to Fia that the air grew colder with each step, and she was thankful for whatever faerie craftsmanship made her thin clothes so warm.

“No, not to sell you, though that was undoubtedly part of it. Do you know of the...the guns.” Elara said the last word like it was foul.

“Guns?” Something tightened in Fia’s chest. She knew the kinds of trade he dealt in, what provided the money for all the things she’d been too vain to give up. But she had no idea it was at a level that he could trade with the faerie king. Surely, he needed more than a few guns. Who was providing her father with enough ammunition to supply what must be an army?

“Rest with me,” Elara said, gesturing to another fallen tree at the edge of the trail. The break was clearly for Fia’s sake, but she was glad for it. She had always tried to stay in shape, but hiking up a mountain was foreign to her body.

She sat beside the Unseelie Queen and took the water she offered. “I didn’t know anything about it. I swear it.” Was that why she had been taken? Was it retribution for her father? She had always worried she might end up hurt as punishment for him, but never had her fantasies included kidnapping by faeries.

Elara cast her eyes to the sky for a moment, thinking. “When humans first invented guns they meant little to the faeries, held no interest for us. What use could we have for such primitive weapons? But their power increased, and there are more than guns now, though I admit I know little about it, but I know you have weapons that explode greater than any of our power, that can kill great numbers in an instant. Until recently I did not worry about their use here. Despite his many, many flaws, Ellio's grandfather banned them." She glanced at Fia, giving her a chance to speak.

But she had nothing to say. "I didn't know," she repeated like an ignorant schoolchild.

"Do not blame yourself. You were not taught because more powerful people did not want you to know. That is their fault not your own."

"Why are you being so nice to me?" Fia asked.

Elara smiled, but it only made her sharp features sharper. "Maybe I will get to those reasons eventually, but for now I will continue your lessons on Daonith." She turned, straddling the log. "The only place to trade between the humans and fae is in the borderlands, the seas of my northern kingdom are too treacherous to sail for most of the year and dangerous even in the summer. Ellio's grandfather controlled the borderlands, as the Southern Court still controls all trade, so his ban was absolute. He believed keeping our lands free of human weapons was for the best of all of us. He wanted the fae to continue to keep out of any human conflicts, of which we have never participated. No one argued, there was little reason. His son was not as steadfast as he was, but his reign was short. Then Ellio became king, and I suspect you can guess the rest."

"He wanted those powerful human weapons?" Fia stretched out a leg and rubbed her hand down it, massaging her muscles.

Elara watched her a moment before dragging her eyes away. "Yes, though few know. But I learned the truth. And he has his ways, which I will explain eventually, that he uses to keep my people less powerful than him, but not powerless enough that he has risked war with us, though I know he desires it. Now he wishes to increase his own power again. And what a lovely way to keep your father's silence, with his only daughter held in his land, now beloved by humans, giving your father an increase in his own social worth, no doubt."

"He does not care enough about me to buy his silence if a better offer comes along."

"Perhaps he does not. But the king believes he cares if you live or die and whatever you or I believe on this front, women have been traded in marriage throughout time, in the human lands and the Seelie." Elara stood.

"Not in yours?" Fia took one last drink of water before handing it back to Elara.

"No. The Seelie—especially the Southern Kingdom—and the humans have much of their cruelty in common. My people...we are not like that. We..." Elara cleared her throat, and her voice was even softer than when she had offered Fia her sympathy. There was pride and love obvious in every syllable. That was a piece of the puzzle, the Unseelie Queen loved her people. "We believe in each other in my lands, we help each other. We are a community. That is our biggest belief and our greatest strength."

Though she knew she was speaking to her kidnapper, her tormenter, Fia could not help but be touched. "That is a beautiful sentiment."

Elara stood, dusting off her legs and swinging her rucksack onto her back. "The next part is a bit grueling. Tell me if you need another break."

And it was. Despite Fia's best efforts, Elara kept gaining ground on her. Several times Elara had to stop when she tried to speak to Fia and realized she wasn't there. But then they would lapse into silence again and Elara would increase her pace, or maybe Fia's was just slowing, and the distance between them would increase again.

The sixth time Fia found herself falling behind, moving her legs only through sheer willpower, she opened her mouth to call out to Elara and tell her she needed another break.

She did not get a chance.

A hand found her mouth, covering it, as another grabbed her waist, pulling her off balance in an instant.

- CHAPTER-
-NINE -

THE ASSAILANT PULLED at her, dragging her towards the edge of the woods.

Not again. She'd had enough of being kidnapped.

Fia bucked against them, digging her nails into the hand at her mouth, trying to plant her feet into the ground, but getting nowhere. Whoever held her was too strong for her to fight and her already tired muscles were useless. Abandoning her attempt to remove the hand over her mouth she grabbed handfuls of the saplings and bushes at the edge of the path, skin ripping with the effort to hold on.

A flash of light and the smell of earth.

The world around her exploded. Whoever held her was flung back and Fia fell to the ground, throwing her hands over her head to protect herself from the explosion.

But the chaos was not a bomb, it was magic and none of it touched her. Breathing heavily, she blinked against the bright, purple-tinged magic that lit the woods around them like a firework.

Elara was standing over the man who had attacked her—a Seelie man—her magic like shards of glass, plunged into his arms, his legs, holding him to the ground. And her face. Fia was not sure she had ever seen such rage contained in one person. Such rage and such power, so much it warmed the cold air around them and lit Elara from the inside.

"How dare you come into my village and try to steal from me?" Elara roared.

Fia stood as the man answered, his voice shaking, breathless from pain. Blood flowed from his wounds, soaking into the packed earth beneath him. "You stole from the king. A pretty penny to return her, one might think."

"Worth more than your life?" Elara took another step closer, all angles and horns. But she waved her hand, and the magic changed, no longer spearing the man but caging him.

He pushed himself off the ground, wincing with every movement, but there was nowhere for him to go, even if his injured limbs would hold him. He was trapped beneath a glimmering web of magic. "You will regret this, dirty Un—" His words were drowned in his scream as his body flew into the air then slammed into the ground.

Fia did not think he would move again, only knew he was alive from the gentle rise of his chest, and she didn't dare move, waiting for his breathing to stop as blood trickled from the side of his mouth.

A crack like a whip sounded and a man appeared. Fia screamed, lunging without thinking towards Elara. The Queen grabbed her, pulling her to her chest. "You are okay," she whispered into Fia's hair, "He is a friend."

The friend was tall and muscled, with skin like birch bark and hair as black as night. He looked down at the bleeding man and then at Elara. "I saw your magic, thought you might need help."

"I appreciate you coming, Kalin. This is Fia."

With a jolt, Fia moved away from Elara, out of the warmth of her arms. Her stomach rolled as the stench of the faerie's blood met her nose. Another body to add to her list.

Kalin looked at the man like someone might look at a dog who had tracked mud all over white carpet. "I can...dispose of him. He does not have long. Not much of a fighter?"

"I did not allow him a chance to show me one way or the other. Foolish either way. I do not believe the king sent him, though if he does not die, I would like to know how he found us."

Kalin inclined his head. "I can keep him alive long enough." He glanced at Fia. "I apologize for frightening you. You must have had enough of that lately. Are you well?"

Was she well? Hysterical laughter escaped her lips before she could stop it, and she was not sure she would be able to regain her composure until Elara's hand tightened around her wrist. "I'm sorry," Fia choked out, choked just as the man on the ground was choking, trying to take his last breaths around a mouth full of blood. "I just..."

But Kalin was smiling, or at the least smirking, it was hard to tell on such a foreign face. "No, a stupid question. Well, I am sorry your hike was interrupted. Elara, I will take care of it and check back when I have answers."

"Thank you, Kalin. Truly."

Again, the large Unseelie inclined his head and then bent low, scooping up the Seelie man as though he weighed nothing and with another crack he was gone, leaving only the bloodstained ground behind.

“Are you okay?” Elara asked, looking Fia over. “Did he hurt you in any way?”

“No.” Fia shook her head. “I am...I do not want to...I don’t think I can...” She looked again at the ground and Elara understood. As easily as Kalin had moments earlier, Elara scooped Fia into her arms. “Do not be afraid,” she whispered and before Fia had time to contemplate they were engulfed in darkness, wind whipped around them, its howl the only sound she could hear. Then they reappeared into the light of the day.

Daonith spread before them, the sun seemed closer, glinting off Elara’s horns. Gently, she placed Fia back on the ground and snow crunched under her feet. She had taken her to the top of the mountain.

Far below she could make out the Village of Frost, nestled between mountains, spanning as far as Fia could see, their wildness punctuated only by occasional wooden houses, smoking billowing out of the chimneys.

“I did not know you could...teleport?” Was that the word they used? It hardly seemed important.

“You barely know me at all,” Elara said softly. “I can do many things, especially here.”

Fia made her way to a piece of jutting rock and sat, her feet dangling off the mountain and Elara made a small noise, but Fia had never been afraid of heights, and she did not think Elara would let her die. Perhaps a foolish thought, but she believed it. Somehow Elara would stop her descent.

Elara sat beside her. "I would not have brought you here if I thought...I did not think they would find my village so soon."

Fia glanced at her, the beautiful Unseelie Queen who would murder in a heartbeat, who had threatened her, who had saved her, who had kidnapped her, who loved her people and this land. Who was she? Dangerous. So dangerous and Fia promised herself she would not forget that, even when it was so easy to do. "They will look for me though, won't they?"

"Yes."

Did she want the Seelie to find her? Did she wish her assailant had taken her away and returned her to Soleil and the King and her arranged marriage? She did not know if she wanted to be with Callum any more than she wanted to be here. "I didn't want any of this."

"We rarely get to choose."

"You made sure of that."

Anger flashed across Elara's face. Already Fia had forgotten, or maybe she had not. Maybe she wanted to prove to herself that Elara was not a danger to her, because if she didn't...if she didn't how would she sleep at night after everything she had seen? How would she breathe? "You will find no regrets in me for taking you, Fia. I have told you I want trust between us, so do not ask me to lie, or offer apologies I do not mean."

A thought, perhaps brought on by whatever had brought on her previous hysteria, occurred to her and a smile pulled at her mouth. "You should be glad it was me and not any of the other girls who might have been selected for the Joining. They would have fainted."

Elara smiled though she quickly composed herself. "You did throw yourself at me with quite a shriek." Her face grew more solemn. "You will find..." She sighed and brushed a strand of hair behind her ear, expertly avoiding her horns. "You will find the awful things you see grow easier. That you can live with them, somehow, each day."

"I do not want to live with them," Fia whispered. "I told you, I do not want this. I do not want to see death." She never had. Not in the human lands and not in the fae, but wherever she went death seemed to follow Fia, tainting her childhood, taking her mother, courting her father.

"Then stop joking about those other girls, Fia, because you have come at the precipice of a war, a war whose weapons your father hopes to supply. So, as I said, you will learn to live with it." Elara stood up. "Take a moment, I'll bring you home when you are ready. I only wanted you to see the view."

- CHAPTER-
-TEN -

THE COTTAGE WAS quiet. Elara had left after breakfast on some business she had refused to give Fia any details about and Aurora was curled up in one of the chairs reading but Fia couldn't sit still.

She'd slept terribly the night before, nightmares of being grabbed, of bleeding men and slit throats. Yet when she'd woken, she'd heard Elara's voice and something had calmed. But the question of why still nagged at her. Why was she here? Why did she feel as if the magic Elara had planted inside her chest with a drop of blood grew each day? Why had her father sold her? Enough questions to drive her insane.

"I need to get out of the house."

Aurora looked up from her book, her hair gilded in the morning sun. "Go, then. Buy something. You know the way to the village."

Fia frowned, and knew she shouldn't say the next words, should just take Aurora's offer, but she couldn't help herself. "Someone tried to kidnap me yesterday."

"A normal day for you," Aurora grinned and shut the book, not even bothering to look ashamed when Fia glared at her. "A fluke. Kalin gave a report this morning before you woke up. He was just a trader. We were able to confirm it. He saw a human with the Queen and assumed you were the stolen princess, thought he might get a reward. And now he is dead, and no one knows we're here. He was not sent by my father."

"Does it bother you? The killing."

The grin faded from Aurora's beautiful face, her lips thinned, and her eyes were far away for a moment. "No, Fia. Maybe it should, maybe long ago it would have. But I have seen death. I have seen countless death, deaths of people who did not deserve it. I have mourned at the graves of good people and cried alone for those I could not be seen mourning. I *know* death. So no, the guard, the trader who wanted to sell you, their deaths do not bother me."

She stepped closer and perhaps she was as dangerous as Elara. She looked it at that moment, razor sharp and ready to strike. "And you know death too, perhaps not as intimately as me, but you know it, Fia. Oh, I could have wept when I met you, because you and I are the same, daughters of cruel men, hardened but not cruel yet. Shallow and vain but sometimes dreaming of better. So, tell me, besides your own fear, does their death bother you either?"

Fia gulped. Did they? How many deaths had she known over the years? She had never stopped a single one. Never even tried beyond the barest of whispers. "I did not..."

The ferocity in Aurora's face faded. "Fia, this is war. Will you be the prize or the weapon?"

Her blood ran cold. The morning sun seemed to dim, but Fia lifted her chin, so tired, so damn tired of being afraid. "You did not take me just to upset the king or to upset my father. You took me for a reason. What is it?"

Aurora looked down at her, appraising, every inch the princess— golden hair, full lips, the ever-playful glint of her blue eyes. But she certainly was not a prize, Aurora was a weapon, one her father had not known was in his arsenal and she had slipped from his grasp just as much as Fia. "Elara has asked me to let her explain, but no, we did not take you to upset my father. We took you because we need a human and you were our first chance in a long time."

Something roiled inside her, hot, ferocious. Fia grabbed her coat and headed for the door, knowing that Aurora would follow her. "Why not one of the other wives from the Joining? I believe the previous one is still alive."

Aurora followed, pushing the door open and allowing the sunlight to stream into the foyer before they stepped out. "Alive and old and very much still in love with her husband, who adores her. They were a good match, and she would not work with us. Nor did we want to kidnap an elderly woman."

Fia scoffed. "But a young one?"

"A young one with much at stake and fire in her veins even if she has not realized it yet. Plus, you aren't my darling aunt. So yes, you seemed a better option." Aurora sighed as they headed down the dirt road that led to the village. She nodded at a passing Unseelie. "What did you want to shop for?"

Fia stopped at a cluster of wildflowers, admiring their tiny spotted purple petals and taking a steadying breath, before continuing on. It was an effort not to wince or cower at each snap of a twig or far-away voice. "I don't know. I just needed to get out."

“You could use a good set of knives—or whatever weapon you prefer.”

Weapons. She thought of the guard, his slit throat, his flowing blood. She thought of her father. The men who worked for him, the sound of snapping bones. Her mother pale. How easily would she die? The guard had been trained. She was barely in shape. Inside her something pricked. She did not want to die without a fight, pathetic and weak. “Yes, I would like weapons.”

“You must promise not to stab me.”

Fia turned to look at Aurora, but there was a playful grin on her face. “Only if you promise to not do anything stab worthy.”

“We will be friends yet, Fia.” Aurora started to say more but a crack broke through the quiet morning, and it took everything in Fia not to scream or cower as Kalin appeared. She could do nothing about her racing heart. Even Aurora’s hands tightened at her sides. “Must you do that?”

He grinned wide, revealing broad, flat teeth. “You are only jealous.”

So, Aurora had no teleportation powers. Interesting. That must be why they had taken the carriage to the village, though Elara had moved Fia with her when they had been hiking. A short distance though. So curious.

"Hello, Fia," Kalin said, looking her over, seeming pleased when he saw nothing amiss. "I am glad to see you well."

She nodded. "And you." To her surprise, she realized it was true. She liked the strange, birch-skinned man.

He grinned again, his happy demeanor at odds with both his size and the fact that Fia knew he had tortured a man the previous day. "You live here?"

"I live wherever the queen asks me to, but I do like the village. It is one of our most beautiful locations." He jerked his chin towards the road, a silent acknowledgement that they could walk again, and he was apparently to join them.

There was so much to learn, and Fia did not know enough to even ask the right questions, but she did her best to tuck everything away in her mind. "You...work for her then?"

Pride filled Kalin's rough-hewn features. "Yes. An honor. My father and hers were very close. There were no two prouder fathers."

Aurora gave a slight roll of her eyes but clapped Kalin on the back. "Keep it together, big guy."

He sent a half-hearted glare at her, but Fia barely noticed. More and more questions rolled into her mind. While she had a passing knowledge of the Seelie, she knew nothing of the Unseelie. She hadn't even known they existed, which seemed like such an oversight it had to be deliberate. Though if they were hiding or being hidden, she did not know. "In your lands the crown does not pass through the sons?"

The humor left Kalin's face just as they came into the village proper, a row of small cottages with unruly gardens greeted them. "No, though it sometimes passes through families, but that is not required, just how it often works. Our kings step down when they are no longer able to do the job to the best of their ability and then we decide on a new ruler amongst ourselves."

A democracy? Or something close to it. Yet the title remained. Perhaps because of the longevity of their rule, or just a difference from the human world. She merely nodded.

"We are going to buy Fia weapons. She has none of her own." Aurora appraised her just as Kalin had done. "She will need training."

Elara's words in the carriage played through Fia's head, her promise to train her so her father could not hurt her again. Something had changed in that moment, her fear of the Unseelie turning into something less sharp.

"I would be honored to help," Kalin said. "Let me go with you to find a weapon that speaks to you. So many people are drawn to the largest one, but it will do you no good if you cannot wield it."

Again, something inside Fia's chest flickered, reminding her of the bond between herself and Elara, but this was different, brighter. Hope? No, but she felt purpose for perhaps the first time in her life.

But that was wishful thinking. Training would not be a purpose and what good would she do really? Even if she wanted to help these people, in whatever way they might need help—which she was not sure she wanted to do—her training would not amount to the power of the fae. It would not stop weapons or blasts of magic.

Still, knowing how to wield a weapon could be useful for whatever happened next in her life. It would be better than not knowing. It would be better to be strong. "The honor would be all mine," she said to Kalin. Whoever he was, whatever his allegiances, it was clear from the size and shape of him that he was a warrior. So was Elara. And Fia intended to learn their tricks.

An hour later she marveled at the weight of the dagger strapped to her leg. It was a beautiful thing, the delicately carved marble handle inlaid with sapphires, the blade long, sharp and shining. She had picked out a sword as well, thin with a sturdy handle, but despite its small size compared to some of the other options, she had still struggled to hold it up and could not imagine doing so for any length of time.

Kalin had noticed as well. He walked close to her as they made their way to one of the restaurants in the village. "Training will be useless until you put some muscle on. We can do some work with the dagger, but your main goal should be strength training."

Her eyes went to his arms—with their coloring they were truly like the trunks of trees. He was huge, putting even the largest human men to shame. "Will it really matter? Against magic?" she asked.

Kalin looked her over, assessing. "You saw Elara's magic, but do not assume all fae have that. Some, yes. We all have the gift of magic, but what she can do is spectacular, usually reserved for the ruling Seelie who have bred it into their lines." He glanced at Aurora who only shrugged. "And magic is not infinite. When the well runs dry it is good to know how to fight."

"Oh," was all Fia could say.

"I can teach you more," Kalin said. "But only over food. I am starving." He rubbed his muscled abdomen. "Unless you need to be back."

Aurora shook her head. "We can eat."

Kalin led them to a small stone building where the best smells Fia had ever encountered wafted out. The food turned out to be even better than the smells, slow roasted meat in savory sauce, tender potatoes perfectly spiced, and endless desserts. She ate more than she ever had in her life until her stomach ached in protest.

When they finally left, Kalin now rubbing his stomach in a satisfied way, Fia was grateful for the walk home. If she sat still any longer, she was sure she would fall asleep.

Kalin walked them to the cottage, making Fia promise three times that she would train with him starting tomorrow, already giving her names of stretches to try before bed that night. In her current state she could barely contemplate touching her toes, but she agreed.

And though she was kidnapped, though she had nearly been kidnapped again the day before, as she fell asleep that night, she found herself looking forward to the next day.

-CHAPTER-
-ELEVEN -

HER EXCITEMENT FROM the night before was hard to maintain as Kalin made her do the same moves again and again, refusing to let her so much as look at her weapons until she'd learned to control her body. She was sure he was right, but doing squats wasn't nearly as exciting as she imagined learning to swordfight would be.

By the time the sun was halfway across the sky, every muscle in her body ached and she wasn't sure she was going to be able to climb the stairs to her room, much less do a push up. Kalin made her personal trainers back in the human world look like amateurs.

Finally, when Fia was fully drenched in sweat that dripped into her eyes and pooled in the curve of her spine, Kalin decided she'd had enough. He looked her over, an easy smile on his face. “You did very good. Better than I thought you would.”

“I’ll try to take that as a compliment.” Fia rubbed her shoulder, but the ache was good, proof of her work.

“It *is* a compliment,” he said. “I have seen faeries give up after less. You will learn quickly if you are still interested after today.”

Fia took a moment to think it over, what the past week had held for her, what the future was likely to hold, the inevitable war that brewed all around her. “Yes, I want to learn.” Plus, she was going to be in the best shape of her life, not an entirely important detail, but she wouldn’t complain about it either.

“Then I will see you tomorrow. And the next day. Whenever Elara does not have need of you.” He gave her a nod and then with a crack he was gone. Her heart jolted. Would she ever get used to that?

Fia slumped into a stuffed chair in the garden where they had been training. She turned her face towards the sky and shut her eyes, letting the sun warm her face while her breathing and heart rate slowed. Her muscles ached deliciously, and she rolled her neck from side to side.

A breeze blew through the garden, whipping up the scent of the flowers...and something else. An unknown scent that gripped her heart like a vital memory she could not recall. Something fierce and unnamed coiled tight inside of her.

She opened her eyes as Elara walked into the garden. She wore wide black pants and a gauzy top that ended a few inches above the pants, leaving a swath of her skin bare. Her silvery-purple hair was loose, falling down her back in gentle waves.

She sat across from Fia, propping her bare feet up on the short table between them. "You surprise me."

Fia shot her a quizzical look, remembering all the magic that lurked beneath her unblemished skin. "You have not yet ceased to surprise me."

Elara chuckled, low and lethal. "I suppose not. But you train impressively. Kalin is...he is a driven man, and he expects it of others. You could certainly learn in an easier way."

"No one else offered."

"I believe I did, though I *have* been preoccupied," Elara said, stretching her arms above her head, her shirt rising higher, revealing more skin.

"With the king who is coming?" Fia did her best to remember. She'd learned so much in the past few days. "Ezriel."

Elara smiled. "Yes, and his wife, Vinessa." She looked around, waved a hand, and the world went still. No, not still. Muted.

She'd put some sort of shield around them, a bubble of shimmering, iridescent purple surrounded the garden, blocking the noises of the outside world.

Fia shivered, as though the shield blocked out the sun too, though it warmed her skin just as it had before. But no birdsong, no wind, nothing. The queen was powerful. Full of wild magic.

All that power and Fia had none. She wished she did, wished for something other than steel to protect her in Daonith because she knew that no matter how much she trained it would not be enough, no matter what Kalin said about steel being there when magic failed. Their power might fail but Fia would never have any in the first place.

And she wanted it. Desperately. She wanted magic in the way she wanted air. She had not realized how badly until that moment, until it surrounded her and thoughts of war entered her head, of the decades she would live here, the least powerful thing this side of the mist.

She did not want to be a useful symbol. Something to be stolen again and again. No, she wanted magic. If only she could reach out and take it, rip and grab and claw it from her enemies until he became hers. Until it swarmed inside her like the bond between her and Elara, like the sense of danger and adrenaline and *want.* And then, at her fingers, so small she was not sure it was real, a dark strand, shimmering. There and then gone in the blink of an eye.

Fia looked at Elara and knew she had seen it too. Those brown and silver eyes were wide and trained on Fia, like a predator on prey, her breathing quick and uneven, mirroring Fia's own. Fia looked back to her fingers, but only for a moment, too afraid to take her eyes off the queen.

What had just happened. She looked again. Her hand was just a hand, but she could feel Elara's eyes on her. Deep inside her something rumbled. The bond between them went taut.

Elara lunged at her, dragging her up by her arm, pulling her close. "Did you know?" she demanded, her voice low.

"No," Fia breathed. "I don't... What is it? What am I?" Her throat was dry and it was hard to breathe.

Elara narrowed her eyes and the shield around them seemed to tighten, grow thicker. "A witch," she whispered. "Tell no one. Not until I can think." Her hand was still on Fia's arm, squeezing too tight, but Fia did not dare to pull away.

A witch. She turned the word over, but it meant nothing, nothing outside of books and movies. A witch was not real. There were humans, there were fae, there were occasional halflings, but never a witch. A witch was a fiction, occasionally written of in history books, but in the same manner as old gods or monsters in the depths of lakes. Something people believed in before they knew better. Fia could not be a witch.

But she had seen it. She had *felt* it. That black strand, like she'd pulled it from the very fabric of the universe, unthreaded it just a bit in her fear and longing, snatched it from the world. "What does it mean?"

Elara let her go and her arm dropped to her side, but neither woman moved back, so close they breathed each other's air. "A witch is..." Elara's head dipped low, her horns brushing against Fia, who still did not dare to move. "It is rare, Fia, so incredibly rare. Though who knows really, when so few humans come here, but none of the other wives, none that I know of." A muscle in her jaw tightened. "Witches are humans who can wield the magic."

"Wield it?" Fia tried to imagine wielding magic, tried to imagine waving a hand and creating a barrier as Elara had done, tried to imagine power exploding out of her.

As if she could read her face, Elara said, "No, not like the fae. It is...different, not entirely understood. Ezriel will know more, his people have some spell magic."

"Spell magic? Like from a spell book?" Fia's voice was strange to her ears, full of both fear and excitement. She could not contain a thought long enough to think this over, to understand how this would change her future. Her thoughts were only for this moment, when it felt like everything had changed, that she had changed. A witch. Would that dark stringy magic keep her safe?

"No, not a spell book. A witch can feel the threads that stitch the world together." Yes, that was exactly what she had felt, a thread. "You can undo magic, create your own, but only so far as you feel the threads, follow them and find what you need. Or take what you need. Come." Gently, as though she was now the dangerous thing, Elara took her hand.

Fia let her, following her as she led her to the large oak tree whose moss-covered branches hung over one corner of the garden, nearly brushing the ground. Elara placed Fia's hand upon the trunk. "Here. Focus on the tree. It is part of the Universe, the same as your or I. Can you feel its roots, the way they run into the earth?"

Fia closed her eyes, and for a whisper of a moment she thought she could. She could see the tree spreading out, roots like spider webs pushing through the earth, feeding from the soil. She could see the worms, their pink flesh wriggling. Hear the song of rain in the clouds, the way it would fall, plunk, plunk, plunk, back to the earth.

A whisper and it was gone. The thread snapped. A crack like thunder. Blinding pain in her head that nearly brought her to her knees. She only remained upright by Elara clutching her.

Fia's heart sank as the pain vanished. Whatever magic she had, controlling it might be impossible, harder than hours and hours with Kalin. All she had tried was to understand it and her head ached like she'd slammed it into something. To actually wield that magic?

Elara eased her to the ground and sat beside her, their backs against the oak. "I should not have asked. It was too soon, it is only..."

Fia understood the unspoken words. A war was coming, and Elara had hoped for a weapon. For a moment, Fia had as well. Stupidly she tried again, placing her hand upon the earth, trying to think of the thread she had summoned, the way she had felt connected.

A flicker. A brief glimpse of something she did not have time to understand before the earth seemed to swell and swallow her whole into its gaping maw.

She screamed out, gasping for air. If before had been a blow to her head, this was as though it had been split. She nearly vomited onto her feet and took deep, gasping breaths, digging her fingers into the cool soil, darkness swimming in her vision. Every muscle ached.

Tentatively, barely pressing down at all, Elara rubbed a circle on her back, snatching it away as soon as Fia looked in her direction. “Are you okay?” she asked.

Fia nodded. A lie, but she suspected she would survive if she did not try again.

For several minutes they sat side by side against the tree, neither of them speaking as Fia’s breathing returned to normal.

“If you do not know anything of magic, how did you summon it before? I saw it at your fingers.” Elara asked.

“Fear. Desire. A bit of both. I have no protection in this world and every need for it. I saw what you could do. “She gestured to the dome of magic that still surrounded them. “I was jealous of your power. No one can snatch you from your bed at night. I wanted to be able to protect myself.”

Elara nodded, darkness clouding her features. “Yes, I suppose that would make sense.” She shifted closer to Fia, their knees pressing together. “Listen to me Fia, I know you have no reason to trust me, I know I stole you away in the night, but whatever comes, whatever happens, do not let King Ellio know about this magic.”

"You think I will go back?" She was not sure she wanted to, not anymore.

The darkness faded slightly in her eyes. "It is a possibility. We will need to go to him again in the future. I came to tell you more about it."

She had, Fia realized. She'd shielded them to tell her things she did not want anyone to overhear. They'd been talking about Ezriel and his wife. And she knew she should still care, that she would as soon as her shock wore off, but those were not the questions burning at her. "Why can I not tell the king?"

"Because it has been a long time, centuries, since Daonith has seen a ruler as power hungry as Ellio. And what you have, it is rare, Fia, exceedingly rare. He will want it in his line, perhaps married to a son, but perhaps for himself."

Fia shuddered at her meaning. "He has a wife."

"And he has had others before."

Others. More than one. What had happened to them, those women who were supposed to be immortal, living for thousands of years? What would he do to Fia if he knew there was magic inside her? She did not want to find out. She raised her chin, meeting Elara's eyes, the silver outline around the brown center nearly glowing. "Did you take me to save me?"

Elara held her gaze, her breathing shallow. "I will not lie and say I did, I took you for my own means, but I hoped they might align with yours. I hoped you would understand. I do not wish to be a monster, but I will become one to protect my people. I will do whatever I need to do."

Keeping her shoulders straight took all of Fia's will, but this moment was important, she knew it even though she would have been unable to articulate exactly why, but the memory of that powerful thread still warmed her fingers, and she knew she needed to pick a side. Even if she lied to others, even if every waking moment was spent pretending, *she* needed to know what side she was on.

"Tell me everything you came to tell me."

Still, Elara held her gaze, and she looked like a queen, even in the garden, without a crown, in common clothes, there was a strength to her, a power that few could hope to emulate. "Before I do, you must believe my earlier words. I will do horrible things for my people. I *have* done horrible things. I am choosing to trust you because I must and because...." She paused, choosing her words. "Because you have given me no reason to not trust you, but if you break that trust you will hurt my people and that blood will be on your hands, but so will your own. If you break this trust, Fia Gray, I advise you to run, as quickly as your human legs will allow, back to your human home."

A chill ran down her spine and Fia swallowed the lump in her throat before she nodded.

A small smile spread across Elara's mouth, and she leaned back against the tree again, her long legs stretched in front of her. "Many years ago, magic flowed freely through this world. The mist between your world and ours was thinner, easier to cross, but humans were advancing and the fae wished to keep them out of our lands. There had been too much fighting between our people, too many deaths on each side. So, the three Seelie kingdoms came together, the largest is Ellio's kingdom, the Southern Court, and they were joined by the Eastern and Western Kingdoms. The Western Court, where Ezriel now rules has always had a bit of the spell magic that you apparently possess, so his kingdom was crucial to their plans."

Spell magic. She had spell magic. She was a witch.

Such a strange word to apply to herself. *Witch.* Fia nodded, eager to hear the rest of the tale, all the faerie history she had never learned in school.

"The third Southern son at that time had a human wife, not for the Joining, but because they were in love, but she had seen the fighting as well, or maybe she just wanted to keep the faerie world to herself, I do not know her motivation, but she agreed to help create a barrier for the humans and eventually the Unseelie joined them. For perhaps the first and last time, all the courts were in agreement. They would work together to strengthen the barriers between the fae and the humans. So, they gathered, one representative from each Court, and they all put in a piece of their own magic. The spells and wards worked, but the Southern King had other magic as well."

Elara paused, her tongue darting out to wet her bottom lip. Fia followed the movement with her eye before pulling her gaze away and back to her face, but Elara had caught her watching and smirked.

"What happened next?" Fia asked, too engrossed in the story to be embarrassed. These were the answers she had wanted for the last week. This was why she was here. In this story was some reason for why Elara had taken her.

"The Southern King took some of the magic from each kingdom, just a little, hardly enough to be noticeable, and drew it to himself. No one knew at first, our magic is all stronger near the border where the mist slows its dissipation and keeps it thick in the air. When they went home, maybe it took a while before they needed any great magic, and then even longer for them to understand what had happened, but eventually everyone realized the king had stolen from them. There was fighting of course, but no one could win against him, he was too powerful, his troops bolstered by the magic he took from us. And king after king, the Southern Kingdom grew their borders, little by little, year after year, until the rest of us were left with scraps."

"You want it back?" Fia breathed.

"Yes, and I will have it back. It took centuries to figure out exactly how it worked. There is no Joining, no human needs to be in Daonith for some of our magic to seep over the border to you. It was all a lie. No, he needs a human in this land to keep the magic of that long ago ruse flowing. There is something in his estate, something the magic is tied to, and I intend to find whatever holds that ancient spell together and break it."

"Aurora wants the crown?" That would explain why she was there.

"Yes." Elara nodded. "She knew what her father was doing, knew about the weapons he intended to bring into our lands, and she knew my people, good people, would be the first to go. We are the weakest against him. She could not sit by and allow it, so she came to me."

Not quite the thread of magic from before but something inside Fia yearned to break forth. No, not her magic at all, but the bond between her and Elara, the constant pull as if she were a compass, made to find Elara. The spell she had cast on their first day together, but different, as if the spell was growing with Fia's magic. She tried to focus on it and follow the magic, but it slipped from her, leaving only an ache in her head. She dug her fingers into the dirt to ground herself. "But you *are* strong. Could it be that hard to fight him?"

"I am, stronger than most of my kind. But not as strong as I could be and not nearly as strong as the king, not strong enough to take on his army on my own. I need to find that object and I need to destroy it." She pushed up off the ground and offered a hand to Fia, helping to pull her to her feet.

"Can I still do it? If I'm a witch, I mean?"

Elara smiled, her teeth sharp, her horns glinting in the midday sun. "You are still human. Your magic is a gift, not a burden. You can still help my people, and now you can protect yourself. And hopefully you will understand a bit better the horror done when he stole our magic."

"Your people have been kind to me," Fia said, thinking of the village, the little shops and the children playing in the streets.

Would King Ellio really use human weapons against them? Would he destroy the peace of this little village?

But she did not need to think for long, because, stomach churning, Fia had her answer. She was here because he would. She was chosen because he would. She had sat aside while her father did all number of unspeakable things, things she could have ended if she had truly wanted. She had never done anything, she had enjoyed the money, the freedom it offered her.

There was already blood on Fia's hands, more than she cared to think about. Blood had watered her family tree for generations. Could she end it?

Again, she caught Elara's eye, resisting the urge to reach up, to run a finger down the horns, onto her skin. "If you are telling me the truth, I will help you."

"Then we must prepare."

-CHAPTER-
-TWELVE -

EZRIEL HAD ARRIVED three days ago, the morning after Fia had sat in the garden with Elara, and she still had not met him. Wandering the Village of Frost, Fia tried not to be put out by the fact that she'd once again been left behind to wander and try to summon magic that made her want to vomit. Tried and, for the most part, failed.

Her only entertainment was her morning training with Kalin and even those had been brief, his mind clearly on other things.

The Queen might believe Fia would help them, but the understanding between Fia and Elara was fragile, both of them relying on faith that neither had yet earned. Fia still wasn't sure if she was being a complete fool—the faerie woman had threatened to murder her several times already.

A fool she might be, but she couldn't talk herself out of helping, especially not when she walked through the village. There was something so warm about the place, despite the chill that permeated the air. Fia was an outsider, so clearly not one of the Unseelie that lived in the stone houses, and she was fairly certain they didn't know why she was there, but when she walked they would wave, smile, they asked how she was getting along. They offered her fruit from their garden and steaming cups of tea. They were kind.

How could she allow the king to hurt these people? Like she had many times before, Fia wished for her phone. She wanted to call her father. She wanted to demand an explanation. A completely foolish thought, the man had never given a single shit about what Fia wanted, not for herself and certainly not when it came to his business.

But she really did miss her stuff. Her phone yes, but also her old clothes—even if the faerie ones were amongst the most comfortable clothes she ever worn—her books, the artwork she'd carefully selected for her house, all the things she'd acquired over the years.

Would she be able to make a home here? She didn't think she'd ever be able to return to the human lands if she did what the queen wanted. Would she live here in this tiny village? She tried to imagine it, a little garden, friendly faces that never grew old even as hers did.

She followed her nose to an open-air market that had been erected in the center of the village on a big, grass square with a gorgeous, well-kept reflecting pond. She wondered if they skated on it in the winter. Elara had given her some pocket money, all of it in copper and silver feather-light coins whose amounts she struggled to remember.

She wandered the stalls, admiring vases, beautiful jewelry and fleshy, ripe nectarines. When she looked up Trillia, the woman who ran the clothing shop, smiled, her cotton candy hair dancing in the breeze. "I'm glad to see everything fits."

"Oh," Fia smiled. "Yes, it's all so wonderful. You are so talented." She looked down at the stall Trillia was standing in front of. Stacks of gorgeous handwoven tapestries, rugs, and blankets in rich colors.

"Let me know if there is anything else you might need."

"Of course." Fia said.

Trillia nodded once and said goodbye, but Fia stayed at the stand, running her hand over one of the blankets. The fabric was thick and soft, designed with thick lines of muted jewel tones that blended into one another.

She ran her finger down a line of woven emerald, thinking of everything that had happened, her own magic and the magic of making this rug, each thread coming together to make something so beautiful out of a tangle of thread. Could Fia make something beautiful out of the mess she was in?

"That is one of my favorites," said the woman behind the stall. She could have been related to Elara, with thick antlers like a deer and light brown skin that shimmered slightly.

"Can I buy it?" A stupid question that made the woman laugh.

"Of course you can." She told her the price. Fia had no idea if the amount was expensive. She grabbed several silver coins and pressed them into the woman's hand.

"Do you live here?" Fia asked, taking the blanket and wrapping it around herself. The blanket was soft and warm and most importantly it was Fia's, something she had picked for herself. Something entirely her own.

"My whole life. You came with the queen, right?"

Fia nodded, unsure of what lie, if any, she was supposed to tell. No one had given her any rules for her outings. "I did. She is..."

"Intense?" The woman offered, laughing again at the look on Fia's face. "I have known her since I was a child. She is wonderful, but she *is* intense. It makes her a good queen. She does not relent, that can be rare among my people. We are not fighters, but Elara is."

"Yes, she is all of that." Fia pulled the blanket tighter. "Well, thank you again." She turned, intending to find something to eat, but instead she found Aurora watching her from across the village square.

Fia headed for her, pausing when a gaggle of children ran by, several of them holding the strings of kites. The children laughed, nearly tripping over each other as they made their way towards an open field, screaming and craning their necks to see the far away shapes of the kites above them.

"They seem so much happier here," Aurora said softly, watching the running children.

"Is that why you did this? It had to be hard to betray your family." Fia spoke gently, worried she was overstepping, but Aurora nodded.

"I wanted to travel. There is so much world I will never get to see because of the politics between our people, so I wanted to see every inch of Daonith, then I came here. I had met Elara a few times before, but only briefly and only within earshot of my father. But one night we happened to be at the same bar. She approached me and I had no idea what she was going to say, but she just sat and started to talk. She was funny, sharp tongued, a little mean to be honest, but I liked her. So, I extended my stay and the longer I stayed in the Unseelie Kingdom the more profoundly jealous I became, not just for me but for my people."

"Why?" Fia asked. She wasn't sure if Aurora realized how much she was talking, she seemed caught up in some kind of nostalgia and Fia didn't want to break the spell.

"The people here are, of course, like anywhere, there are good people and...less good people, but they care for each other. My people are raised knowing they may one day be called to fight for the empire and that if they please the king they can get land and riches. They hurt each other for opportunities. Children are sent away to school, put to work. The children in my kingdom do not run through the streets laughing."

"And you wanted that for them?"

Aurora laughed. "I wanted it for *me*. When you're raised like these children—raised to care about the people around you, raised to help, it creates a different kind of person than the people in the Southern Kingdom. I know I sound like a naïve fool. They are not all good here, or all bad where I am from, but they are different and it is generational. But I think my people can be good too. I think they deserve that."

"The thought of it makes me jealous too. Our fathers are a lot alike." Fia's childhood had not been one of laughing and running. It had been strict private schools, stricter nannies, and very few friends, none of them genuine, only the children of her father's associates, forced proximity while they dug into each other's wounds, looking for weakness. What kind of person would she have been if she had been raised differently, raised to care about the people around her? What if someone had cared about her? She would never have been on her knees, hoping not to be chosen by a man she'd never met, all in a desperate attempt to please a father who could not be pleased.

A breeze blew through the square, setting off distant windchimes and Aurora cleared her throat. "King Ezriel and his wife Vinessa would like to meet you."

"Oh," Fia squeaked, she had been so lost in her thoughts she had forgotten all about the mysterious king.

Aurora looked her over, the dreamy, faraway look gone from her eyes, the stoic princess returned. "And maybe loose the blanket, you look like a vagrant."

Heat flooded Fia's cheeks. "It was so beautiful." She lowered her voice. "I wanted something I chose."

Aurora smiled. "Keep in on until we get there."

She led Fia to the same carriage they had ridden in when she had been stolen and brought to the Kingdom of Frost. The inside was toasty. She folded the blanket on her lap and watched out the window as they passed through the village proper and onto a small, two lane road, flanked by tall pines and the last straggling wildflowers.

"What am I supposed to say to him?" Fia asked as a pasture full of large spotted cows passed by outside.

Aurora shrugged. "Just talk to him. He wants to know who he is working with." She unwound the braid in her hair, letting it fall in loose, golden curls around her shoulders.

The two women fell into silence as the carriage continued on, driven by the magic of the world, a fact that still seemed near madness to Fia, madder still when she remembered the dormant magic in her veins.

What had it been like before? There was still enough magic to power the carriage over hills and bridges, so what had the world been before the Seelie king had stolen the bulk of it away, leaving only the dredges?

The world outside the window was beautiful, pine-green mountains giving way to bald peaks capped with snow, a woman putting out her laundry to dry, a field of speckled horses, tiny waterfalls running down the side of the mountains to feed the creeks that lined the road.

Could the woman putting out her laundry feel the loss? Would the barren fields they passed be full of crops if the magic had not been taken or was it simply too late in the season? And more questions. What of her own magic? How many more witches might there be if more humans came to this world? Were there hundreds of people in the human world, magic rumbling within them, never to emerge? Could Fia make a life here? And the biggest question of all—was this her war? Was it worth the danger she would be putting herself in?

She had no real answers by the time they pulled up outside a small but beautiful inn made of white stone. Manicured vines grew up the front, pruned back from the wide windows and the expansive porch. The carriage slowed to a stop and Aurora got out first, holding the door open for Fia.

Elara appeared in the doorway of the inn, her silver-purple hair pulled back, her clothes simple and black, but on her head sat a small tiara, inlaid with amethysts and tucked between her horns.

She made her way down the porch, looking Fia over and wished she had worn something else besides the tight pants and overly large sage green sweater she'd picked out, lounging clothes, not meeting a king clothes.

"Is it soft?" Elara asked, as though she could read Fia's thoughts and Fia nodded, the sweater was the softest thing she'd ever worn. "Then it will be just fine. Vinessa will love it. Ready?"

Was she? She wasn't sure she would be ready if she had a million lifetimes to prepare. Not ready for war, not ready to try to be someone different, someone braver than she was. But she nodded and Elara led her up the worn stone steps.

-CHAPTER- -THIRTEEN -

THE INN WAS quiet, their footsteps echoing off the polished wood floor as they made their way to the back, into what must be some sort of conference room and Fia had to stifle a laugh at the thought of faeries having conferences.

The laugh died when she beheld the two people sitting behind a long, sturdy-looking table. The man was large and lean, though clearly muscled underneath his clothes. He was also beautiful, one of the most beautiful men she'd ever seen, putting even Callum to shame. He had warm brown skin, deep blue eyes, so dark they were almost black and a mass of dark curly hair, though a streak of silver ran through it, right at the front.

But it was the woman beside him who drew Fia's attention. Vinessa was obviously Unseelie. Her skin was palest pink, and her hair was thick and dark green, the strands more like vines than hair. Her face was small, her chin pointed, and she looked like a doll, with perfect, tiny features and well-shaped lips curved into a smile.

But her beauty paled in comparison to the wings at her back, iridescent pink, only a few shades darker than her skin and shimmering even in the low light of the room. They were long and thin, reminding Fia of a dragonfly. She looked wild, but in an entirely different way than Elara, more like she belonged perched on a flower, an ethereal thing of storybooks.

Both the king and queen were flanked by several guards in pewter gray clothes, large swords at their sides. Most had the same dark skin as Ezriel, though one looked to have some Unseelie heritage and was a deep burnt orange.

The queen stood, squeezing her husband's arm as she did and her smile grew. "Fia, it is so wonderful to meet you." She came forward and grasped Fia's hand in her own, but before Fia could shake it she pulled her into a hug. "What a time you have had." She pulled away, running her hands down the sleeves of Fia's sweater, as though they had been friends forever. "Oh, the Village has the best clothes for miles and miles We will have to go shopping sometime." She dropped her arms but continued to smile.

Fia tried not to gape, unsure of what to say to such a force of a woman. She was saved by King Ezriel standing, his smile as warm as his wife's and Fia couldn't help it, she liked both of them immediately.

"She should come with us," Vinessa said gently, quietly, to Elara.

Elara did not take it gently, her lips pulled back into a snarl, exposing her canines. "She will not."

Ezriel moved closer to his wife. "She means no disrespect, Elara, but you took her, and Ellio knows it. Now you are here, in your own lands. *We* are here. I know you believe in your people, and we arrived with as much stealth as possible, but if Ellio shows up here it will be your people who suffer."

The Unseelie Queen did not look convinced, her lips still pulled back, the silver rim of her eyes like molten steel. "We have already discussed this."

Vinessa swept thick strands of her hair over her shoulder, acting as though she had not heard Elara. Maybe Fia did not like them as much as she thought. "And if she is taken, do you have another human? Shall we take Beatrix and hope her heart does not give out? She's quite old. Would you have Fia, and our hope, die for your hubris?"

Elara took a step closer and so did the Western guards. Fia only gulped, though they fought over her she was not stupid enough to put herself between faeries who looked ready to rip each other's throats out.

But Aurora had no such qualms. She stepped between Elara and Vinessa, hands up in supplication. Her voice was level, calm, and Fia wondered how many arguments she had come between in her own home. "Perhaps we all go to your Court. We still need to speak to Queen Seera and it will be best if we present a united front. Your Majesty, would you be able to accommodate us all?"

Ezriel dipped his head, a twinkle of mischief in his eyes. "Yes, if Elara puts away her fangs and promises not to disembowel any citizens of my land."

"And what do you think?" Vinessa asked.

Everyone in the room looked towards Fia. She nearly laughed. Imagine that. Being asked where she would like to go. Vinessa was returned to her good graces. "I would not mind seeing more of Daonith and I was nearly kidnapped in the village, though that has not been particularly different from my experiences anywhere else since my arrival." She looked at Elara, who did not seem the least amused, though Vinessa beamed at her.

“You put yourself in danger,” Elara said, her eyes still molten, though she was no longer snarling.

“I am already in danger,” Fia said quietly, moving closer to her. And then more words tumbled from her lips, though she had not planned to say them. “I won’t go if you don’t want me to, but they are right, this is a small village, and everyone has been kind to me. I do not want to bring the king and his armies here. Maybe Kalin could come as well, I could continue my training.”

For a moment Elara and Fia stood looking at each other, their orbits pulling them close as it had from the first time Fia had seen her. There was a tug on the link between them and Fia’s own magic responded, a dark thread winding its way from her palm and around her wrist before it extinguished. She gulped, but it had happened so fast, and no one seemed to notice. Surprisingly there was little pain in her head, only a slight ache behind her eyes.

“I want her guarded,” Elara said, pulling her eyes away from Fia after what felt like an eternity. “And I will bring my own guards as well.”

Ezriel clapped his hands together, grinning, though it did not reach his eyes. Had Elara told him about Fia’s magic yet? Is that why he wanted her to come to his kingdom? “Excellent. I will send word ahead to prepare rooms for you and your guests. We can leave whenever you are ready. Once we are settled, we will invite Seera to our kingdom and hope she agrees."

"She'll agree to come," Aurora said. "She cannot stand to be left out but getting her to agree to your plan will be much harder. She has allied with my father in the past. She is a risk."

Fia wished she knew more of their lands, of the ties between these people and the centuries of politics that ruled them, but all she had was Elara, the woman who had stolen her. But the fear that once had gripped her heart, oily and slick, vanished with each passing day, though she knew it would return when she learned the details of their plan to free themselves from Ellio.

Still, curiosity and wonder had replaced her fear, and she grew stronger with each day spent training with Kalin. There was even a chance she might master her power, maybe find a place among the faeries. She was not sure she could ever go home, wasn't even sure if she wanted to, really. Not now that magic flowed inside her.

And the human world had never been her home. She'd never had a place she felt safe and loved. There was no one to miss, no nostalgia for much except a life she had understood a bit better than this one. At least in Daonith she mattered, she stood among kings and queens, she had an opportunity to help people, to become someone she wasn't ashamed of.

So, she had to travel, get to know as much of Daonith as she could, because if they won she would no longer be engaged to Callum, but Elara wouldn't need her either. So, while the faeries schemed and plotted, Fia would try to find that elusive home, find a place where, when the dust settled, she could settle as well.

Planning to travel to the Western Kingdom took several days. Teleportation, she had learned, was a rare faerie gift and took a lot of magic. Trying to transport dozens of people in such a manner would be impossible. She wondered if she had any special abilities, any gifts rare to even witches?

While Ezriel and Elara planned—which she noticed involved a lot of yelling—she continued to train with Kalin every day and was finally starting to see results, mostly in the form of sore muscles when she awoke. But he had let her hold weapons that morning, not for long and only, he said, to get used to moving with the extra weight, but still, she'd gotten to hold a sword. She'd loved the weight of it in her hand, how solid it felt, but it *had* made it harder to move.

Her favorite part of training was going on runs and getting to stretch her legs through the mountains while the cold air pulled at loose strands of her hair. Each day she moved faster, each day she went further from the village. Despite his size, Kalin never seemed tired and when they stopped to rest, he was always willing to answer any questions she could think of, though she didn't dare try to get him to reveal anything too juicy, especially not about Elara.

Fia liked him, he was a giant of a man and ridiculously muscled, but he smiled easily, more than Fia thought she would smile if she tortured people for the queen. Maybe that said something bad about him, but Fia didn't think so, not anything more than he loved his people and would do unpleasant things for them. She'd known people to do unpleasant things for far worse reasons.

"So..." Fia tried to time her words with her breathing as they made their way along a fairly flat part of the trail. "The Unseelie...you all look different and the Seelie look mostly the same...I mean not the same but..." She was rambling and possibly saying something incredibly rude. She clamped her lips together.

"The Unseelie are composed of several races, though the names of many have been lost to time and interbreeding whereas the Seelie are all one race and it is rare they have children with the Unseelie." Kalin passed a water bottle to Fia and slowed his pace. She was happy to do the same.

"But Ezriel's queen is Unseelie."

"The union is not beloved by everyone in his kingdom. She is the first Unseelie to sit on the throne of any kingdom except ours, the Northern Kingdom. Do you need to rest?"

Fia shook her head as they started up an incline. If she stopped moving she wasn't sure she'd be able to start again. "I didn't even know the Unseelie existed before I got here."

"The Southern Kingdom has controlled the border for thousands of years. We are told the humans are kept in the dark to keep us all safe, but the real reason is to control trade. Ellio controls all the goods that come from or go to the human world. To trade without permission in his kingdom is seen as an act of sabotage against Daonith and is punished severely."

Fia was quiet for a moment, considering his words as she focused on getting up the mountain. The air smelled of pine and each step seemed to make the air colder than the last, but she enjoyed the burn in her calves and knowing each day she was stronger than the day before.

For a while she lost herself in the hike, forgetting any problem except the incline, then they were at the top, the whole world seeming to spread out miniscule beneath her. Fia braced her hands on her knees, drawing air into her lungs. She had climbed to the top of several of the smaller peaks now, but this one had the best view yet, miles of wilderness, punctuated only by small cabins and plumes of chimney smoke. She could just made out the inn where Ezriel and his entourage stayed at the edge of the Village of Frost and the lake behind it, glittering in the morning sun.

"You are strong, Fia," Kalin said, resting against a tree.

"I'm not so sure," Fia said. "My whole life has just been a series of things that happened to me. I don't know if I've ever actually decided anything for myself." Her cheeks burned at the shame of admitting it, but she was glad she had. The words melted into the mountain mist and with them part of her, a small, scared, jagged piece of herself she had carried since childhood, melted too.

"That may be true, but I cannot judge your past. I have been alive for centuries and made many decisions that I wish I hadn't, but now you are willing to help my people. The Queen kidnapped you, many would refuse, perhaps you should, what she did was not a kindness, but still, you are willing to try to free my people's magic. That is strength, strength of character."

Was it true? She desperately wanted to believe him, but the words had not landed like Kalin must have hoped they would. Was she a fool? Working with a woman who had kidnapped her—who did that? An idiot.

Her mind spiraled down and she felt the thread, the tie to the world, and she tried to grasp it. Visions hit her like bricks, the mountain, the lake, flashes of faces with strange features, laughing, crying, a babe in someone's arms. The visions grew darker and Fia gasped.

She was on the ground, Kalin's face hazy above her, fear in his eyes. He exhaled as his features came into focus. "Fia? Fia, are you okay?"

"I don't know if I can wield this magic, Kalin. I'm afraid it will wield me." She pushed herself onto her elbows but didn't dare try to stand up yet.

He shook his head and sat on the ground beside her. "You only feel this way because the Southern King stole your magic from you. You should have had this magic since childhood, it should have grown slowly. You are trying to learn in a week what it takes fae decades to master, but you *are* its master. You are only late to the craft."

Again, kind words, meant to soothe, but did they matter if she fainted every time the magic hit her? She'd almost controlled it before, she'd had that thread come and go and been fine, but she hadn't meant to do that either. What good was magic she couldn't wield?

She eased herself into a sitting position and wiped the dirt from her clothing. Enough lying on the ground feeling helpless. Whatever Kalin said, it would consume her if she let it, but she wouldn't. She wasn't that scared helpless child. If she could climb mountains, she could master her own power. Most importantly, she would be no man's pawn, not anymore. "How do I learn to control it?"

"There you go, that's the attitude. But don't ask me, ask Elara, she has more magic than any of us. And the Western Kingdom has spell magic. Ezriel and Vinessa may be able to point you in the right direction."

She nodded, though the movement hurt her head. A knot was forming at the back of her skull, where she'd hit the ground, but she was pretty sure she wasn't concussed. Nothing felt truly damaged. "And when we go to the Western Kingdom, you'll keep training me?"

"Of course. I wouldn't let you off that easily." He grinned. "I know I said you are strong but physically..." He blew out a breath. "You have a long way to go."

Fia swatted at his arm. It was like hitting a tree or the mountain itself. "That is rude."

He laughed as he stood and offered her a hand. "And don't think you can just faint to get out of it."

Warmth that had nothing to do with magic filled Fia. All her life she'd wanted a friend, a real friend. And somehow, in a strange land, with a man who looked like a tree, she'd found one. "You're an ass."

"And you're weak as a baby deer. Now, quit dawdling. We need to make it back down the mountain and I'm not going to carry you."

-CHAPTER-
-FOURTEEN-

OVER THE NEXT few days Fia saw little of Elara or Aurora. The two women spent all their time at the Inn planning with Ezriel, but she did have company. The cottage had gained a terrifying new occupant, a dark-haired woman with pale skin and nails that looked suspiciously like claws named Saskia. She barely spoke and when she did it was only to Kalin, who might as well have moved in for as often as he was at the cottage.

Fia had taken to spending most of her time either in her room or not in the cottage at all. When she wasn't training, she continued to wander the village, eating lunch at a tiny restaurant tucked between the grocer and a glassware shop so often the small, winged faerie who ran it no longer let her order off the menu but would bring out whatever she thought Fia might like. So far, she hadn't been wrong.

Maybe she would do that today. Or she could visit the tea shop. Or just walk. There was a path beside a small creek lined with smooth stones and she wanted to know where it ended.

Her door banged open and she nearly jumped out of her skin, the brush she'd been using on her hair clattering to the floor. Elara stood in the doorway, not looking the least bit sorry.

Fia was only wearing pants and a bra, hadn't gotten to her shirt yet. "Excuse me."

"You are excused." Elara headed for her bed and sat, picking up the shirt she had laid out and looking it over. "The Unseelie style suits you."

The shirt was fairly simple, not much more than a cropped t-shirt, though looser and gauzier than what was in fashion for the humans. She didn't point that out to Elara though, not wanting to get into a discussion on human versus faerie fashion. "Some might consider it rude to come in unannounced."

"Some might," Elara conceded. "But this is my house."

Fia couldn't help but roll her eyes. "Are there other options? Might I arrange for somewhere else to stay?" She didn't know why she was poking at Elara, she absolutely believed the faerie woman could be lethal. She'd *seen* her be lethal.

Irritation flashed in Elara's eyes. "No, you may not acquire your own residence but thank you for bringing it up. That is what I came to speak to you about. We leave for Ezriel's kingdom this afternoon. Are you packed?"

Fia glanced around her room. She hardly had anything to pack but she was surprised to feel a tinge of sadness at leaving the cottage, even more at leaving the Village. "Will we come back here?"

The irritation disappeared, Elara's face softening. "Would you like to return?"

"Perhaps." Fia tried to imagine the future, what her life might look like one day. It was a nearly impossible task, but... "If we win, I will need somewhere to live. I know I've seen little of this world but here might not be so bad." She took her shirt from Elara. "In my own residence, of course."

"Of course." Elara cleared her throat. "Fia, I..."

She pulled her shirt over her head. "Yes?"

A moment passed. "I think this would make a wonderful home for you if you desire it. You should see the world though, before you make any permanent decisions."

"And win, right?" Fia smiled. "What about you? Where will you live? Here? Maybe we'll be neighbors." She was rambling, but inexplicably it seemed to be getting under Elara's skin and maybe she shouldn't, but she liked watching her squirm, even if the source of the squirming was the thought of Fia being her neighbor.

"I have a different home," Elara said, looking up into Fia's eyes. "I will show you it sometime. It is beautiful, often cold, but beautiful. It is near the sea." Those eyes, deep brown and bright silver. Maybe she wouldn't mind Fia being her neighbor, maybe they could find a friendship if Elara never found a reason to kill or maim her.

Fia sat on the bed beside her, close enough that their knees pressed together. Fia didn't expect it to make her breath catch in her throat, even with two layers of fabric between them. "You didn't come to talk about our houses."

"No, I didn't." Her fingers were splayed on her thigh, long fingers. "Most of the group will travel by carriage, but I am worried about us being followed and if we are, I would rather find out when you are not around."

Fia pressed her leg into Elara's for a moment. "Well, it would be rather hard for me to help if I'm taken or murdered, but I won't let your protection go to my head and think you care about me."

She was only teasing but Elara's jaw tightened, and it was several long moments before she spoke. "The two of us will travel by porting. My magic cannot make it in one go so we will have to take breaks, but we will be impossible to track. We hope anyone watching may believe Saskia is you through the window and we can make sure we are not being followed. Once we make it to the Western Kingdom, we will go to Haveneze, where Ezriel lives. I do not think Ellio is bold enough to send spies to another king's home yet.

She nodded but honestly it didn't matter much to her. She would go where she was told. She did not know enough about Daonith to care where the destination was. "So, I'll still be allowed to wander?"

Since they had decided they would leave the Village of Frost, Fia had worried she would truly become a prisoner, that the faeries, in the name of keeping her safe, would lock her up, unwilling to lose their only human. The faeries seemed to want her willing participation in their plans, but how far would that get her if she refused? And willing was not always wanting. She'd seen many people, after spending time with her father's men, make choices they did not want to make at all.

Elara stood, the warmth of where their legs met leaving with her. "With modifications. Ezriel will place a glamour on you to appear Seelie, so no one will report a human amongst his lands. A silly plan, but he insists and it is his kingdom."

A lump formed in her throat. "Will it hurt?"

Elara shook her head. "No, though it may...tickle at first. But you will still look mostly yourself, that will require less magic. We would like to do it now, before we leave."

Now. Did she want to look Seelie? What would happen if she said no? But there would no doubt come a time when she did refuse to do their bidding. The glamour seemed harmless enough. Better to agree and save her fight for another day.

She gave her approval and Elara left to fetch Ezriel. There was not enough time to become afraid before they returned.

The king stood before her, such a solid presence, examining her face in a way that made her want to shrink from him, but she held her chin high. Did the Western Courts choose leaders as the Unseelie did or was it birthright like in King Ellio's kingdom? Though she had only known him for a few days, Fia could understand why someone would choose Ezriel to lead them.

"Are you ready?" he asked, his voice gentle and reassuring. Fia gulped and nodded. The King took her head between his calloused hands and breathed deeply. Gentle, white magic spread over her, starting with her head, trailing down, cold like being plunged into a bucket of ice. Then pain, sharp and quick enough to make her gasp. There and gone in an instant.

From the doorway, Vinessa clapped her hands together and Fia looked to see her and Aurora grinning. Fia brought her hands to her face, much the same, then her ears, pulled into points. Then she noticed her hands, her long fingers, the somehow more elegant curve of her wrist.

"You look lovely, though no lovelier than before," Aurora said, taking a step towards her. "Would you like to look in the mirror."

Did she? It had seemed like such a small thing, but it was her face, her body. *Her.* She nodded and Aurora placed a hand on her back, walking her towards the mirror.

Everything was the same and yet not. Her eyes were brighter, her skin smoother, her hair sleeker. Aurora and Elara stood in the mirror behind her, the women who had stolen her and yet, maybe, they had freed her, because she would have married Callum, she would have borne his children and lived in his country estate. The fae features in her body were not the only changes, the muscles that had only begun to grow under

Kalin's tutelage were more pronounced and her gaze held a strength she had never managed as a human.

Maybe being in this kingdom wasn't a choice either, she had been stolen for exactly this purpose, but this she wanted. She wanted to help. She knew what it was like to live under someone's thumb, to have it all and yet have nothing, no true freedom, no real choices. And she wanted to help herself, free the magic beginning to sing inside of her, create something beautiful. She wanted a life full of friends and laughter. She wanted to know her own power.

And that was the biggest change of all, the stirring inside her chest, the growing of her very soul. Staring into the mirror as Vinessa and Ezriel slipped away, leaving only Aurora and Elara, she thought of her old life, her too big house, her friends who never called, her nice car, her phone that she had treated like a lifeline, and she could not imagine herself back in it. To fit into that world would be shrinking, becoming so much smaller than she had become roaming the hills and mountains of the Village of Frost.

"Are you okay?" Elara asked, the silver of her eyes shining.

"Yes," Fia said, because somehow she was. Her body was strange, changed in ways she was not sure she liked, but inside the strange body she buzzed with life. She turned, looking over both women and asked Aurora, “Do you second guess it? Standing against your father?”

Aurora’s eyes flicked towards the ceiling, and she tucked a strand of blonde hair behind her ear. “Yes, of course. And it took many centuries to gain the courage.”

Fia reached out, taking Aurora’s hand into her own, it was warm and soft, her own new calluses catching on Aurora’s soft skin. Had she ever really wanted more than to be a princess? Had she wanted to be a rebel or had she found herself in an enemy kingdom looking at the truth and knowing what was right. “I never thought I would thank someone for kidnapping me but thank you—though you could have been gentler.”

Aurora’s face brightened. “For all my own reasons I could not watch you be forced into a marriage, sold from one brutal man to another’s son.” She squeezed Fia’s fingers. “I will see you in Haveneze.”

“That was...nice,” Elara said, looking her over. “And you make a fetching faerie.”

Fia rolled her eyes, moving away from the mirror and grabbing the hooded jacket on her bed. “You also could have been a *lot* nicer. You were an ass. You scared me on purpose.”

Elara shrugged. "You would not have trusted me if I had been nice. It would have been a lie. My kingdom is full of kind people. Kind, starving people. They need me to be frightening."

Fia pulled the jacket over her head, and the fabric brushed her now-longer ears. Perhaps it was true, Fia had seen the queen spill blood without a second thought, she'd seen her send a man to be tortured, yet she had people who would die for her, she had Kalin and Aurora and Saskia. The last was terrifying but had done nothing truly unkind to Fia and had come the moment Elara had asked her to put herself in danger as a body double.

They were not so different, Fia and Elara. They had both been forced into lives and actions they did not want by horrible circumstances. No, not circumstances. The greed of men. But was Fia as strong as Elara? Would she rise to the occasion or cower as she had so many times before?

"It is time to leave." Elara said, looking her over again. "On second thought, I believe I prefer your human body. I don't need another fucking Seelie around." She put out her hand out to Fia and Fia took it. Strong and warm.

-CHAPTER-
-FIFTEEN-

DARKNESS PRESSED IN on them as they ported through Daonith, away from the Village and towards Haveneze. Wind roared around them, whipping at Fia's hood and pulling strands of her hair to lash at her face. She clung to the woman beside her, pressing their bodies together, Elara's horns hard against her face, their fingers intertwined.

Then quiet. The world was still dark, though the twinkling stars seemed near enough to touch. Around Fia stretched open rock, then a plunge before more mountains, their peaks jagged and sharp. She stepped away from Elara, taking in the beautiful, hostile landscape.

"The Broken Teeth," Elara said as an explanation. "No eyes here to see us."

"Yeah, but it's fucking freezing." Fia wrapped her arms around her torso.

"You will be fine. We won't be here long. I only need a short rest." But snow started to fall as the words left her lips, fat flakes that quickly grew in intensity. The queen shivered. "It is a bit chilled. Come." She grabbed Fia's hand again, tugging her.

There was a cave not far from them, barely ten feet deep but enough to get them out of the elements. They moved to the back wall and Elara took sticks from a stack against the wall and expertly built a fire. How often had she hidden here? With a wave of her hand, purple tinged flames left up, bathing Fia in warmth.

The heat was welcome and she rubbed her hands together. The flames illuminated the cave but there was not much to see, plain gray stone, utterly unremarkable. Except Elara, lit only by the candlelight, the rest of her face in shadow. Fia had forgotten earlier, forgotten just how dangerous the Queen was. She was built for violence, not her body, though it was tall and tight with muscle, but her magic, still so powerful. Powerful enough Fia could sometimes feel the magnetic pull of her. How powerful would she be once King Ellio's hold on her was released? How deadly? Fia shuddered.

"Teleporting....porting." Fia corrected herself to the faerie term. "It takes a lot of power?"

Elara rested her head on the cave wall behind her, closing her eyes. “In a way, especially when carrying something. To move ourselves over great distances takes a lot of will. It is not only the power but the mental drain. It’s hard to explain.”

Fia thought of the headaches that plagued her whenever she tried to call upon her own magic. “I think I understand, at least somewhat.” But Elara didn’t respond, only kept leaning against the wall and Fia let her rest.

Outside the wind roared past the opening of the cave, blowing snow inside. How high up were they? She wished it was day, wished to see the land below them, to see if they were amongst the clouds. How could they not be when the stars seemed close enough to touch? She pushed past the fire, allowing it to warm her back as she gazed out the cave and into the heavens.

Fia had spent her life in cities where the night sky was an endless inky black, only the moon strong enough to shine, but here, peeking out from between the clouds as they blew by, by the stars were bright and endless.

Suddenly a memory of her mother came to her, some kind of trip not long before she killed herself. She had dragged Fia out of the villa and onto the deserted beach until they were nearly to the water. Then they'd laid in the sand, their shoulders pressed together, as her mother pointed out constellations.

"The mother," she had said, her arm raised and dangerously thin. Her mother had been all bones before she had slipped away completely. But that night she had looked over at Fia, smiling. "If you ever miss me, you can look for the mother."

"She's not my mother, you are," Fia had said, snuggling closer to her as the tide came in, lapping at their bare feet.

"Fia?" Elara said, making her jump. The snow had stopped as suddenly as it had begun. "You ready? We should go before another storm starts. The Teeth are always like this, some meteorological oddity I never understood."

She shook away memories of her mother and the guilt and anger and longing that always came with it. "Yes. I'm ready."

Between them, Elara reached down twining their fingers together. The darkness surrounded them and there were no longer stars, in the emptiness of magic there was only Elara, her long fingers tucked between Fia's.

The next place was warmer, though not by much, at the edge of a small lake that reflected the moon overhead. Beyond the lake, hills rolled towards the midnight horizon, their graceful curves broken by the outline of tall trees like fingers reaching to the sky.

"When we get there..." Elara said, looking down at their still intertwined fingers and pulling her hand loose, though she did not step away. "You are disguised, and I will not cage you, but you must be careful. I would prefer we go to my home, Niveren Gap, but the others are hesitant to go there. The trust between us is minimal and hard won, not to mention Niveren Gap is furthest from Ellio's power. There is some umbrage over it."

They walked along the edge of the lake together, only the noise of the wind in the trees and the occasional call of an owl to keep them company. "They think he takes less of your power?"

"Yes, but there is barely any more magic for us. We lost it the same as everyone else. They do not say it but they also wonder if that is why I am so strong, if I somehow took more than my share, but I took nothing. I am Unseelie. We do not steal from our neighbors. My strength is only the luck of genetics. But there are many people in Niveren Gap, many bodies for magic to emanate from, and after the initial purge we were able to direct it to our crops, and they grew a bit better than other places. And the city is on the sea, we have always fished. So, there were years where my people ate while theirs starved. I understand why they are upset, but my people have been hungry too, even if I kept one city fed, and only barely at times."

"The magic helps the crops?" The thought had crossed her mind, there was so much barren land in Daonith, but she had never asked. Fia was once again struck by how much she had to learn and how she may have never known any of this if she had married Callum, only what was fed to her by the tyrant king.

"We have never had the benefit of electricity We used our magic for everything before it was stolen. And we had a population that had grown in a well-fed kingdom where people rarely wanted for necessities, so when it was suddenly taken, when our crops died and our reserves dwindled to nothing it was gruesome. To watch my people....to watch *children* starve and I could do nothing..." Elara's hands tightened into fists and magic sparked around her, reflecting off the surface of the lake before fizzling away.

No words came to Fia, but her heart ached. Her mother's death had been sudden and she had barely survived. What Elara had endured was unimaginable. So, she stepped closer, letting their shoulders brush together, their shadows merge into one.

Without a word, Elara took her hand again, this time more roughly than before, no intertwined fingers, only palm gripped in palm. Neither spoke until they came upon the outskirts of civilization.

Smoke billowed from the chimney of a small cabin and faelight lit the windows of several others. Not even a village, only a few houses huddled together at the far end of the lake, but she suspected there would be more once they crested the small hill beyond the cottages.

“Why did you not port us the first night? It would have gotten us out of the city faster.”

The anger twisting Elara’s features at the memory of her people starving eased and the magic that bound them stirred inside Fia. Elara must have felt it too because she tightened her grip on Fia’s hand. “Ellio does not know the extent of my powers. I did not know if you would run, if you did, I did not want him to know what I can do. I have always taken a carriage into his city, I am careful he does not see me using magic. Most likely he has heard rumors but nothing he can be sure of.” Her fingers clamped like a vice. “He will not see it until I use it to destroy him, just as he destroyed my people.”

The Queen had worked so hard, planned for so long, and yet it all hinged on Fia, on the hope that a woman stupid enough to pledge herself to a world she had never seen would fight for a rival kingdom. Would any of the other women who had knelt in that room be where she was? Fia swallowed the lump in her throat. She had been chosen and suddenly it felt like fate.

And it could not be fate because if she was meant to be here then the burning flame of hatred in her heart for what her father had done might flicker out. No. She shook her head, drawing Elara's attention. There was no fate, only people making choices. Her father had not known about these people. Even if the universe, or fate, or whatever she wanted to call it had nudged her towards the fae, even if, by some miracle she did not die but helped these people, her father would get no credit for that.

No credit for the weapons and who knew what else he smuggled in. No credit for the plans he had made with a man even worse than he was. No credit for the way he had sold his only child, a child he had never loved. A child he had not even comforted when he'd come home to the flashing lights of ambulances and a little girl covered in blood, but instead told her he hoped she'd never be as stupid as her mother and then poured himself a drink.

The only thing her father had ever been proud of was her beauty. *My beautiful Fia, lovely enough to be a weapon.*

Fia needed to be back around people, not under the open night sky. There was too much space for her mind to wander, for her to think and hate and harden her heart. "What makes men so willing to sacrifice children for power?"

"Would you want to kill him?" Elara asked, never one to shy from violence, a trait Fia was coming to appreciate. Hand in hand with Elara, Fia felt many things, but always safe. The only thing that could hurt her was the queen herself.

"I don't know if I could," Fia said. "But maybe now if I wanted to I could." Heat built inside her and her magic weaved with the small, simple thread between them, winding and twisting until they were one, and somehow, with all the stars to witness the bond grew.

She knew Elara felt it too. Surprise sparked in her eyes, but all she said was, "I could kill him for you, Fia. Him or any of your enemies. Anyone who has hurt you."

Heart in her throat, Fia stopped walking, taking in Elara, her horns nearly glowing in the moonlight, her eyes alight with silver flame. She held those eyes in her gaze as she brought Elara's hand to her mouth, pressing her lips to her knuckles. "You have my loyalty. You are my Queen." Her magic weaved again, black threads wrapping around their hands.

Elara's breathing was shallow as she placed Fia's hand on her chest, right above her pounding heart. A moment that could have been a second or an hour passed before Elara spoke. "Welcome to my court, Fia Gray."

-CHAPTER-
-SIXTEEN-

THE WESTERN COURT Palace was beautiful. Cream stone towered above gray stone cliffs, tall pillars hung with billowing gold curtains that flapped in the unending sea wind, colored glass, shaped to look like crystals and filled with faerie light hung from the ceilings so colored danced across every surface. The entire outer edge of the palace and most of the hallways were open air, ceilings but no walls, until you were well inside the space.

Fia was to share a room with Elara, but their suite was as big as the entire cottage, made of a large sitting room, a dining area, two large bedrooms with their own bathrooms, and an enormous balcony connecting the two rooms.

The balcony was at the back of the castle, overlooking the jagged cliffs and the sea beyond, dotted with rocks that jutted above the ocean's surface, ready to ruin any boat that made it past the enormous coral reef spreading like the web of an enormous spider. Beyond the reef the view was marred by the same thick mist that lined the bottleneck of land between the faerie lands and the human.

No wonder ships did not try to make it, even if they sailed through the mist and the reef and the rocks, they would have to scale the cliff face to make it to the city beyond. Trade would be impossible, invasion stupidity.

A beautiful, isolated land, like all of Daonith, cut off by an unjust king who hoarded magic like a dragon. Fia had seen the thin children, the women washing threadbare clothes in the small stone houses that lined the road to the city. The dragon must be slayed, the people freed from tyranny.

She woke early the morning after their arrival, hoping to train with Kalin but a quick walk through the palace did not reveal him and she was afraid to explore further, not yet familiar enough with either the kingdom or the king to wander into spaces she could not easily identify.

By the time she made it back to her room Elara was awake, her hair a tangle around her horns. A silk robe was cinched at her waist but open enough to reveal more of the Queen than Fia had seen before, every bit of it toned. "Glad to see you did not run away." She attempted to rake a hand through her hair and frowned at the result.

"I wanted to train with Kalin," Fia said, wishing for a cup of coffee. "I didn't see him though."

Elara sat on a sage green couch, tucking her legs beneath her. "I got word after you went to sleep that the caravan was stopped on the way. No one was injured but Kalin and Saskia doubled back to see if it was just beggars as they said or if they were followed."

"And if they were followed?" Fia might be pushing her luck to ask such a direct question about Elara's plans but after last night things had changed between them. She could still feel Elara's beating heart and when she sat beside her on the couch her scent filled Fia's nose, fragrant and musky yet feminine and something else, something...something that tickled Fia's mind, a memory she could not grasp.

"If they were followed then I do not care what the others say, we will be going to the Niveren Gap and Queen Seera will just have to lower herself to meet us there."

The door to their suite banged open and Elara was up in a moment, her hand going to a dagger Fia had not noticed strapped to her leg. And she *had* noticed the leg. "Shit, Aurora. Are you trying to get stabbed?"

"Oh yeah. My greatest desire… or I was coming to see if the two of you wanted to join me for coffee. Some of us arrived here later than others." She gave Elara and Fia a pointed look.

Elara's grin was deadly. "Blame your father for your diminished powers. It is not my fault you cannot port."

Aurora bared her teeth, snarling at the queen. "Risky, risky words before coffee."

"Enough of this," Fia said. "I was wishing for coffee, and Aurora has appeared like a very loud angel. To deny me would make you my enemy. You wouldn't want *that* would you." She winked at Elara.

Elara fought a grin that Fia had rarely seen, but then her gaze changed, soft and hard all at once and Fia knew she was remembering the pledge from the night before. "No, I would not want that."

Aurora cleared her throat. "Weird energy in here." She looked Elara up and down. "Will you change?"

"Yes, give me a moment." Before Elara left she inspected Fia's outfit, flowing pants and a tight-fitting sweater. "You will be hot when the sun comes up."

Fia doubted it. She did not have Elara's mountain-born blood. When the Queen returned, she was in a pair of small black shorts, the dagger on her leg now extremely visible, and a loose black top with gauzy sleeves.

"Subtle," Aurora said, before leading them out of the room.

The dining area was enormous and open on three sides, the ocean breeze pulling at golden curtains. Beneath Fia's feet the cream stone was sun warmed where it wasn't covered with plush rugs. There was a slight chill to the wind blowing from the sea and she wondered what they did when it grew too cold to eat here. Another area or magic that kept them warm?

Wide, plush fabric chairs in gold and cream were situated around low tables where Seelie fae she did not recognize sat, eating breakfast from the vast array laid out on a long wooden table. It was not just Ezriel and his court but staff and their families, the children all comfortable in the space, laughing and talking to each other.

Ezriel and Vinessa were at the buffet table loading plates and Vinessa smiled, waving them over. “I hope you slept well. I know the first night in a new place can be strange.”

“Oh, I did. The bed is wonderful,” Fia said, grabbing a plate of her own and piling it high with faerie fruit, some of which she knew and some she did not but was excited to try.

“Any word on who stopped the carriages?” Elara asked, getting right to the point. She put a piece of unbuttered toast on her plate, tapping the crust against the porcelain and making crumbs.

“Yes.” Ezriel jerked his chin towards a grouping of chairs near the corner, away from the crowd, and once they were done getting their breakfast and coffee they followed.

Aurora sat next to Fia, passing the creamer to her and leaning close. “Best to let the two of them argue,” she whispered, eyeing Ezriel and Elara. Vinessa seemed to have the same idea. She smiled gently and focused on her plate.

“They were not simple robbers, as I suspected. No one stops a royal caravan to steal from them.” Ezriel said over a steaming mug.

“Risky though,” Elara said, emptying a surprising amount of sugar into her coffee. “They must be close to the king if they were willing to risk their life just for information. Such a small group could not have hoped to take Fia if we were both there."

"Instead, they were brought here," Ezriel said, his brow furrowed. "And they achieved what they wanted, a bit of chaos to see who was truly in that carriage. And now there are two men loyal to the Southern King in my prison. I can kill them, which I hate, or let them stay and gather more information, which I also hate." His jaw was tight.

"Then we should leave," Elara said, looking like she might jump up and do just that. "I told you the first day, Niveren Gap is much safer than anywhere in your lands."

Vinessa's grip on her fork tightened and she looked up. "Our lands are safe."

Elara sat her coffee down hard enough that liquid sloshed from the sides. "What was your plan in bringing Fia here? Did you think I would be so grateful at staying with her that I would give in to anything you asked? Did you hope she would stay?"

Ezriel shifted closer to his wife. "You agreed to bring her. Whatever your misgivings, it is safer than her wandering your village and Niveren Gap was never an option. You know this."

"Only because you do not think of the Unseelie as equal to yourself. But there was an attempt—"

Ezriel cut Elara off. "There was an attempt to steal Fia from your lands as well. Do you really think staying with her, when Ellio knows who took her, is what is best for her safety?" He glanced at Fia and she couldn't decide if she wanted to interject or sink into the cushions of her seat. Aurora shifted closer to her.

"You speak to freely about what you do not know. Ezriel married me, an Unseelie –" Vinessa began.

"Marrying someone does not mean you respect them or their people," Elara said through clenched teeth.

"I hardly think it is time for that argument. Surely there are more important matters," Fia said, forcing confidence she did not feel into her voice.

The silence that filled the space was tense. Elara's fingers brushed against the knife at her thigh then she placed a hand on Fia's shoulder, warming her skin. "Fia is a member of my court. I will *not* leave her behind and I will certainly not ship her off to a foreign kingdom."

Vinessa's green eyebrows shot up and she coughed several times. Her wings tightened and eyes moved to her husband, but she was the only one looking at him, everyone else's eyes darted between Fia and Elara.

"She is a human," Ezriel said, his voice dangerously low. His nostrils flared as though he could smell something other than their breakfast and his eyes narrowed. "This is dangerous territory, even for a Queen."

Fia cleared her throat. "You want my help, but you speak as if I am not here, as if I am incapable of deciding my own loyalties. Only one queen came and took me from a forced marriage, only one kingdom has trained me. Would you have come for me, or would you have continued to allow your people's magic to flow from their own land?"

When she had pledged herself under the stars, she had also made a promise to herself, to mean her vow, to make it worth something. She would not sit idly by, no matter how uncomfortable she felt, while her Queen was insulted. Even if the King looked like he wanted to reach across the table and strangle her.

Despite the ache it caused in her head, she let her powers unravel from within, black threads danced across her knuckles and wound their way around her wrist. She could feel the power slide from her, reaching towards the cliffs and the sea beyond, the deep depths, the life and power within it, the sand beneath. The ache turned into something sharp and threatening and she pulled the magic back into her, shoving it down in the blink of an eye. Searing pain shot through her skull, but she held herself steady.

The King watched her display, muscles tense. No one seemed to be breathing at all. "You would do well not to speak on things you do not understand. You know nothing of our land, of what has been done to our people. You are not fae, no matter what tricks you might have, so do not presume you understand me or my people."

Elara's fingers returned to her weapon, but Fia laid her hand gently atop the queen's. "I am not fae, but you need me. Since the night I arrived I have been asked for things that seemed beyond my reach. I am not fae, but you need me, or you will continue to live under the thumb of those border lands. We both know Ellio is not amassing human weapons just for protection. And since I was taken, I have been willing, I have listened and trained and found my own power and I am ready to help. You all ask so much, you want me to go back into the castle with powers I barely understand and free magic and I am willing. But when you speak about what happens to me next, you will include me in those choices because that is what I have earned."

"We use some spell magic in our kingdom," Vinessa said. She stabbed her fork into a piece of lavender-hued melon. "I will find someone to help train you."

Fia nodded. "Thank you, your Majesty." She started to pull her hand away from Elara's but the warmth and strength of her was nice so she left her hand on the Queen's but returned her gaze to the king, while his wife's words were kind, she needed his respect. If he did not agree, none of this would work.

He stared black with midnight blue eyes, assessing Fia as though he could see into her very soul. Let him look. No longer would she cower. She might die when she returned to the Southern Kingdom, she would not do it with the same fear in her heart as when she left. She would not die a coward.

"Very well," the king finally said. "Is it your wish to stay with Elara when King Ellio knows she took you and very well might know she is here?"

She looked at Elara, her straight shoulders, her eyes of steel. Fia's magic surged in her veins. "Yes. Everyone who undertakes this should be present for the planning."

"That is not how wars work," Ezriel said. "Everyone cannot plan."

“This is not a war, Ezriel,” Elara said. “Not yet, not until we complete this task. Until we free all magic it will be a slaughter. We cannot fight him without our magic at full strength. Eventually there will be time for soldiers and generals, but it is not now. Not yet.”

“Well, if you want us all here, it is worth noting we can’t free magic without a representative from all the kingdoms. We will need Seera and she has not yet answered any of my letters,” Ezriel said.

“Demand it,” Aurora said, looking at the group gathered around the table of forgotten breakfast. “Sign both your names to a demand.”

“She will be furious,” Vinessa whispered.

“Yes.” Aurora nodded, a smile pulling at the corners of her mouth. “Make her furious, furious enough to act. Call out her honor, her people’s strength. Make it a challenge she cannot resist. That is the way to deal with Seera.”

Beneath the table, Elara’s fingers wrapped around Fia’s hand. “Nothing else has worked, Ez.”

The king nodded. “It’s worth a shot.”

-CHAPTER-
-SEVENTEEN-

THE LETTER WAS sent that afternoon. After breakfast there had been nothing pressing for Fia to do and she had not seen Elara in several hours, so she wandered the castle.

Maybe she was not yet as brave as she hoped to be because she did not dare leave the estate ground or maybe it was not cowardice but intelligence. Someone had tried to take her from the Village of Frost, the carriage had been attacked, and she had, after all, been successfully kidnapped her first night in Daonith.

She made her way down a set of wide stairs towards where she believed the garden was when a familiar voice caught her attention. She spun, taking in the large form of Kalin turning a corner. A sword hung at his side and there were bags under his eyes, but he was whole and unharmed.

Without thinking Fia ran to him, nearly knocking over a courtier. Kalin's face broke into a grin at the sight of her and he spread his arms, catching her and wrapping her in a bone crushing hug. "Wow," he laughed, his booming voice filling the hall. "I can feel muscles on you for the first time."

Fia pulled away to playfully slap his shoulder. It was like hitting a boulder. "I'm glad you're okay."

"Me? Of course. Many men have tried to kill me, those were nothing." He waved his hand as though shooing away a fly. "But look at this." He touched his finger to her glamoured ear. "You fit right in. Better than me I suppose."

Indeed, he did stand out at the Western Court, much more than even Elara. "It's different here than the Village."

"If you miss the Village then I cannot wait for you to see the rest of the Unseelie Kingdom." He turned to the Seelie man beside him. Fia had barely noticed him in her excitement over seeing Kalin. "This is Lord Gavin, an old friend to the Queen and to myself."

Fia extended a hand to the brown-haired man. He had a pleasant look to him, a warmth in his eyes that made her want to trust him. "Do you live in the city?"

He shook his head. “No, my lands are near the border of the Unseelie Kingdom. You will have to visit sometime if you enjoyed the Village of Frost. The rolling hills near my home are some of the most beautiful lands in Daonith.”

“I would love that,” Fia said. “Well, I won’t keep you, but perhaps you’ll walk me into the city sometime soon, Kalin? I’d love to explore the city.”

“Of course. After training tomorrow, we’ll head out.”

The palace garden was beautiful, full of tall hedges, cut into intricate designs that lined twisting paths. Arches, hung with vines, marked dim alcoves and each turn seemed a world to itself, blocked by shrubbery from the rest of the estate. A garden to get lost in.

Winter was nearing. The garden must be even lovelier in the spring, but the reds and oranges and browns that surrounded Fia held a magic all their own, one season drifting into the next, on and on toward eternity.

Fia took her time meandering through the winding paths, pausing at a pond full of fat purple and yellow fish.

"This is one of my favorite spots," a voice said behind her, making her jump. Elara leaned against a tall tree whose branches nearly brushed the surface of the pond, her hands in the pockets of her shorts. Always shorts when Elara wasn't required to dress up. She'd said her home was cold, it must be for the chilly autumn day to seem warm enough for bare legs.

"I have never seen fish like this," Fia said, not that she was particularly acquainted with fish. Still, these looked particularly magical with their bright glimmering scales and pale, fanned tails.

"I don't believe you have them in your lands." There was a twinkle in Elara's eyes, promising mischief and Fia wished that look could stay forever, that Elara would never need to look icy again. "You were brilliant with Ezriel earlier. He will not forget you standing up to him anytime soon. He's a good man but centuries as king have made him used to getting his way."

"I know I'm a pawn, but I'm tired of feeling like one." Fia sat on the stone edge of the pond, letting her fingers trail in the cold water.

Elara pushed off the tree and came to sit beside her. "I wish I could assure you that you are not a pawn, but you are right, they will see you that way. But I can assure you that your pledge to me will never be forgotten. You are a member of my court, a soon to be powerful witch, and we will keep reminding them of that. They will realize you are much, much more than they think. More than we hoped."

A fish swam near the surface, looking up at them with pale eyes. Fia searched for words, something to say, but nothing seemed right. She was thankful for Elara's trust but still unsure if she deserved it. Would she be powerful? Would her fledgling magic matter at all when face to face with fae centuries older than she was?

The Queen moved closer, until their legs nearly touched. She was surprised how much she wanted Elara to close the gap, to feel the heat of her bare thigh against her.

"He is also afraid," Elara said, her voice low. "Everything we are planning is so dangerous. We have to go in without knowing much and what we do know has taken decades to learn. And after..." She sighed, a bone-tired sound. "After could very well mean war if anything goes wrong. No, after will probably mean war even if everything goes right. A good king does not want to lead armies."

A rustle of skirts on stone and the clearing of a throat drew their attention. Vinessa stood with Gavin, the man Fia had met earlier with Kalin.

"I ran into Vinessa in the hallway a moment after I left you and we got to talking. I think I might be able to offer you assistance, Lady," Gavin said, pushing a strand of dark hair out of his eyes. Though fae he appeared older than Fia, but still retained a boyish charm, one Fia suspected no amount of years would ever dull.

"Oh?"

"Yes. Vinessa said you have recently acquired magic, or rather, have recently been allowed access to your own magic and wished to learn more. That is where I may be able to help. My grandmother was a witch." He smiled. *His grandmother.* Not like Fia's grandmother, a still living woman, someone who had lived very long ago.

"Saskia offers her help as well," Elara said, glancing at Fia. She knew why the Queen had not mentioned it yet. The wraith-like fae terrified Fia. But she was a member of the court now and so was Saskia. Still...*the claws.*

Gathering the skirts of her pewter gray dress in her hand, Vinessa stepped closer. "May I speak to Fia alone for a moment?" Her words were to Elara.

The Queen looked at Fia, offering her a silent choice and Fia nodded. She may have butted heads with Ezriel, but Vinessa had been nothing but kind to her.

Gavin offered his arm to Elara, flashing another brilliant smile. "May I escort you on a tour of the grounds?"

The look on Elara's face was not one Fia was soon to forget. Confusion, irritation, amusement. "You are bold, sir."

Still, he grinned. "I have heard it is one of my best qualities and the one most likely to cost me my life eventually. Still, I would offer the walk."

"Fine. Put your arm down," Elara said, with a final glance at Fia before she left her alone with Vinessa, who took the seat Elara had vacated, trailing her fingers through the water as Fia had done minutes ago.

"I have something to say, but it is only advice, Fia, please do not take it as a demand or an order or even an attempt at one. I understood you clearly earlier and you are right. These are not your people, yet you have promised yourself to them. And as they are my people, I can offer you only thanks for such a generous gift."

Such sweet talk. What on earth did Vinessa want to say to her that she needed to butter her up so thoroughly before she said it? Intrigue gripped Fia as the faerie's wings expanded and fluttered at her back. “I would be happy to hear any advice you might give me, Your Majesty.” Was that right? Your Highness? Fia had no idea, but Vinessa’s expression didn’t change so she continued. “Despite my earlier words, I hold no ill will towards either you or your husband. Especially you.”

“I appreciate that more than I can say.” Vinessa smoothed her skirts. “My advice is to take your time, Fia. The thing between you and Elara...she is a good queen, and she loves her people, but they have suffered, more than perhaps any other kingdom, they have suffered. There is a darkness in her.”

What was she talking about? Fia struggled to keep her face neutral. Of course there was a darkness in Elara, she’d watched her people starve for no reason other than Ellio’s greed. She clenched her teeth rather than respond, she wanted to know what Vinessa would say next but had no kind words to urge her on.

“When magic was taken, she was just a girl, coming to power. I was barely older than her and our kingdom knew that the niece of the king had more power than the rest of us. They were scared and she was strong, so when the king could not save them, they looked to her, the powerful, beautiful, horned princess. They gave her a larger burden than such a young woman should have shouldered. She has tried to fight before, tried and been squashed before she could even act. These things leave scars on a person."

"Excuse me?" Fia said, moving slightly away from Vinessa.

She kept talking. "There is a wall around her heart, built over centuries. You are young and you have made a promise that will be hard to take back. I know what it is like to be seduced by someone more powerful than yourself—"

"That is enough!" Fia stood up. "I don't know what you are talking about." And even if she did, she didn't want to hear it. Didn't want to think about the things she forced to the back of her mind.

Vinessa stood as well, a phantom, summer-scented breeze ruffling her dress as her wings pulled tight behind her. "As I said, it is only advice. But be careful of the promises you make, Lady. Be careful of how you become indebted when you have not been here long enough to know much of our world. When you are so young."

"With all due respect, I am not a child." She was nearly thirty. Not as old as the fae, but not a child. "And my heart remains, alone, in my chest, unburdened."

"Of course," Vinessa said. "Perhaps I am mistaken."

"Perhaps you are."

Vinessa shrugged and started to walk away but took only a step before she stopped. "I said that wrong. I only want you to live, Fia. I know what we are asking you is so vast and you signed up for none of it. I know the horrors of this world, I have watched my people die from the time I was a little girl in that Seelie village to now, when I am their queen. I will watch more of them die if the King comes to us with those human weapons we don't know how to fight against. But I see you, so young, so human despite the magic in your veins and I worry about your future—that even if everything goes right, if we, by some miracle from the gods win, you will spend so many of your young years, when you should be enjoying your victory, trying to love a heart that has been broken beyond repair. I hope I am wrong, in so many ways, I hope I am wrong. And beyond all else, in gratitude, I wish you only the best." With a sad, gentle smile she was gone, lost in the labyrinth of the hedges.

There was nothing in her words that Fia wanted to contemplate, yet they echoed in her ears. Elara was terrifying, dark and capricious, quick to anger. To love her would be dangerous, always coming second to her people, to the power that already flowed in her veins, power that was soon to grow larger. Before Fia loomed a war, one that was not her own, yet she had joined, perhaps not willingly, but with little other choices, not if she would live here, not if she knew the truth.

There would be no going back to Callum, no pretending she didn't know the things she knew. The lie of the Joining. How she had been sold to keep needed magic from others—both the humans she had come from and the fae she had promised herself to. The knowledge she might have lived in some country home, rich and spoiled as a princess, while in other kingdoms people starved as once fertile fields refused to yield crops made her sick.

Each day she was told this was not her war, but maybe it was. Humans had waged war for centuries over spots at the border land where a fraction of magic could be found to power equipment to save lives. People paid their last dimes for spots at the hospitals. Each day people died for lack of space or money while magic that should be saving them was held back by King Ellio. And her father had known, and if he, a dangerous gangster knew, how many others knew the truth? Her father was never sick, she couldn't remember him so much as coughing, and his drugs and weapons never sat for long. Did Ellio give him magic? Did he buy her father's poison for years before he'd bought Fia, treating her like a promise between them, not a person at all?

Magic lashed at her fingertips, twisting around her wrists, strands and strands of it that longed to go further, to dig into the garden soil. The magic she had not known was hers. Did it come from her mother? Would she have been stronger if she had been allowed access to it? Would she have lived? Lived to shield Fia from so many horrors that still haunted her, that lurked in the shadows of her mind that she did not dare investigate?

Fia, her mother, those small, thin children in the village, Elara's childhood. So much lost. This was Fia's war, as much as it was anyone else who fought it. She had not asked for it, but who asked for war? Never those who would fight in it, only those who would send others to die to get them power. Men like Ellio.

A hatred she had never known burned inside her as she thought of her mother, her beautiful mother who loved stars, who her father had watched waste away. Her mother who had tried to take her, who she remembered shoving clothes in a suitcase, dragging her to the car, her fingers bone thin in Fia's small hand, going too fast to the airport and getting out of the car only for her father to be there.

Then her passport had been in his safe and men had been at the door and the skin around her mother's eye had been purple. She'd gone into the bathroom and only her body had come out.

If Fia died killing Ellio, the only thing she would regret was losing the chance kill her father next.

-CHAPTER- -EIGHTEEN-

"YOU ARE TOO tense," Gavin said.

They'd found an open area outside the palace proper, but still within its walls, a small field surrounded by trees with a golden statue of a goddess Fia didn't recognize in the middle. She knew nearly nothing about the fae gods. Religion had long ago faded for most humans. It was hard to worship invisible gods when magic itself sparkled on the other side of a misty wall, controlled by beautiful immortal beings.

"Hard to be calm when my head is throbbing." Fia rubbed her temples, but it did little to ease the pain. There was a small patch of half dead wildflowers under the trees not ten feet from her. Gavin wanted her to find them with her magic. Eventually he wanted her to make them bloom, which seemed impossible, but for now just to find them with her magic. That task seemed equally impossible. She could feel the earth, the grass beneath her feet, but when she tried to stretch toward the flowers the magic snapped, leaving her shaking like she'd exercised too long.

"My grandmother said it was worse when she hadn't used it. She said it was a muscle."

His grandmother—Fia would give her left tit for an actual witch who could tell her more than what some six-hundred-year-old man remembered from his dead grandma.

But Gavin was what she had. She tried again, pulling the magic from inside her, deep in her veins and imagining it moving away from her, searching, searching.

"Shit." The magic collapsed back into her and Fia fell to her knees as something wet trickled down her face. Her nose was bleeding.

"Maybe we should take a break."

"No." She pushed herself back up and wiped at her nose. The blood smeared across the back of her hand, and she grabbed a handful of autumn leaves from the ground to use like a rag. "I need to get this, even if it sucks."

“I don’t disagree,” Gavin said, taking a tentative step towards her. “Do they really intend to free all our magic? That is what the whispers say.”

A slight incline of her head was all Fia offered. “Has it been awful? Truly?”

“Not only the loss, we have found ways around that in the centuries since it was taken but it is the knowing, knowing what we could have and that we do not. To feel enormous power in your veins and be unable to access it without burnout, to know the Southern Kingdom rules us all through treachery, by stealing what we create. Yes, it is awful.”

“I’m sorry I didn’t know before.” There was guilt where perhaps there should not be. “And for the weapons,” she whispered, unsure of if he knew, but he should, all of them should know the danger they were in. But there was no surprise on his face.

“I do not blame you or seek your apologies, but some will hold you accountable if he uses them.”

The magic inside her pushed against her skin and threads of it inched, dark and shimmering, along the forest floor. “Perhaps they should. I never stood up to him. I could have ended it long ago, but I was afraid.” The magic kept moving. Her joints ached but she stayed upright.

"That *is* a burden to carry, but you were young, only a child for much of it." Gavin took another step closer, watching the magic, the dark webs disappearing into the earth. "You can protect these people, even if you did not protect your own."

The words hit her like a fist but still she stood, sweat gathering on her brow as she stared at those wildflowers, felt their own threaded magic, the autumnal death that slithered through their cells. She willed them alive.

They obeyed.

Fia fell, her knees digging gouges into the soft earth, dirt lodging under her fingernails. Blood dripped crimson onto the browning grass.

Gavin let out a whoop of triumph then offered her a hand. "I know it's hard, but if you face your demons they cannot dampen your magic."

She let him haul her to her feet, her vision going black at the edges. She stumbled against him, and he wrapped his arms around her.

"Fia, are you okay?"

Her magic was still out, threads of it moving away from her, dancing up the trees, rustling the leaves. Strong, ancient beings, their armor of bark, readying for winter, for cold and sleep.

She could not pull the magic back. Her efforts did nothing.

Birds in the sky, wings beating, wind like something solid around them. They would leave soon.

Her vision grew darker.

"Fia?" He was so far away. The trees and the birds and the universe itself were around her. Or nothing was. Was she nothing? "Fia?"

Nothing.

The air smelled like the ocean. Her head hurt. Her head always hurt lately. She opened one eye, peeking up at a smooth, cream-colored ceiling.

Beside her someone moved and long fingers pressed against her forehead. "I'm going to kill Gavin," Elara said.

The magic. She'd actually used her magic. And then passed out. But she'd done something with it, something real. Above the bed Elara's face came into focus. Her silver and brown eyes were wide and her hair looked like she'd been running her hands through it, leaving it tangled around her horns.

"I'm okay," Fia said, wincing. She motioned to the pitcher of water on the bedside table. Her throat felt like she'd been swallowing sand.

Someone knocked on the door. Before either of them could answer Saskia came in, a small linen satchel dangling from her clawed fingers. "I thought this might help." She held out the satchel to Fia.

The smell was pungent, floral, and woodsy all at once. She opened the drawstring top and peered in. Crushed something. "What is it? Is it drugs?"

Saskia raised one dark eyebrow. "Medicinal drugs, yes. If you would prefer more psychedelic drugs I can acquire some."

"She would not," Elara said, plucking the bag from Fia and dumping the contents into a glass of water. She twisted her finger and the water and herbs mixed, turning the water a bright fuchsia.

"That is a common mix for your ailments. We use it when children go through puberty, and their power grows. It eases the transition, helps with the pain."

Great. She was getting medication for children. But she took the glass from Elara and drank deeply. The flavor reminded her of the lavender lattes she'd get occasionally in the human world. The pain in her head dulled.

"I'll let you talk," Saskia said, nodding at Elara before she left.

The Queen perched on the edge of the bed, power sparking around her as though she could not contain it. "Please don't kill Gavin," Fia said, not sure if she had been joking. "I need to learn. He was only trying to help."

Something fierce and feral shone in Elara's eyes when she looked at Fia. She exhaled and it eased but the spell connecting them was tight and Fia could still feel her magic swirling around the fragile thread, strengthening it. She fisted the sheets beneath her hand to keep from reaching across the space between them. "Will Queen Seera answer your letters?" She pushed herself up and situated her pillows behind her back, scooting over to give Elara room.

A moment passed before the faerie queen moved fully onto the bed, half sitting, half lying beside Fia, their legs stretched out in the last of the dying sunlight. "I do not know. If she doesn't there are other options we can pursue. I would rather Seera be on our side, but she is difficult."

Big words from Elara, who was certainly not easy by anyone's standards. "What, exactly, are we going to do? What's the plan?" She held Elara's gaze. It was time—past time—to know the truth.

Without hesitating Elara answered, the feral look back in her brown and silver eyes. Her magic fanned out as it had in the garden, creating a shield around them, a bubble with only Fia and Elara inside. "We will find whatever talisman holds our magic to Ellio and we will destroy it with a contingent from each of the groups who were there when it was formed, you, Aurora, Vinessa, and Ezriel."

Fia's heart skipped a beat and the sunlight faded, leaving them in shadows with only Elara's sparkling magic to light the room. Her hair shone and her horns became iridescent. "Not you?" She would be doing all of this without Elara?

"I will be there, providing backup."

"No." That was idiotic. "It will take power, you know it will. You are stronger than Vinessa. Why would you not do it?"

Elara shrugged. "Ezriel suggested his wife. I do not think he will ever fully trust me, and I needed him on our side. It is a small thing."

Fia pushed herself to fully sitting, her muscles barking in protest. "It is not a small thing, Elara. This is *your* plan. I'm not doing it if you aren't." She didn't know exactly what breaking the talisman would entail but it couldn't be easy and judging by how using her power had gone so far it would probably hurt.

Slowly, as though the queen was afraid she would bolt away, her fingers settled over Fia's hand, warm and callused. "For the plan to work, someone needs to watch over you and make sure you are not interrupted. I will keep you safe."

Fia turned her palm over, pressing it to Elara's and intertwining their fingers. "You are the *Queen*, Elara. You should not be stationed as a guard. Your people chose you. You have more right to rule than Ezriel or Vinessa. And with those human weapons...Ellio will retaliate when you take your magic back."

"What is your point?" Elara asked gently.

"My point," Fia said, dropping her hand and choosing boldness. She took the Queen's chin in her fingers, staring into those beautiful eyes. "Guards die and when this war comes we will need you, your strength, your power. I love Kalin, he has become a true friend, but he should be waiting outside. War is coming and we will need you."

The thread between them lurched as Elara moved, pushing a piece of hair behind Fia's ear, her fingers lingering, tracing a line down her cheek, her shoulder, to the arm still holding the Queen's chin. "There is nothing you say I disagree with, though putting Kalin in danger instead of myself revolts me. But let me think and maybe I will speak to Ezriel. If nothing else, Vinessa would be better here, watching over her new people. If things go wrong leaders will be needed so our kingdoms don't fall."

Fia moved her hand, letting it fall to Elara's knee, somehow they were sitting face to face on the bed. She barely remembered moving. "Good. And the talisman, do you know where it is?"

"No," Elara breathed. "It is in the castle, but we have never been able to find it. I believe he moves it."

The air smelled like her, each inhale breathing in a piece of Elara, of her queen. But it was something else, a realization she did not want to have that made Fia's heart pound in her chest, made her want to close the space between them, press herself into Elara and lay in the queen's arms until the sun rose. "I..." She swallowed and reached for the water, taking a long drink before she spoke again. "You trust me? You once said I must earn it. Have I?"

The queen's head dipped, nodding. "Yes, Fia. I trust you."

"I could find the talisman if I went back. With a little more practice, I'm sure I could do it. If I returned to the Southern Kingdom, I could spy for you."

-CHAPTER-
-NINETEEN-

"NO." ELARA GRIPPED Fia by her shoulders. "I will not send you back into that place, Fia. Do you hear me?"

Fia reached up, removing the Queen's hands and putting them in her lap. She looked over her face, full of outrage. And the horns. For nearly a month now Fia had wanted to feel those horns and if she went back to Callum and her engagement perhaps she never would. She would never do so many things, but she could do this.

Slowly she reached up, almost in a dream. The pads of her fingers brushed against Elara's horns, hard and solid, like the queen herself. Fia traced their shape, the grooves in the surface, the swirling turns, until the queen's hand darted out and grabbed her by the wrist. "You will not be a spy. It is too dangerous."

"Who else could?"

"Even Aurora was unable to find it."

Fia moved closer, spreading her aching legs until she surrounded the queen. Above them her magic grew thicker, bathing them in purple and silver. "Aurora did not have my magic. Give me a bit longer to train, to learn to control it, and then let me go back. I will find whatever binds our magic and I will return to you. I will come back, Elara."

Elara's chest moved rapidly and Fia could hear each breath, the quick inhale and exhale. "If you go..." the words seemed to pain her just to speak them. "Fia, if you do this, he cannot know you're a witch. Not him, not his charming son. And I will be nearby. Locate the talisman then leave and I will come for you. We are connected, I will know."

"You can't do that. You need to be here. You need to convince Seera, not wait for me."

"*That* is nonnegotiable. I will not leave you alone there. When I met you, Fia, you were meek, but I could see in your face that it was not who you truly were. You were only acting out a part you had been taught. You are strong and vibrant. You are a fighter. I will not send you back there to forget all you have become. You lie to those bastards, find what you need to find, then you leave, even if you have to blow up the whole fucking city to do it."

From the look in her eyes Fia knew that Elara *would* blow up the city if it came to it. She would use every ounce of her magic to drag Fia away from those people. The knowledge stirred inside her and she did not know how to feel. Vinessa's earlier words came back to her.

And her own words bubbled up from her chest, threatening to spill from her lips. But she couldn't say any of those things now, could speak none of her truths. Not when she would leave soon, not when there was no future promised to them. She could not say the things she wanted to say to Elara then return to Callum. There were lines she could not cross, not yet, maybe never.

"We will need a plan. It has to look like I escaped. They need to trust me, especially Callum." The next words tasted like poison. "He wanted to love me. I can get him to show me things."

Curtains fluttered as a breeze blew into the room and Fia thought of the wildflowers, of the way they had bloomed and she had bloomed too, no longer in her father's shadow. To go back to that world where men passed her like a prize. Her heart ached.

She took another drink of the tonic, letting it ease the physical pain inside of her. “I can’t believe for all your swagger you were going to stand outside while everyone else dealt with the talisman.”

Elara huffed. “They would have called me in eventually. Vinessa is lovely but not particularly powerful.” She looked into Fia’s eyes. “Can you feel this?” A tug on the bond between them. Fia nodded. “Do it back.”

Power stretched like a cat in the sun inside Fia, dark threads that danced along her bones and reached for the bond. She imagined the power wrapping around it, grabbing it like hundreds of midnight fingers and pulled. Elara’s pupils flared and she nodded.

The fingers softened to tendrils, swirling and dancing with the bond, caressing it softly like a lover. Beside her, Elara swallowed hard and released a slow breath. “Fia...”

At the sound of the queen’s breathy voice, Fia pulled back her magic, rolling it into herself. “I will tug when I have found the talisman and again when I am free of the estate. Will you be able to track me by it?”

“Yes. That was the idea, remember?” Elara stood. “I will check in with you later, Fia.” She disappeared with a soft crack, leaving the room much colder than before.

The next few days were spent training with Kalin in the morning and practicing her magic with Saskia and Gavin in the afternoons. Gavin did most of the instruction, while Saskia sat nearby, watching them, cleaning her nails, and occasionally offering a suggestion.

“You can pull it back if it starts to overwhelm,” Saskia said, as Fia panted, hands on her knees. “Or use less magic. Have you tried separating it, keeping some buried within?”

“I have tried. I have not been successful.” Fia took a breath, ready to try to pull leaves from the tree above her but stopped at a strange sound approaching.

From above, Vinessa fluttered down, her wings flapping gently, and landed on the soft earth. “It seems to be coming along well.”

Fia had known she could fly or at least assumed so because of her wings, but watching it was something else altogether. The other two seemed to feel the same, Saskia's lips were in a thin line that Fia couldn't decipher, and Gavin looked absolutely spellbound.

Vinessa only smiled. Clearly, she knew what she was doing, what her beauty combined with those butterfly wings did to people. A different kind of queen entirely than Elara. "May I speak to Fia alone for a moment?"

Gavin gave a bow and started gathering his things but Saskia stood, looking to Fia. For the space of a heartbeat, she considered shaking her head. She did not want to hear Vinessa's speech again.

The heartbeat was too long, Saskia tensed. "I will stay."

"It's okay," Fia said. Saskia still did not move. Relations between the Kingdoms were tense; a month in their lands had taught Fia that. She did not want to add to it. "Truly."

"I will let Elara know you are finished with your training for the day," Saskia said, leaving Fia and Vinessa alone in the forest opening. Fia waited, refusing to fill the silence. Whatever Vinessa had to say, she would let her say it.

The faerie looked up at the trees, their autumnal leaves swaying in the wind. She was out of sorts with the season—

her green hair, her pale pink skin. Spring personified. “A secret to stay between us?” Vinessa’s lips curved into a delicate smile.

“Unless it is too deliciously juicy, I believe I can keep a secret.” Fia smiled back, some of her dread at the conversation melting away at the faerie’s easy demeanor.

Vinessa stepped forward, her wings fluttering like the leaves, until she was within whispering distance. “I am grateful to you for whatever you said to your Queen that made her demand to replace me when they go to the Southern Kingdom.”

Fia knew she was gaping like a fish, trying to find words that refused to form. Grateful?

“Yes, shocking, but these plans were formed long ago, when Ezriel felt he had a score to settle, and I was his very new wife. It was a move meant to intimidate but the better I got to know Elara the less I agreed with it. She has power I cannot dream of, power that will only grow when her magic is freed. And I am a coward. I do not wish to be there at all.”

“Ezriel does not seem like such a proud and spiteful man that he would risk something like that.”

Vinessa sighed. “He is a good king and a wonderful husband, but he risked a lot by taking an Unseelie wife. I think at the time it was less to do with Elara—though she is quite skilled at getting under his skin—and more to do with proving that I was capable. He wanted me to be a hero to our people."

When Fia first met Vinessa, she had liked her instantly and now she knew she had been right, despite their previous conversation. The Queen was good, flawed but good. "And you do not want to prove that?"

"I think I prove myself to them in many ways. I have worked hard for our people, opening new schools, working on social projects, making sure they are fed. I will never prove myself to them through strength. And Ezriel knew, I think he was only waiting on Elara to ask."

Fia rolled her eyes. "Then I am also glad I pushed as well, if only to save our king and queen from themselves."

Outside the clearing someone cleared their throat and Fia stilled for a moment, but it was only Kalin. "Queen Elara has sent me to walk you safely back to the palace."

"I will leave you," Vinessa said, taking a few steps away before flapping her wings.

Fia watched as she disappeared over the trees before turning back to Kalin. "Porting is really cool, but I think I'm more jealous of flying."

He shrugged. "It has it's uses. When the power returns, I would like to build an aerial unit of Unseelies. Vinessa is not the only one who can fly, and I believe they would be useful in battle." He offered her his thick, tree trunk arm and she took it. "Perhaps you will help me talk the Queen into it, since she is so amenable to your charms."

"As are you." Fia grinned up at him sweetly, squeezing his bicep.

He covered her hand with his. "I have heard your plan to go back. It is brave and I am proud of you. I also do not like it. I have grown very fond of you."

"You're going to miss me?" The thought warmed Fia's heart. She wondered if anyone in the human world missed her. She doubted it.

"I will miss you and I will worry like a mother hen. It will be quite unbecoming." They cleared the forest and the land opened to a vast cliffside, the ocean roaring below. A few houses dotted the land and though the bulk of civilization was beyond another copse of trees and out of sight, she could hear noises from the city nearby.

"I will miss you too," Fia said, trying to sear the moment into her brain. The smell of the ocean, the sounds of the city, and the warmth and strength of Kalin's arm in hers.

Elara waited for them not far ahead, completing the moment. Fia would hold onto the memory when she went back to the Southern Kingdom. She would remember Elara, the wind whipping at her hair as she waited for them, the friendship she had found in Kalin, the secrets shared between Vinessa and herself. All the things she had wanted without knowing she wanted them. And she would find her way back.

-CHAPTER-
-TWENTY-

NOBODY WANTED HER to go back, but everyone agreed to let her do it, knowing she was their best shot to free their magic and the only way they wouldn't go in blind. What had been a hope had become a reality. They had needed a human to free their powers but Fia having magic was beyond their wildest dreams. She could see it on their faces, fear and anticipation, a wild, rebellious plan had become something real, but they weren't imagining their magic flowing free, their people laughing, no they were thinking of war.

But before anything could be done, they had to figure out how to get Fia back to the Southern Kingdom without the King becoming suspicious.

Aurora paced the palace hallway, golden curtains billowing around her on a chilled breeze, while Fia leaned against one of the pillars. The faerie muttered to herself, her brow knitted together. Every few minutes she would stop, tap her toe against the floor or stare out at the horizon, sigh loudly, then continue pacing.

"We don't have to figure it out today," Fia said when she could no longer stand watching her walk back and forth.

"I know that," she snapped then grimaced. "Sorry, I'm just stressed. I can't find an angle that gets you back in the castle. It's so unlikely you would make it through these lands by yourself without dying."

"Gee, thanks." Fia pushed off the pillar, looking out towards the sea, sparkling in the setting sun.

Aurora shrugged. "I should have given you more days there. Taking you immediately was foolish. Now they won't trust you, they have no reason to."

"Yeah. That was a bit rough." Fia thought of that night, waking up from her sleep, watching the ruby shine of the guard's blood in candlelight. "Why *did* you take me so quickly?"

A wave, larger than the rest, crashed into the cliffside, drawing their attention. Aurora stood beside Fia in the open hallway. Another wave hit and they both took a step from the marble floor to the loamy soil of the cliffside, entranced by the ocean.

The crystalline fae lights in the open-air hallway blinked to life as the sun sunk further on the horizon, casting the world around them in blue, green, and orange. Fia pressed her lips together, waiting to see if Aurora would answer her, if she had an answer at all.

Elara was impatient and rash, Fia understood why the Queen had been impatient to take her from the Southern Kingdom, but Aurora was more calculating, slower to act. Had she simply allowed Elara to force her choices as she often did or had there been another reason?

Dolphins crested above the reef, their silver skin like moonlight in the fading sun. Perhaps Aurora would not answer and in the end it would not matter.

"I was afraid you would fall in love with Callum," she whispered so low the wind nearly stole her words.

Would everything be different if Fia had been given more time with Callum? He had been kind, maybe not the partner she would have picked for herself, but if he had been her lifeline in a strange, new world would she have clung to him?

When she had first arrived, she had told herself she would find a way out, but throughout her life Fia had told herself many things—many lies. They were just ways to get through the day, words that allowed her eyes to close at night. The Village of Frost was the first time Fia had ever felt bravery rush through her veins, lighting her from the inside, making her not only want, but reach for more.

She watched the dark threads twine around her fingers before blowing away in the breeze. She was full of magic and life and desire, and she didn't want to go back to her old life. She didn't think she could shrink herself enough to fit even if she did want to. She'd grown too big, too wild.

"I don't think what I felt for him would have been love, but you were right, I would not have left as easily. I think after my father forced me into marriage any freedom he gave me would have seemed like a miracle."

"I told you before, in some ways we are a lot alike. I know the way it feels to be away from your father for the first time—truly away, not just in distance but away from their control, their power over you. I like you, Fia, and I worry about you going back, that you will find it hard to resist becoming who you were before, falling into old patterns. And I worry even more that they won't believe you and you'll be hurt."

Fia kept her eyes on the dusk-dark sea below, not daring to look at Aurora, to see herself mirrored there. "I have my magic now. I will not forget who I am. I won't forget any of this. I won't go back to sleeping through my life."

"I was unable to either. Elara has that effect on people. You want a minute before we head in? We have about an hour before Ezriel's shindig." Fia nodded and Aurora squeezed her shoulder before heading back through the curtains and into the heart of the palace.

Earlier in the afternoon, Ezriel had announced he was hosting a get together in his private apartments for everyone, that it was past time they figured out how to get along, and that he looked forward to their alliance.

Fia suspected that Elara asking to be included, finally, made him realize just how stubborn the two of them had been, even while working together. No one said it, but Vinessa winked at her when he made his announcement. She hoped she was right. The faster Ezriel swallowed his pride the better.

Still staring at the waves, she tried not to think what would happen if things fell apart. The cushy but cloistered life she could have had with Callum truly would be a dream compared to what would happen if they realized her treachery. Would the king kill her? Would her father allow it? Would he know at all? Would he care?

And Fia had seen enough in her life to know there were things worse than death. If King Ellio decided to keep relations up with the humans, to parade her out every few years as proof of goodwill between the fae and humans, she knew her life would be hell between those appearances. There were ways to hurt people that didn't show on the skin, ways that eventually would make her a much easier symbol to wield.

She shuddered, wrapping her arms around herself, though no wind made it through the fabric of her jacket. There was nothing to be gained by those thoughts, only fear, and fear would not control her any longer.

With a final look at the reef, and a wish she could see beyond the swirling mist to the horizon, she turned and headed for her room.

The door to Elara's chambers was closed but Fia could smell her in the living area, her earthy scent permeated the space. Fia headed for her own room to change into something more formal, but Elara's door swung open and Fia's breath caught in her chest.

The Queen's gown was gold, a harsh, regal contrast to her silvery hair, curled and pinned around her horns, between which sat a delicate silver crown made of impossibly thin threads of metal twisted together, amethysts tucked between the strands. She grinned a feline smile at Fia and stepped forward, the tight gown hugging every curve of her honed body.

"I put something on your bed, but you don't have to wear it." Her voice was low, husky, made for a bedroom.

Every inch of Fia burned as she made her way to her room. Her gown was a near match for Elara's, cut low in the front and lower in the back and above it...Oh gods, a tiara, not nearly as elaborate as Elara's but a *tiara*.

The Queen stood close enough that her breath fluttered Fia's hair. "I did not want them to forget whose court you are a part of."

Everything in Fia was both too tight and too loose. "This may send an entirely different message." One she was not sure she was ready to send, one they had not spoken of at all, though they traveled together and shared rooms, and made promises in the dark of the night. Not yet, not when she was about to leave.

"You do not have to wear it," Elara said, moving impossibly closer, her body pressing into Fia's side, her horns scraping against the side of her face.

Fia took a step away because if she didn't she would move the other direction, let herself fall into the Queen's arms. A perilous move, not only because she was leaving, but because of the Queen herself, who had so much darkness in her. Vinessa's words had been true, even if Fia had not wanted to hear them. To love the Queen was dangerous, an abyss Fia didn't think she'd be able to crawl out of if she let herself fall in.

So, she stepped toward the dress, letting the soft, smooth fabric move through her fingers. Elara's dress was daring but Fia's was scandalous. She loved it. She would have picked it for herself, enjoying all the eyes on her, secure in the knowledge no one would dare touch her, not with the dress a claim from the most powerful among them.

Would she allow herself to be claimed?

As though sensing her hesitation, Elara stepped around her and plucked the tiara from the bed. She ran her fingers over the single amethyst in the center then placed it on Fia's head. Her silver and brown eyes dropped to Fia's mouth, catching there. "I know what it says, Fia."

Fia's throat was dry, her magic roared inside her. "I'm leaving, Elara. I'm going to Callum, and I don't know how long I'll be there. I don't know what will happen."

The queen's eyes dragged from her mouth, higher, to look in her eyes like she was the only person in the world. "I am immortal, and you will have decades and decades if you stay here, all that magic in your veins. You'll live a long life. I can wait if you want me to wait."

Her heart pounded. "Elara...." The Queen stepped closer. "I would not leave. I could not leave." Because for all the darkness, what truly scared her was the possibility she would find something she had been looking for without knowing she was searching, and it would not be long enough. There was a war marching toward them. Death and destruction. What if she found Elara and then lost her so soon?

"I expect nothing, Fia. I have asked for nothing. Just a golden dress for a beautiful woman. A promise and a threat. You will be away from me, I do not want any of the other Kingdoms to get ideas about where you might return, about how they might claim that power inside you."

"Do you want that power?" The tiara was heavy on her head.

Again, the Queen's eyes dropped. "Among other things, Fia Gray." She brought her thumb to Fia's lips, running the pad of it along the seam. "But it will always be yours. Your power is not mine to have but I do find it...intoxicating."

Fia pulled Elara's thumb into her mouth, and the wildest urge came over her. Without thinking she bit down on the Queen's thumb and Elara pulled back, eyes wide. "No. Not yet." She took another step back, her chest rising and falling rapidly, though she quickly regained her composure. "Wear the dress, Fia. I want to see them squirm."

Fia had no idea what had happened, the strange urge that overcame her or Elara's even stranger reaction. She also knew the Queen was not going to explain. She'd spent enough time with her to know that if Elara wanted her to know something she would tell her. Maybe if she pushed, maybe if she stepped closer, made her voice breathy...

Yet she didn't. Instead, she nodded. There was already too much, so many things to consider and plan for, so much to fear. Let Elara keep her distance. Everything would be easier with the Queen at arm's length. "Of course I'll wear the dress."

Elara's swagger returned as she headed for the door, pausing only once to look over her shoulder at Fia, dragging her eyes down her body before pulling the door shut.

-CHAPTER-
-TWENTY ONE-

THE HALLWAY TO the Ezriel and Vinessa's personal apartment smelled like sandalwood and lilac. The windows were wide, all the way down to the floor and glassless with the same golden curtains as the lower levels flapping in the ocean breeze. Fires burned in fireplaces tucked away in alcoves, keeping the air warm with the help of, Fia suspected, a bit of magic.

Aurora had gone before them in a short, pale green, gossamer gown, flowers braided through her golden hair like a nymph or a salacious goddess of spring. She'd grinned wide at the sight of Fia and Elara in near matching dresses before practically skipping away to leave the two of them alone again, though not before blowing a kiss.

The length of Aurora's skirt made Fia feel much better about her own dress and the amount of skin on display. She hadn't noticed the long slit up one of her thighs when it had laid on her bed. The thing was practically three pieces of fabric held together with a prayer, and though she still loved it just as much as when she'd first seen it, she wasn't sure what the usual attire was for a faerie party. Most of the clothes she'd seen in Daonith had been lovely but practical.

"You look beautiful," Elara said as they neared the doors, manned by a single guard as though Ezriel had no worries at all that someone might find all the royals gathered together an easy target. She hoped he was correct, not foolishly naive, or at least had other guards hidden nearby.

"You did dress me," Fia said, smiling at the Queen. "It seems you like dressing me."

"I have other interests besides freeing magic, you know, and you're a very nice model."

"I didn't peg you for someone who cared about fashion," Fia teased.

Elara frowned. "Not even with my tiny little shorts? I had them custom made, Fia. They have holders for weapons. I was hoping you'd be a bit more perceptive if you were going to try to find the talisman."

Fia did her best to look affronted though she wanted to laugh. "I'll have all your threats to keep me focused."

The humor left Elara's face and Fia worried she had pushed too hard. "You should not trust me so much. It is foolish."

Part of her wanted to agree, to placate the Queen, but only part of her. "I remember your threats, Elara and I have taken them seriously, but I believe I have earned your trust, and I will continue to earn it. These people mean something to me. The Village means something to me. I don't take helping them—protecting them—lightly."

Elara's face softened and she moved towards Fia at the same moment the door opened, and Ezriel's voice reached them, freezing them both in place. "Welcome to—" He looked Fia over or might have if his eyes didn't stop on the tiara on her head.

"Good evening, Ezriel," Elara said, grabbing Fia's hand and pulling her over the threshold and into the enormous apartments beyond.

Vinessa's touch was evident in the decorating, the space was regal, yet soft and inviting, with room for large gatherings and smaller areas, perfect for only a few people, tucked away in candlelit corners. Soft chairs and tables full of pastries and candied fruit beckoned guests to forget who Ezriel was and spill their secrets like he was a friend.

A quartet was playing live music, a quick song that Fia didn't recognize but made her feet want to move. She knew most of the people there, including Kalin who was having some sort of argument, or at least heated discussion, with Saskia and one of the men who had stood behind Ezriel when she had first met him, but there were others as well, beautiful Seelie fae who must be part of Ezriel's court.

Did they know who Fia was? Did they know she was a human wrapped in a fae's body by their king's magic? They certainly knew who Elara was and everyone in the room seemed to be trying and failing to look at her without being obvious.

Elara's hand snaked around Fia's waist, and she thought of her earlier words and what they meant in this room, all the beautiful faces who would want her if they knew what lurked beneath her skin. And that lurking magic wanted out, wanted to slither across the room and wind around all the fae, learn what secrets they held deep in their chest.

The human guns and bombs were not the only danger her father had brought to Daonith. Fia could become a weapon. All she had to do was learn to control her magic.

Elara's fingers tightened on Fia's waist. "Easy. They do not need to know what you can do. Your once in a lifetime power."

"Not once I free the magic. There will be more witches," she whispered, pulling Elara towards toward one of the smaller seating areas so the music could cover her words.

The Queen smirked, settling into a dusty-pink loveseat and pulling Fia down beside her "Do you think every human witch possesses even a kernel of the magic in your veins? You are here because you are strong, because your soul, your destiny, knew where you belonged."

Was it true? "You are strong too, even with Ellio's leash you are stronger than anyone else here. I think they hate you for it, even if they don't want to."

"What a pair we could be." Elara's leg was hot against Fia's thigh. "How they might hate us both. But they will yield. I will take you home to Niveren Gap and they will know how foolish it would be to touch us. A new era for the Unseelie, an end to being second rate."

Saskia sat beside Elara on the arm of the loveseat. "You are drawing too much attention and Ezriel wants to see you. He is practically dancing with the anticipation of it, like a child who needs to use the bathroom."

Elara clicked her tongue. "Do you worry about me?"

"It is my job to worry about you, and I would hate to spill blood in this place. It is clear his pretty queen spent many hours decorating it. They very well may bill us for it."

Fia let out a bark of laughter before she could stop herself, but Saskia was right. This was a party to get to know each other, but they were tucked away like lovers, discussing the faults of the other kingdoms, as though Fia had any right, as though she knew these people at all.

Across the room, she caught Vinessa's eye. She smiled as she made her way to them and offered Fia a drink. "Have you had faerie wine before?"

Fia shook her head. "Not yet. I have heard great things." She took the glass and sipped slowly. The taste was divine; sweet and tart and rich. She took another drink.

"Easy now." Saskia said, standing.

"Oh, let her have fun." Vinessa waved a pale pink hand. "She deserves a night of fun, doesn't she, Elara?"

Elara turned to the Western Queen, her eyebrows raised near her hairline. "Have you forgotten all the fun you had in the Unseelie lands already, Vinessa? Or is your King that exciting?"

Vinessa blushed, turning her skin crimson. "I do have fun with him, though I know he might not seem that way."

Fia took another sip of her drink. "No, I find it easy to believe he can be *very* fun."

Vinessa laughed, her wings fluttering and gestured to her husband, who disengaged from the group he was talking to and made his way over to them.

There was a haze to the king's eyes, and his lazy smile grew wider as he took in his wife. He wrapped his arm around her slender shoulder. The king, it seemed, also enjoyed faerie wine. "Is she not the most beautiful woman you have ever seen."

"She is certainly up there," Elara said, glancing towards Fia.

The King turned his sights on Fia, looking her over, his eyes snagging on her crown. "Elara, I am weary of the way things are between us, the hostility. We have grown too old for it. Though we may never see eye to eye, I cannot imagine a future where I forget what you have done for both our people. We each have played our parts in creating this, but I hope, going forward, we can work together more easily and consider each other more than just reluctant allies."

The group surrounding them went silent except Saskia who made a strange clicking noise.

Elara stood and Fia shoved her hands beneath her thighs to keep from reaching for the queen. Across the room Kalin stood alert, his attention no longer on the conversation he had been having with Aurora but focused on the queen.

The two monarchs stared at each other, Elara nearly as tall as Ezriel. Her chin dipped and she extended her hand. "From this day forward the Unseelies and the Western Kingdom will be allies." A rare grin spread across her beautiful, sharp face. "Now, I am tired of looking at Fia in this Seelie costume and she will not be here much longer, despite all our worries. Can you please return her to her own face. I trust no one in this room will betray us."

Ezriel continued to grin sloppily. "I planned to suggest the same. What future do we have if we cannot trust each other?" He looked around the room, where everyone was looking back. His shoulders straightened, firelight setting his brown skin aglow. He had never looked more like a king. "You have all proven your loyalty to me time and time again, now we will prove it to each other. Let us all honor Fia as we have honored few humans. She was forced into the Joining, but her heart was not given to the third son, but to Daonith and all its people."

Fia resisted the urge to roll her eyes, sweet words if a bit verbose for the situation. The king was most certainly drunk. She smiled at Vinessa but she had eyes only for Ezriel, smiling at him as though he had created all the stars in the heavens.

Ezriel raised his glass, turned his attention to Fia and a cool sensation rolled across her, followed by a sharp sting, and then her body was returned.

She stood, looking down at her hands then moving them to her ears, nearly disrupting her tiara in the process. Round human ears. She grinned and held up her wineglass, letting black threads of magic weave around the stem, then up her arms. “To the future of Daonith!”

Faerie wine was delicious and Fia quickly learned to sip it slowly. Despite everyone’s proclamations of goodwill, she had grown up around power and did not want to lose control of herself in such a viper’s den. Still after a few cups, her head swam and the edges of everything grew soft, from the wine and the faerie lights to the breeze drifting in from the open balcony door.

Across the room, Elara leaned against the wall, talking to Aurora, the conversation making her both laugh and scowl. Fia wished she could hear the words.

"We have had an idea," Kalin said, drawing her attention away from the queen. Gavin was beside him, handsome in a tight, dark outfit, his hair brushed away from his face, silver woven through like gossamer threads.

"I think it is a good idea," Gavin said, moving close to her and keeping his voice low. "But you will need to trust me. I have brought Kalin as a character reference."

"And because it was my idea," Kalin said, frowning at the Lord and mumbling, "Seelies."

Gavin looked up into Kalin's pale, birchwood face. "Now, now."

"What is the idea?" Fia asked, uninterested in waiting for the two of them to be done irritating each other. She dared a look at Elara, glad the two of them had come to her first. Whatever the idea, she appreciated the chance to decide her own future.

"I have kept up a relationship with the king," Gavin began.

-CHAPTER-
-TWENTY TWO-

THE AIR WAS colder away from the braziers that had lined the walls of the King's apartments. In the open hallways, with most of the fires extinguished for the evening, the wind bit at Fia's exposed skin and she pressed against Elara for warmth. "What do you think?"

"I think it is a decent plan, and you seem to like it. You will be the one in danger, so the decision is yours."

Not at all what Fia had expected. More than she could have hoped for, really. Threads of magic wound around the bond between them and something heavy inside Fia lightened, the air no longer seeming so cold.

They walked the rest of the way in silence, their bodies bumping against one another, golden fabric sliding against skin. The interior of the palace was full of staff and court members, but as Fia and Elara walked they moved aside, leaving the hallways clear until they came to their own room.

Elara pushed the door open, allowing Fia to step inside before following. They parted, each heading for their own room and the thing inside Fia squirmed.

Halfway across the living area she paused, reaching up to trail her fingers along the tiara on her head. Elara was almost to her own door, her arm reaching to open it when Fia spoke.

"I am glad that it was me and it was you. Despite everything, I'm happy for maybe the first time. And I will miss you. Constantly." More than miss, she would ache. The thought of leaving Elara, of knowing she would be out there, alone, waiting only for her...Fia's magic roared, a wild animal in her chest.

Elara was frozen, staring at Fia, nearly making her regret the words and then within a blink she ported, reappearing inches from Fia, sharing her air. The hand that had reached for the door settled on Fia's side, pushing her back, back, until she was against the wall and Elara's fingers tightened, her other hand reaching up to brush her knuckles against Fia's skin.

Electric magic of a different nature sparked in every spot they touched and Fia's breathing shallowed until she was not sure if she was breathing at all.

"Then don't," Elara said, her voice low and husky. "Stay here, we will find the talisman when we go together. I have asked too much."

"Yes," Fia's hand trembled as she reached up, tracing the curl of Elara's horn with her fingers then running them through her hair. "You have asked too much, but I will not stay. I have to go. I have sworn myself to you, to your people. I will do this and then, maybe, I can have all the things I want."

Elara pressed her palm to the bare skin of Fia's chest, right above her wildly pounding heart. "They are already yours." Her eyes fell to Fia's mouth and she leaned in.

The door banged open. "Are you fucking serious?" Aurora yelled, the door banging again as she shoved it closed behind her and threw up a thick shield of magic around the room, trapping their voices inside.

Elara did not kiss Fia, but she did not let her go either, keeping her trapped against the wall, but her now deadly focus was on Aurora. "Leave."

"No," Aurora said, taking another step closer and Fia hated her, just a bit, for her refusal. "Is this what I signed up for,

Elara? Is this why I left my kingdom? Why I betrayed my family? For you to fuck some human girl. All the years you have worked for this, and you would throw it away?"

Oh. Fia blinked against the sudden tears in her eyes. What was she doing? How could she ever think a queen could be hers? Had she thought so highly of herself because the prince had chosen her? He never would have without the deal between their fathers. She never would have been picked, not out of all those lovely girls.

Even if Elara wanted her and Fia was sure she did, her kingdom would never accept Fia. She pulled the tiara from her head.

Elara took a step back, looking at the tiara with growing horror on her face, as if she too realized what she had done.

"I don't..." Aurora sighed. "Fia, no. I didn't mean that." She took a small step closer. "But you *smell* like each other. If you do this, they will know the second you step into my father's estate." Gently, she took the tiara from Fia and handed it to Elara. "You should—"

"Thank you for stepping in when my judgment failed, but you will stop there. I still do not answer to you, Aurora and I will continue to make my own decisions in this regard."

In what regard? Fia looked between the two of them, trying to decipher the words Aurora had been about to say.

The princess's mouth was a tight line and a muscle in her jaw twitched before she spoke. "I only meant to say you should let Fia sleep in my room and stay away from her before she leaves. Let your scent fade. It will be nothing more than what is expected from two women in close proximity."

"No," Elara said, practically pushing Aurora to the side to put the tiara back on Fia's head. "Tell him I kept you close, Fia. It is no lie. But you will stay here. I will make sure you are safe for as long as I am able."

"I can keep her safe," Aurora said, once again moving her body between them.

"Stop it," Fia moved from between both of them. "I am so sick of being a pawn. I am sick of having no choices. My whole fucking life I have been agreeable and often still got knocked around for it. I have been used my whole life. Even now, that is why the two of you brought me here, to do your bidding. At least Elara has the decency to talk to me like I am a person, to consider what I want. You say you are my friend Aurora and sometimes I believe you are, but I know you would slit my throat to advance your cause because for all your pretty reasons you are not helping your people as Elara is, you are freeing yourself. I do not fault you for it because in that we are the same, but talk to me like I am here."

Aurora took a step back, fury twisting her features. "I would slit your throat? Do not presume you know me so well, girl. I came here because I knew you would fuck your deceptive queen and my father, my brothers, the whole fucking Southern Kingdom would smell her all over you and know you for a liar. *He* would slit your throat and send Helio across the border to find some pretty, stupid girl to drag back for Callum." She threw her hands up. "I could have had my freedom years ago, Fia. I could have left and lived whenever I wanted. I am the daughter of the most powerful man this side of the mist. The lack of power means nothing to me. I would never starve, never need for anything. How dare you accuse me of working only for myself?"

Shame, thick and oily, coated Fia's insides. "Still, the way you speak to me..."

"In that you are correct and I do apologize. But to me you are so young, you know nothing of our ways. And I am deeply, deeply grateful that you have chosen to work for us. I appreciate all you have done and will do, but now you are chiding me because I do not treat you the same as a six-hundred-year-old queen?" She laughed and ran a hand through her hair, leaving it tangled. "Gods. I am *so* sorry, Fia." She laughed again, so loud Fia worried she might be growing hysterical. "We have thoroughly upended your life. What you must think of us."

Elara laid a gentle hand on Aurora's shoulder. "Perhaps it is time to leave. The moment has passed. We will be fine."

Again, Aurora laughed but her shield faded from the room. "The two of you? Unlikely. But fuck if I want to be in the middle of it any longer." She looked Fia up and down. "Callum would never have survived you."

Fia lay in bed staring up at the ceiling, replaying her conversation with Aurora, trying to keep the moments before it with Elara out of her mind.

They could smell her? And there it was again, the phantom shadow of Elara's fingers against her skin, her palm above her heart. The all-encompassing desire to touch her, to taste her, to have her. The ache that had grown so slowly she had not noticed it until it was too late. How had she ended up here, half in love with the woman who had kidnapped her? The nearly sacred bond between them had been a threat in their first days together—she could still remember her fear when the Queen warned her not to run.

But only weeks later she had been swearing allegiance to her under the night sky, not yet admitting what she felt. Horny, if she was being honest. Maybe she should sleep with someone else. Anyone had to be better than Elara because the thing between them was explosive. She would not fall into bed with the horned queen and find her way back out. That would be it for her, the place she came to rest.

The thought scared the shit out of her because she had no idea if Elara felt the same way. Perhaps she did this to many women. Perhaps there was a string of them scattered across the faerie lands, lying in bed just as Fia was, wondering what had happened to them, how they had lost themselves in someone so dark and harsh and terrifying. What if Elara was it for Fia and Fia was not it for Elara?

Or what if it was nothing at all? What if this was just her addled brain trying to make sense of the last month of her life? Easier to desire than to spend each day terrified of the woman she had seen slit a throat, the woman who had threatened to slit hers.

Her thoughts drifted back to Aurora and the accusations she had flung at her. And maybe they were more true of Fia. Yes, she had loved the Village of Frost, yes, she was irrevocably drawn to the woman two rooms away, but was she only agreeing to help because for the first time in her life freedom was on the horizon?

Her father had kept her caged her whole life, made her terrified to step out of line, knowing punishment would be swift and harsh. Callum would be another kind of leash, a nice man who would fill her womb with babies and keep her in some country house, turning these magical lands into anything but an adventure.

But Elara...somehow being with her did not feel like a cage nor a leash. Elara was open skies, the stars so close she could almost reach them. If they made it through this, she knew Elara would never hold her back, she would let Fia spread her wings because Elara was a wild thing and wild things did not dwell in cages or at the end of leashes or clip the wings of their lovers.

At least that was how she imagined it would be. The possibility she was the idiot so many had accused her of being occurred to her. There were so many ways to be wrong, not only about Elara not loving her back, but about trusting her.

Fia had made roads she could take, and Elara might be the worst option of all. Fia did not truly know her, all of it could be an act. Elara could be cruel and callous and only hiding it to make Fia want to do her bidding.

Anything else she could live with. If Elara did not want her, she would cry and cry and then she would survive, maybe a little heartbroken forever, but alive. If their plan did not work and she never left the Southern Kingdom, she would dream of these days as she held half-fae babies in her arms, but she knew she would love them and she would make it through her long years.

But if everything was a lie, if she did everything she promised and they won their fight and in the end she found herself at the other end of Elara's wrath, if all her threats became reality—that Fia could not live with, not with her trust in herself completely broken, because she was choosing Elara, making the first real choice for herself and it if it was the wrong choice—

A knock sounded on the door, and it swung open. Elara stood in the doorway, her hair unbound, in the shortest nightgown Fia had ever seen. "I can feel you."

"Excuse me?"

"Through the spelled thread between us, I can feel your panic. Are you that frightened to go back to Ellio? As I said, I will not force you. Not if you are truly afraid."

Fia sat up in bed, pulling her knees to her chest, aware of how short her own nightgown was as Elara's eyes snagged on the back of her thighs. "No, it's not that. Would you like to know the truth?"

"Yes." Elara kept her fingers wrapped around the doorknob like it was an anchor.

"Well." Fia sighed, bracing herself. "I am scared of you, that all of this is an act. That you saw me for who I am, saw what I needed and used it against me. That you will hurt me when this is over."

Magic sparked at the doorknob, making the metal sing. "How do I prove myself to you, Fia? Do you want me to crawl into your bed? Do you want me to stay away entirely? Do you want me to get on my knees and swear to you on my kingdom? Because I will."

Fia did not know what to say, her muscles ached with the desire to go to Elara. Before she could find the words, the queen came to the side of the bed and dropped to her knees, a look in her eyes that set Fia's very soul on fire.

"I will not hurt you, Fia. More than that, I will not let anyone else harm you while I breathe. I swear this to you on everything dear to me, from the Village of Frost to Niveren Gap. And I swear if we free my magic, they will not be able to stop my breathing and I will destroy anyone who has ever hurt you. Make me a list, Fia, of all who have wronged you and they will not walk the earth."

Move. Her brain screamed at her to move, to grab, to take, to taste. But Aurora's warning kept her frozen in place. Still, she did not dare move a muscle for fear she would not be able to stop. "I will find everything the king hides from you."

The queen stood and reached across the bed to drag her thumb across Fia's mouth, pressing down on her bottom lip. "Do it quickly."

-CHAPTER-
-TWENTY THREE-

THE SUN WAS up and had been for some time. Fia was sure Kalin was waiting for her, Gavin as well, but she was scared to leave her room. Scared to face Elara. She needed to rush their plans, to get the hell out of the palace, and put distance between them until she could act on everything she wanted to act on.

Otherwise, she was going to combust.

A knock barely finished sounding before the door swung open and Fia wasn't surprised to see Kalin, a frown marring his features. "Are you ill?"

"Yes," she lied.

Stepping into the room, he sniffed the air. "No, you aren't."

"Gross." Fia got out of bed and went to the window, pulling open the curtains and letting the sun stream in. "It's incredibly gross to sniff at illnesses. Do you know that?"

"I think your wormy little hairs are gross."

"I don't have wormy little hairs. Feel it." She shoved her head in his direction. "Soft as silk. Besides, you look like a tree."

"And you look like a hairless monkey."

"You just said I had wormy hair." Fia grabbed her robe and pulled it on. "You're just trying to piss me off. Why?"

"Well, you did call me gross, but mostly to get you to stop sulking in your room. You're supposed to head out at the end of the week. You need to get some more training in."

The end of the week? A flash of the queen on her knees filled Fia's head. "I want to leave today. Please arrange that."

Kalin's booming laughter filled the room. "Who do you think I am? I don't make the plans, I just make sure the plans happen."

"You make plenty of plans for me." Fia knew she was being petulant, but she couldn't stay another day. She wanted to do exactly what her queen had asked and get things done quickly. Again, she went to the window and looked out at the spread of gardens and ocean beyond. She was not entirely selfish, she had meant what she said, she wanted to free magic.

She thought of King Ellio, his pretty wife, Calliope, and the beautiful Southern estate. She thought of the humans, flocking to the border hospitals for a chance at curing horrible diseases with the trickle of magic that made it to them. It was not only the faerie's magic he had stolen, it was her magic as well. Nearly thirty and she had not known.

A dozen women stolen for a lie. Generations of witches who thought the power had gone extinct centuries ago if it had ever existed at all.

"Do you know where Aurora is?" Fia asked. She needed to apologize to her.

"She left this morning to visit with The Eastern Queen. Her reply to our request arrived late last night. I don't believe Aurora will be back before you leave."

Shame filled her chest. But there were so many things in her life to be ashamed of. She would add her words to Aurora to the list of things to atone for. And if she survived it was one thing she would actually be able to fix. "How about Vinessa?" Anything but seeing Elara.

Kalin huffed. "You need to train, Fia."

"I need to leave!" Her voice was high. "Please, Kalin. I cannot...I have to leave."

"These are the words of a fool. You want to run from her so badly you do not notice the den of vipers you run toward."

She balled her fists so tightly her nails dug into her palms, but she did not want to say more hateful things to Kalin who had done nothing wrong. She took a breath in through her nose, thinking over her words. "I will not argue that point, I could not possibly know all the ways King Ellio might punish me, all the ways this might go wrong. But I am not running for the reasons you think."

He laughed and pushed past her to sit on the edge of her bed. It looked small beneath him. "I am an old warrior, Fia. I know what it means to care too much, to need to leave because otherwise you might not. That I can respect. But there is so much danger, and you are just a girl."

"I am not that young." She looked him over. The first time she had seen Kalin he had been so foreign to her, now he was just a friend. How quickly her world had changed, her life had expanded to include more than she had ever imagined.

"You are young to the fae and not terribly old for a human either." He smiled gently at her. "I must confess I argued to keep you longer. I am scared for you, I wanted to train you more, make sure you were ready."

Sitting beside him, Fia breathed him in and let her head fall onto his shoulder. "I don't think you'd ever train me enough I could physically fight the King, but my magic is ready, ready enough for me to find the talisman. I don't faint anymore and he doesn't know I have magic, so I'll have the element of surprise." She didn't believe in her words for a second but didn't want Kalin to worry the whole time she was gone.

He wrapped his arm around her, pulling her tight to him and kissed the top of her head. "I thought the Queen's plan was stupid when I first heard it, I thought you would just be some dumb girl, too terrified to be any help. I underestimated you and it seems your father did too—even more foolish on his part as he had decades to get to know you. But if you get into trouble do not think of us, think only of yourself and get away. We have survived this long without all our magic, we will continue to survive and find a new plan. You must survive as well."

When she stood, she felt stronger, less panicked but still determined to leave. And she knew leaving was right when she ran into Elara in the hallway.

The Queen swallowed hard, but her eyes were soft. "Fia..." Her name was sweet on Elara's lips, a prayer, a promise. Her eyes flicked to Fia's mouth, the brown dark, the silver molten, and Fia was not as strong as Kalin thought because she wanted to fall into her.

But Elara would never let her fall. She was a Queen, she had made promises and oaths long before Fia had been born and would keep them long after she was gone. Again, doubt crept in, strengthening her will to leave, because the queen could look at her with lust, but she did not know if it would ever be love, if it could be, and Fia could not know the answer before she left. Everything else was so much more important but if she stayed it would not seem as if it were, there would only be Elara.

"I want to leave. Today, if possible," Fia said.

Elara took a step back, crossing her arms. She frowned. Slowly, her arms fell to her sides. "Give me a few hours. I need to make arrangements so I can stay nearby."

Fia was not fool enough to argue. "I will find the talisman as quickly as possible. I only saw the estate briefly, but it did not seem well guarded. He is too confident. I doubt it is hidden well."

"I suspect the same, but we were never allowed to roam the grounds and had no way to find the talisman. If he doesn't know about your magic, he will not put extra protections around it. I believe he moves it, but that is only conjecture."

Gods, Fia wanted to reach for her, but Aurora's words rang in her ears. Another reason to leave. If either of them gave into temptation it could ruin their plans. Stupid fae sense of smell. "I hope I can figure out how exactly to sense it."

"You're one of only a handful of humans in our lands and, as far as I know, the only witch. It will want to draw on your magic."

Another thought came to her and she grinned. "If it is easily snatched, should I take it?"

The Queen did not smile back. "Take no chances in taking the talisman. Take it only if you are utterly alone and absolutely certain you can get away with it. If you attempt to take it, if you are caught in any way, he will know our plans, and all of this is for nothing."

Right. Of course. Still, the idea of stealing from the man who had lied to the entire world and conspired with her father to sell her like a prize cow warmed something in her. She was glad all the years she had spent around her father's awful associates gave her the ability to keep her face neutral when she needed to. "I appreciate you letting me leave."

The Queen let out a long breath. Fia was always making her sigh. "I try, very hard, to let you make your own choices. I took enough of them away from you already. Meet me in our room after lunch and I will have plans ready." She nodded and left.

When she rounded the corner, Fia let a single sob escape her throat before clamping down on the magic threatening to explode out of her in its wake and, for just a moment, let herself feel the pain of the last few months, of the years before that, of how every fucking moment of her stupid life had belonged to someone else and what a coward she had been.

And then she clamped down on that too. Enough. No tears or screaming would make any of it fair, none of it would bring her mother back or give her a better father. No amount of wailing would fix any of her problems. There was only Fia. Maybe this was her punishment for ignoring everything she had seen in the human lands, or maybe the world was random and she had just been dealt a shit hand. None of it really mattered, none of it changed anything.

She headed for the kitchens, her stomach rumbling. Hopefully there was some plan, some path forward that gave her a life she could be proud of. She liked that version better, that something had led her here, that all she had endured had brought her to Daonith and she would be able to help these people in a way she had never helped her own.

The kitchen staff was putting away breakfast, but they left a few pastries and links of sausage on a plate for her. She thanked them profusely, headed out to the cliffs, and ate, sitting on a rock, the wind whipping at her hair.

The world was beautiful, cruel and capricious but beautiful, full of wonderful people doing their best. After everything, she still believed most people were good, a few hateful men did their best to change them, to make everyone as dead inside as they were, but the dolphins still swam and the waves still crashed and children sang songs and women danced and each day families woke up and smiled at each other and all of it was beautiful.

She was only alone for a few minutes when Gavin sat beside her and set his sights to the ocean.

Neither of them spoke but she was glad he had joined her. There had to be a plan, to put all these people before her, to let Gavin be here when she needed him, both to train her and to help her. She glanced at him, hoping she was right. "I hope this is not a mistake."

"Me too." He kicked off his shoes and leaned back into the short grass. "Because I'm fairly certain this is the stupidest thing I have ever done. I should go back home, hope to finally meet a nice girl and live out my extended years. I don't know why I'm volunteering to trick the most powerful king in these lands."

"You and me both." Fia leaned back as well, watching the clouds overhead, puffy and white against the blue sky. "I could just marry Callum, you know. Live out my extended life as well. Instead, I'm doing the stupidest thing I have ever done. I'll probably be caught and who knows what the king will do to me."

"Nothing good."

"Do you think maybe we are both enormous idiots?"

"I think it is a real possibility, but if we pull it off, imagine all the tales they will write about us. We'll be heroes. You more than me, but I'll be there."

A great gust of wind blew over them and the clouds shifted. "There will be lots of girls then."

There was only the sound of seabirds for a long moment before Gavin answered. "For you as well, if you wanted them, though I suspect you do not."

But Fia did not want to talk about that, so she let the silence settle and Gavin understood. He stayed beside her for a while, just the two of them on the cliffside and somehow when she finally made her way back to the bedroom she shared with Elara her heart was lighter.

-CHAPTER- -TWENTY FOUR-

PLANS HAD BEEN made. Elara had told them to her quickly the night before, her shoulders tense, her words clipped, then she had retired to her room. There were no sultry looks, no more falling to her knees, just simple facts and no emotion.

Things were easier that way, but Fia hated it. She wanted to touch her, to cry how much she would miss her. She wanted and wanted and wanted but wasn't that the problem? So, she only stared at the queen's closed door for a minute before she went to bed.

The next morning the room was quiet. She couldn't help herself, Fia went to Elara's room only to find her things packed. No sign of Aurora either, though she hadn't held much hope for a chance to apologize.

They were gone, and again she supposed it was easier. No weeping or wailing. So, she was left with the wanting. She told herself everything was for the best.

Breakfast was waiting for her on a tray. Before she could finish, the door to her apartments opened and Kalin and Gavin entered.

"You ready?" Gavin asked. He was in simple clothes, light linen pants, a loose shirt, and a dark blue tailored jacket, unassuming yet handsome. Perfect for travel.

"I came to say goodbye," Kalin said, nodding his head to her and then squeezing her shoulder. "Be safe."

"I will do my best," Fia promised, smoothing her own leggings for something to do with her hands, then thinking better of it, she stood and pulled Kalin into a tight embrace. "I will miss you dearly, friend."

"You as well, kiddo. Remember who you are, which Court you belong to." He leaned down, pressing his lips to her cheek before leaving her alone with Gavin. The want was not nearly the same, but the thought she might never see Kalin again sat heavy in heart.

Neither Fia nor Gavin spoke much for the next half an hour. Fia's thoughts were full of Elara. She wanted to see her, to breathe in her scent one last time. Instead, she crawled into a simple carriage, her stomach aching, and watched the palace and the cliffs disappear behind her.

"Will we pass through your lands?" she asked Gavin as they rumbled along through the city surrounding the palace.

"Just the very edge of them. I have far more than anyone could ever need." Gavin smiled. "And you will always be welcome in every acre."

He meant it. Another friend. Whatever happened with Elara, Daonith had given Fia plenty to be thankful for, but also plenty to lose. "Thank you. I'd offer you the same but I'm afraid I don't have much."

"No, but you'll like Niveren Gap when you get there, as long as you don't mind the cold. There are penguins."

Fia sat up straight. "You're lying."

He laughed as they passed under the city gates, the same beautiful white stone as the palace. Even in the morning sun, colorful faerie lights floated in the space like a curtain, parting as they passed. "Well, they aren't walking through the city, but if you go to the coast, you see them sometimes."

Fia leaned back in her seat, watching the autumn leaves fall to the dusty road and thought of what the Niveren Gap might be like. Better than the Village of Frost? She had a feeling her imagination was falling short of what she would find. But eventually her thoughts wandered toward the kingdom she was heading back to.

She thought of her first night there, how she had been dragged from her bed, the dead guard, the flight through the city to keep the full extent of Elara's powers from her. All she had wanted was to go home.

Now she just wanted to see her queen again. Everything in front of her, the good she might do for so many, all her righteous reasons, but she also did everything to get what she really wanted—what Vinessa had known she wanted before she had been willing to admit it to herself.

Around lunch her stomach started to rumble but Gavin said they had to keep going. They did not want to be seen in any town, did not want to answer any strange questions. The King needed to believe Gavin had seen her in the Western Kingdom and stolen her away. It all depended on the years of fake servitude he had offered to the king—originally as a favor to Ezriel to keep an eye on Ellio, now something he did for all of the faeries.

Finally, when the small village they traveled through faded away to farmland, Fia recognized, or thought she did, where they were. The mountains she had ported to with Elara, The Broken Teeth, rose in the distance. Gavin ushered the carriage towards a smaller road heading into the forest that grew at the foot of the rugged mountains.

Finally, when she was sure they were deep in the wilderness, they stopped and sat out a picnic beneath two pines. The air was colder than what they had left behind, wind whipped down from the mountain and all the deciduous trees had been stripped bare.

If Gavin's earlier words were correct, she needed to get used to it. She would spend her life in the cold if she got what she wanted. A Queen. A crown of her own. The thought sent a shiver through her that had nothing to do with the wind.

She wrapped her hands around her steaming mug of tea. "Can I ask you something? As a friend."

"It would be my honor, Lady."

"Don't call me that." She narrowed a stare at him over her cup. "And don't judge me."

"Never." He pushed a strand of dark hair out of his eyes and leaned back on the blanket spread beneath them to rest on his elbows.

"Vinessa told me to beware of the Queen. Not in those words, but she worried I would only get hurt." She looked him over, choosing her next words, but he knew. Everyone had seen her in the golden gown. "Am I a fool to want her? What can there be between us?"

Before answering Gavin cleared his throat and looked towards the sky. "I cannot presume to explain Vinessa, or claim to know Elara well, but I think two things; one, Vinessa may have the same fears that you do, that the two of you are very different, that someone doing so much for us, someone just learning about her magic, and with centuries of life ahead of her should not begin those centuries with heartbreak. Two, Vinessa has her own love story. She was a poor Unseelie villager when she met Ezriel, and he looked at her and knew of their mating bond immediately. So few of us get that. But it does lead those who do experience it to have fanciful ideas about what the rest of us should do."

A mate. How nice it must be for faeries to know for sure. "You never found your mate?" She started on the turkey sandwich he had packed, wishing it was also warm.

"No, lady, I have not. But I am not so old yet. I believe she is out there. Now finish up, we do not want to be caught out here or someone else may drag you back to the king."

Though he was joking, the weight of his words fell on Fia, and the sandwich became dry and hard to swallow. Only another day and then she was back and there was so much King Ellio could demand of her, so many ways he might want her to prove her loyalty. So many ways she might fail.

"I'm sorry," Gavin said, sitting up and putting his hand atop hers. "Is the human world better than this?"

A bark of laughter flew from her throat before she could stop it. "I do not think so, but I am not the one to ask. I have lived under a terrible man's thumb my entire life. But no, I do not think it is so much better, but I like to think everywhere could be better than this."

"So do I." Gavin said, tightening his grip of her hand. "It is my defiant hope. While I watched my people starve, while I felt my own magic curl and wither in my veins, I thought of how the world could be better. So I lie to the king, and I overcharge him for the food my people grow, and now I take him a traitorous, brave woman and I hope that one day we will all be free, that our crops will flourish, and our hills will be alive with animals, our streams will run heavy with fish, and that the next person who comes to power is kinder."

"And yet my father has sold the King human weapons." They did not mention it often, her metal and gunpowder dowry. No one speculated on what the king might do with it or how badly they might soon need their magic at full strength, but it lingered in every conversation, and she knew she was responsible, in so many ways, for all the times she could have stopped him, could have cooperated with the authorities at her door, could have worn a wire or snapped a picture and had not. This would be her repayment.

"All the more reason for our defiant hope," Gavin said, withdrawing his hand and returning to his lunch. "If I am to die, I would rather not do it kneeling but fighting."

Fia thought of her own life, so short compared to his. She was not sure she wanted to fight, but no, she did not want to die as a coward or live as one either.

The mountains faded into hills and snow fell as the sun set over the faerie lands. That night they slept in the carriage, not wanting to risk the exposure of an inn as they got closer to the Southern Kingdom. She was still a prize that could be returned to the king, but there was no guarantee how someone else would treat her, even if they did take her back.

When she woke the carriage windows were frosted and the fields they passed were dusted with snow, though she was toasty tucked inside a knitted blanket.

She wanted a shower, definitely wanted to brush her teeth, but that would wait until she made it back to Ellio's estate and her waiting fiancé. She watched Gavin sleep on the other side of the carriage. His features were soft, his hair fanned across his face, and his chest rose and fell gently. His words the night before came to her and she smiled, certain he had a mate out there somewhere. They would be lucky to find him.

Fia pulled the blanket to her chin and thought of Elara, the silvery purple of her hair, the way her nose scrunched when she laughed, all the things she didn't want to forget. She tried to imagine another life, tried to imagine what could be with Callum, but no matter how she tried, all she could see was the Queen.

-CHAPTER-
-TWENTY FIVE-

WITH EACH MILE they traveled into the Southern capital city of Soleil, Fia's skin grew tighter, the magic inside her twisting and turning. Was it the amount of magic in this land or something else? Could her magic sense the danger she was putting herself in?

She could barely focus on Gavin as he prattled on and on about their meeting with the King. She knew it was important, but her magic was restless and all her energy went to soothing the darkness within and forcing away the memory of Elara's face.

The tether between them went taut.

Relax. Give the King nothing to be suspicious about.

She was a stolen human, eager to be returned to Callum and the safety of an estate she had barely known, but she knew would be better than the horrors of the Unseelie Kingdom. She could do this. She knew plenty about horrors.

Finally, the estate came into view and the carriage pulled to a stop. There were more guards than before and parts of the fence looked freshly redone, fortified after their escape. She looked at Gavin, who nodded once before the stress pulling at his features melted away, and he became the picture of ease. "Ready, Lady?"

Fia thought of her childhood, her father, his friends, his associates, her mother dead before Fia reached double digits taking all the light in Fia's life with her. She let all of her past weigh on her, let it pull her shoulders down and seep into her pores. She remembered palms slapping her face and fists in her stomach and let them steal the light from her eyes.

"Yes, I'm ready." She did not allow herself to think of Aurora or Elara or Kalin except to miss them, to long for what had so quickly become familiar.

Gavin's hand stayed on the small of her back as they walked toward the gate that separated the estate from the rest of the city. When they got close the guards came to attention and one broke from the others, blocking their path.

His mouth opened then snapped closed when he realized who was standing before him. "Has this man been holding you?"

Fia shook her head, only allowed herself to meet the guard's eyes for a moment. "No, he is returning me. He...he found me."

The guard motioned over his shoulder and one of the other guards left. "Come inside." The gates opened on silent hinges and Fia followed the guard in, forcing her feet to move against every instinct in her body.

Her magic, bolstered by the abundance of its kind in this kingdom, threatened to explode from her. She would need to move fast or she would give herself away.

Someone was running, metal hitting metal, and Gavin stiffened at her side as guards surrounded them. Inside the estate people were shouting.

"Is it really you?" asked a familiar voice and Callum's guard Fermir parted the crowd and stood in front of her.

She looked into his eyes and her magic roared again. She shifted her gaze to the ground. Demure. Broken. "Yes," she breathed.

This had been a mistake. She was too different from the woman who had left. She had not expected the way her power would feel here. Rage filled her and it took all of her will to keep it off her face. The talisman was nearby. The King was not just keeping the power in the Southern Kingdom, he was keeping it here, in his estate. How much had he harnessed for himself? And with guns and bombs and who knows what else on his side?

Her throat went dry.

She had to find the talisman. Then, one day, she would make her father pay for his crimes. Make the King pay. But all of that was second to finding the talisman and going home.

"Fia!" Callum was holding her face in his hands before she saw anything more than a blur. "Oh, gods. I am glad you are whole." He let her go and stepped back.

She threw herself at him, wrapping her arms around him, letting herself shake as though it were sobs and not fury.

He ran his hands over her hair, her shoulders, making soft noises. "Lord Gavin, I was told you found her. You have all of my gratitude. The crown owes you a debt."

"Yes, I found her, Highness." He bowed low. "She was in the Western Kingdom. I was able to sneak her away two days ago. She says she is unharmed. She is a good woman and thankfully trusted me."

"I had to take a chance," she murmured into his shoulder, making her voice soft and broken. "I don't want to be the reason for a war. I don't want...I just want to..." She made a distraught noise and sniffed loudly. "I know I was not pleased at first, but I did not want this, Callum, please believe me." She gripped the fabric of his shirt.

He tightened his arms around her. "It is okay. I do believe you. That is not in question." He looked around. "Thank you, Lord Gavin. Fermir, please make sure a room is made for Lord Gavin. I know my father will want to meet with him and there will be the matter of a reward."

"Oh, I do not require a reward, Your Highness." Gavin shook his head as if he could not imagine such a thing.

"Nonsense," Prince Helio said, pushing through two guards to stand in front of Gavin. "And not another word of it. You will allow us to show our appreciation for the future Princess Fia's return. I assume you have a day or two to stay?"

"Yes, Your Highness." Gavin bowed again and Fia pressed further into Callum to keep from wincing. Everything was so formal here, Lords and Highnesses and incessant bowing all while they stole and plotted war. Gavin's reward would be the same as the rest of Daonith's, rule by a handsome tyrant, a land always on the brink of starvation and war.

"You're shaking," Callum whispered. "Let me take you inside. We do not have a room made for you, but you can come to my residence until my father returns, that is, if you would like."

"Yes, please." She gave a final glance to Gavin and sent a prayer up to whoever was listening. Let him survive. Let him find the lies he needed and say them smoothly and then return to his lands.

Sun-kissed balls of faelight bounced through the halls of the estate, warming and lighting their path. Was the talisman nearby? Would she pass it? She did not dare use her magic to feel for it as she allowed Callum to lead her to his rooms, making small talk.

Guards trailed behind them, hands on swords. How would she free herself of them? A problem for tomorrow, for today she just needed to continue to be the traumatized fiancé. Callum was being sweet, would the king as well? Maybe if she did this right, if she fully convinced his son she was only a victim, the king would believe her as well. After all, she *had* been stolen.

At his door, Callum turned to the guards. "Do not interrupt us until my father is here. She needs to rest."

Fermir looked at him as though he wanted to argue but nodded. "He should already be on his way home. We sent a messenger to him. And if your brother comes?"

"Tell him I am asking for an hour with her before she is bombarded with their questions, but do not argue with him." Callum did not wait for an answer before ushering Fia into his room and closing the door.

His residence was vast, twice as big as the apartment she and Elara had shared, yet not as opulent as she had imagined. The space was warm and cozy, wood and soft fabrics. An entire wall was taken up by a built-in bookshelf, filled with not only hundreds of volumes but trinkets as well, little crystals, small hand carved boxes, paper chains and a stack of letters.

She let him lead her to a chair and sank into it, thanking him when he placed a blanket around her shoulders and again when he lit the fire with a swipe of his hand.

Tears formed in her eyes, and she let them fall, let him make assumptions. It was not far from the truth. Being here, letting herself fall into old habits, into subservience, brought back more memories than she had expected. She never wanted to be that weak human woman again. She was a witch. She would not forget.

But the memory of that human would always be inside her. Fia would never forget all the things that had been done to her and all the people like her. She swore to herself to honor it, to remember and fight to never return.

“Oh, Fia.” Callum pulled a chair in front of hers and pressed his palms into his knees. “I can still smell them on you. Do you want to talk about it? We knew she was dangerous, but we never imagined the lengths she would go to....and my sister.” He sighed and shook his head. “I’m sorry, I do not mean to push you. Tell me what you need.”

“I don’t have much to tell you,” she said, pulling the blanket tighter. She missed her blanket from the Village of Frost. Would Elara remember to pack it? “I wish I did. I wish I had secrets to share. Elara took me to the Western Kingdom, and I know she was meeting with King Ezriel, but I didn’t hear anything. I tried to keep my head down. I wanted to gain her trust so I could get away.” Some truth in the lie. Without knowing what King Ellio and his family knew about her time away she did not want to stray too far from the truth. Getting caught in even one lie could ruin everything. “She threatened to use a blood tie on me if she caught me trying to leave. I was too scared to even try but she did it anyways. After, she said she could use it to track me. Please tell me she won’t come back for me.” The bond between Fia and the Queen tightened. Could Elara feel it too?

Callum frowned, moving closer to Fia, his muscles strained at the effort he was making not to touch her. The concern on his face made her feel sympathy for him. None of this was his doing. Fia had no idea how much he even knew. He might be ignorant of all his father's wrongdoings, his only sin being born third. "There is no blood tie that I know of unless it is strange Unseelie magic."

What? Then what had Elara done to her when she had drunk her blood. "There isn't?" She did not need to lie. Her confusion was real.

He shook his head and strands of golden hair, so like Aurora's, fell into his eyes. He brushed them away. "No, the only blood magic within the fae is the mating bond."

Fia's blood ran cold, the words stealing the breath from her chest and she struggled to keep her face neutral, struggled and failed because concern twisted Callum's features. Another lie. She needed another lie. "Oh, then I could have left sooner." The words placated him but not Fia.

Mates.

The only blood magic for the fae was the mating bond and Elara had drunk her blood that first morning. She had known the whole time.

The tether between them purred. The bond. The fucking mating bond. How had she not known? And yet, she had. In the ways that counted, she had always known Elara was hers. She had felt drawn to her since the beginning, even now being away from her was a physical thing. She had needed to flee because each day near Elara without being with her was too hard and it never lessened, only got harder.

She had not known because she was not fae, was not raised wondering if and when the bond would hit her. But Elara was and she had known. Did the others know?

"Are you okay?" Callum's nose twitched. He was sniffing her.

Terror gripped Fia and she forced herself to nod. "Yes." She needed to get away from this, draw Callum's thoughts from why she smelled of the Unseelie Queen. "Do you think you and I might be mates?" She did her best to smile sweetly at him.

"Perhaps." He smiled back, but there was little kindness in it, the happiness did not reach his eyes.

"How would we know?" A stupid question but she wanted answers.

Callum shrugged. "I don't know. I have heard you can just feel it, a draw to the person, not unlike regular love but strong, a physical pain to be away from them, to be without, and worse once the bond is accepted. That's the blood magic. Each faerie must drink the other's blood, just a drop, taking the other into them."

"So, then we couldn't be mates. I am not fae."

He put a gentle hand on her knee. "You are correct, it is a magical bond. I am sorry for the lie, I just didn't want to disappoint you. It does not mean we cannot be happy together."

"I'm sorry that I might keep you from your mate." She didn't need to lie about that. He was in an impossible situation.

He shrugged, removing his hand. "Many faeries do not ever get a mate. At least I will get a beautiful, kind wife."

Oh, poor Callum. How fiercely would he hate her when he found out the truth? She would make a fool out of him. She wished there was another way. But Elara was out there. Her mate, who she wanted to strangle for her own lies, for not telling her. "I think we might be very happy together. I wish I had not been taken."

Before he could respond the door opened and Callum shot to his feet, opening his mouth to yell at Fermir, but the guard put up a hand before Callum could speak. "Your father has returned and had demanded the Lady Fia come to the throne room immediately."

"The throne room?" Callum looked down at Fia. "Why?"

Fermir shook his head and lowered his voice. "I don't know. You know how he is. Go quickly, he is furious."

-CHAPTER-
-TWENTY SIX-

THE THRONE ROOM was dark with tall ceilings and heavy chandeliers, the biggest room Fia had seen in the estate, big enough for all the Lords of the land to gather if the king needed to give some proclamation.

Now King Ellio sat above Fia on his massive golden throne, his pretty wife Calliope beside him. Fia's nose nearly touched the ground and her legs ached from holding her bow, but she would do whatever it took to appease the king.

"Rise," he said, his voice booming across the nearly empty room. Callum stood beside Fia and his older brothers, Helio and Cyrus, stood near the throne, a step below where their father sat. Each of them as beautiful and blonde as their father, a whole family of gorgeous, gilded fae. How many of them knew of the theft of magic, of the arsenal of human weapons their father hoarded? Were they all in on it?

Fia held her hands behind her back and tried to look contrite as she gazed up at the king. Soft face, hard heart. The man was a liar and a murderer responsible for starving all the other kingdoms, of keeping lifesaving magic from the humans. He was the reason Fia had not known she was a witch, had been forced to cower to her father her whole life. She could not wait to rob him.

She hoped she could watch as Elara killed him one day. Hopefully before he could start the war he no doubt was planning. Did he plan to stop once he ruled all the fae kingdoms? What about the humans? What had he promised her father?

"I apologize for my absence, your Majesty," Fia said, letting her voice tremble. "And I am so happy to be back in your kingdom with your son." She reached for Callum's hand and he allowed it, moving closer to her, his smoky scent filling her nose.

Beside the King, Queen Calliope shifted, leaning to look closer at Fia. "You look well enough. Unhurt."

"Yes," Fia said, moving her gaze to the floor. "I was not tortured, only taken." Best to not appear too broken, to not have to pretend anything more than necessary. “After we left your kingdom, I was generally kept in Elara’s chambers. I was lucky to meet Gavin. I had worked to gain Elara’s trust, hoping she would allow me more movement, and it worked.”

Calliope nodded and settled back in her chair, looking at her husband. Would he be as easily convinced?

“And is there anything to report? Do you know what she meant by taking you? And was my daughter with her?” Emotion tugged at his last words, the betrayal by his only daughter. Let him feel it deeply. Let it haunt him.

Fia shook her head, pushing down on the magic inside her, so strong in this kingdom, and let her body tremble. “I do not know. I wish I did, your Majesty. I do know Elara keeps bodyguards with her. We went to a small village where the people knew her well and then we left quickly for the Western Kingdom. She seems to have some business with Ezriel. Some plan. All I heard them talk about was Niveren Gap, the sea beyond.” Let him waste his resources looking into lands far from his own. The people in the most fiercely guarded Unseelie city would be safer than any of the villages. It was the best she could do. She had to offer him something.

He nodded. “I am sure more memories will come to you in the next few days. Please tell them to my son, he will report to me. Your father worries for you, but I have sent word you are back. We will hold the wedding at the end of the week."

Horror filled her chest. She could not marry Callum. Quickly, she shoved the emotion down. Not now. "I would like...if it is not too much to ask...can I help with the planning?" It would give her a reason to move about the castle and hopefully figure out how to escape when the time came.

"Of course, you are the bride." The King smiled. He would be handsome if she didn't hate him.

"We will work on it together. I will meet you in the morning," Calliope said, standing and making her way down the dais towards the guards waiting for her.

Fia squeezed Callum's hand, hoping he would get them out of this room, but his brother spoke.

"Father," Cyrus said, "Certainly, you have more questions for her."

"Do I?" The King lounged in his seat, looking down his nose at his second son. "She was here a day, she knows nothing of our ways or our kingdom, what exactly do you think she learned in the time she was gone."

"She learned more than she lets on," Helio said.

Fia made a small noise, moving closer to Callum. "I was only there...they did not tell me anything."

"She wasn't a spy on a mission, brothers," Callum said. "And she was held by Elara herself, with the help of our sister. That she learned little is hardly a surprise, whatever those women may be, they are not stupid. They would not have let her hear anything that could be used against us."

The king stood, clearing his throat and bringing the room to a thick silence. "I have heard enough from the three of you. If she lies, we will learn of it soon, I am sure. But she is just a human girl, and I will not terrorize my future daughter in law on her first day back." He stopped in front of Fia, he was nearly as tall as Kalin. "I trust you because I trust your father, but our alliance will only go so far." He lowered his voice, though everyone could still hear him. "If there is a war brewing, you can be assured I will win it. So, if there is any confession you need to make, I will take it and you will find me fair and forgiving, but only if the confession comes from you. Any tricks discovered will not be treated with the same kindness."

Fia nodded, dread building. He was easy to hate, and it was easy to imagine fighting against him, but this man would kill her with only a moment's thought to her father and Elara would never arrive in time to save her, not if he caught on to any of her plans. "There is nothing to confess, your Majesty. I wish I was not coming back useless to you, but I cannot pretend I tried to spy. I was afraid and wanted only to leave, that is the only goal I worked towards."

"We are to believe that Zachary Gray's daughter is this meek girl before us?" Cyrus said, stepping closer and raising his chin to look down upon her.

The king chuckled. "I will not raise another of my daughters to be fearless and bold. No, I believe Zachary had the right idea. I was acquiring your brother a wife not a sparring partner."

Blood trickled down the inside of Fia's cheek where she bit it to keep from speaking. Let him think whatever he needed to think to believe her. She dropped her gaze to the floor and pressed her body into Callum's side. He wrapped a protective arm around her, and she melted into the touch.

"Father, can I please return her to her room. She knows nothing that will help us."

"Go." Ellio waved his hand. "And rest girl. Calliope will be in to see you early tomorrow."

-CHAPTER- -TWENTY SEVEN-

SURE ENOUGH, THE QUEEN arrived early the next morning, accompanied by half a dozen maids carrying trays of breakfast and bolts of fabric.

The next three hours were spent planning a wedding Fia would never attend. By lunch her cheeks hurt from smiling, but Calliope was happy. With a final note jotted down on sizing, she dismissed the maids.

"Let's take a walk around the castle, get to know each other. Besides, you look like you need some fresh air, maybe some peace and quiet," Calliope said, her smile never seeming to falter.

Fia nodded and stood up, stretching her hands above her head. How to nicely ask Calliope to leave her alone? She needed time alone to figure out how she was going to search for the talisman without notice.

She'd played with her magic until well into the night, letting the dark strands furl and unfurl in her hand then dance across the room, pressing into the panes of the window before she recalled it, until she was sure she could control it well enough to not be immediately caught. But even with her practice pressure built inside her head, her magic was wild and wonderful in the Southern Kingdom, but it also demanded to be used.

She'd spent a couple terror-filled moments imagining what would have happened if Elara had not come for her and her magic had exploded out of her in front of the king. Would she be staring down the barrel of a marriage to Helio instead?

The Queen checked her reflection in one of Callum's many mirrors. "Do not hate me for henpecking you, dearest. The King and his sons are still worried, but I thought you would prefer my company to theirs until they fully trust you again."

"I understand." Fia allowed the queen to put her arm through Fia's and lead her into the hallway, past guards and onto the estate grounds.

Guards stood around the walls that enclosed the garden and courtiers she didn't recognize sat under trees or walked in groups. Fia had underestimated the task. She had known it would be hard and dangerous, but her main worry had been the king and how she would escape once she found the talisman. She had not worried about how impossible it would be to get a moment alone to even search for the thing.

"We have several gardens," the queen said, continuing a conversation Fia hadn't been listening to. "I'll show you the largest next. I think it would be a lovely location for a wedding. There is inside as well, either of the ballrooms would work, or the chapel if you want something more traditionally human, though it would need to cleaned. The King's family do not worship the old gods often, but I hear humans often marry in their temples."

"Yes," Fia nodded. "Lots of them do, but I've never been very religious. Outside would be perfect. And Callum will look so lovely under the sun."

"Oh, he will," Calliope smiled. "He is a sweet man. You will grow to love him, I am sure of it."

Did Calliope love the King? What was this woman's story? How had she become married to him? Where was Callum's mother?

"Oh, your Majesty!" A maid skidded to a halt in front of them, her chest heaving. "The healer you requested is here, ma'am. She was already on her way to meet with the humans and got your letter. Her reply must have been lost, we did not know she was coming."

"Oh!" Calliope's hand flew to her chest. "Here? Now? For how long?"

"I am not sure. I apologize, your Majesty. I wish we had known."

Something horrible flashed across the Queen's face, longing and desperation, hurt, and something so raw that Fia nearly reached out to comfort her. "I...Fia could you...I only..."

"Go!" Fia said. Whatever the reason that the Queen needed a healer, she did not want to deny her. Something told her that the Queen was not nearly as awful as her husband, probably did not even know his plans. "I will be fine, I promise. I will not run away or do any subterfuge."

"Oh." Calliope's hand lowered to clutch at her throat. "I...You will find the next garden if you follow the rose lined path just ahead. Would you wait for me there? I should not be too long."

"Yes. Honestly, I could use a moment alone to think and breathe and try to come to terms with the last few months. It would be a blessing."

"Oh, thank you," Calliope said. "I will explain all later, I promise. This will forge our friendship. I am sure of it."

"Yes, Majesty, I believe it will." Fia smiled and watched as the Queen and her maid hurried away then followed the path toward the other garden. There was no point in being caught where she shouldn't be on her second day and the garden was as good a place as any to begin her search.

What was the Queen up to? Was she sick? Buying poisons? Fia liked that idea best. Hopefully the poison was for both the king and his obnoxious elder son.

The path clung to the brick and stucco side of the estate as it curved, until it opened to a garden, the front dominated by a hedge maze and enormous rose bushes in every shade of the rainbow, the far side was a large, manicured lawn with some sort of game set up, nearly like croquet, except the balls were huge and the wickets more like tiny soccer nets.

A wedding could easily be held on the lawn, the guests romanced by the scent of the roses. Fia would tell Calliope she loved it. In another life she might. But instead of heading for the lawn, she headed into the maze, until vast shrubs rose on each side of her and she was protected from prying eyes.

With a shuddering breath, Fia knelt on the ground and let her magic thread out of her, reaching and stretching through the soil, though she wasn't sure exactly what she was looking for.

Then something tugged on a thread, a wild thing, grasping and scraping against her magic, demanding it come closer, that it give and give. But where had it come from? Nearby, but not close enough, and Fia was reluctant to let her magic stretch further, not knowing her limits or if anyone would be able to sense a magic unlike their own prowling the grounds.

She coiled the threads back toward herself and the wild thing protested, scraping phantom claws against the dark strands, drinking in her power, something it had not tasted so powerfully in so long. Fia stood, stumbling into one of the bushes, her heart pounding as she snatched her magic into herself, slamming an invisible door. Bile rose in her throat and she clenched her teeth to keep from vomiting, breathing through her nose.

Her dreams of destroying the talisman shattered. She was not nearly strong enough to take on the ancient, clawing power. The talisman would destroy her. And Ezriel had been a fool to ever try to stop Elara from fighting it.

She wanted out, wanted to go to the woman who was her mate and the safety she offered. She was not made to fight, so many times in her life she had wanted to be stronger, but she never had been and now she had promised to take on a wild beast of an object with magic she had only begun to control.

The tether between them tightened, as though Elara was tugging on it. Fia swallowed, willing her heart to calm because if she continued to panic she would get her wish, Elara would come for her. But there would be no safety, Elara would return, even without knowing where the talisman was, even if Fia didn't want to go with her.

For Elara she would fight. She would find the talisman, and she would return to destroy it to keep her mate safe. For once in her life, Fia would not cower. She would be better than she had been raised to be. Not meek. Not anymore.

She made her way out of the maze, smiling sweetly at two passing ladies and scanned the area for Calliope, but the Queen had not yet returned from visiting with the healer for whatever reason. Was it worth it to keep searching? The talisman's snatching power was not hard to find, but she was no closer to knowing its location. She weighed her options.

Seldom did it bring her pleasure, but she was Zachary Gray's daughter, and she knew a thing or two about deception. It was too early to show her hand. If she earned the royal family's trust, the rest of her lies would be much easier. Plus, she wasn't particularly keen to feel the grimy tug of the talisman again.

So instead of searching, she wandered the garden, taking in the walls, the exits, how many guards were stationed and how alert they looked. More than before, Ellio had increased his security. As a test, she wandered near the far side of the garden, where an open gate led to a wide street and the city of Soleil beyond. Slowly, casually, she moved closer, never letting her gaze settle on the guard.

He came to attention, moving his body into the open space of the exit. "Afternoon, Lady Fia. Do you need an escort back to your room?"

"No." She smiled sweetly at him. "Just waiting for the Queen. I barely saw the city when I was here before."

"Soleil is a beautiful piece of land, Lady. I'm sure the prince would be happy to escort you through it anytime."

So, they were under orders not to let her leave then. How far would they push it? Would they actually stop her? Grab her and drag her back? Probably. "Yes, I'll have to ask Callum to take me out soon.

"Perhaps sooner than you think." The guard smiled at someone behind Fia and Callum's smoky scent hit her nose.

"Dearest, what are you doing here?" He led her away from the gate with a hand on the small of her back. "Did you give Calliope the slip?"

Fia forced herself to laugh. "Of course not. She had to run inside for a moment. She will be back soon."

Callum looked over his shoulder, yelling at the guard to let his stepmother know he was with Fia. "Did you have a good day with her?"

"Yes, it was pleasant enough. The lawn would be a lovely place for a wedding, don't you think?"

He paused to consider it. "Yes, it would be a perfect spot. But do not get too attached to this estate, your country home waits for you. I am so eager to show it to you and get you away from here, let you settle in and feel at home."

Fia leaned her head on his shoulder, hating herself, just a little, for what she would do to him when she left. He was good, better than the rest of his family, but she did not have time to build trust with him, to see if he could join her cause. Aurora must not have thought so, and her judgement had to be good enough for Fia, even while some small part of her imagined the country home, the ease of not fighting in a war.

But the war was coming, whether Fia wanted it to or not, and she would not be on the wrong side of it. Not again. She would not give up on this second chance to be a good person, because her life would be long, much longer than she had dreamed of before she came to Daonith.

There would be many years Fia would have to look in the mirror and live with herself and her choices. The way she had spent the first three decades of her life betraying the humans, allowing her father free reign to hurt people from behind a desk would always weigh on her. Maybe she could take some of the stain from her soul by helping, as best she could here.

And if things were better in Daonith she could help the humans. She would be mated to a Queen. She would have power. She could free the human magic, let witches return, and with them healing magic, for both humans and the overworked earth.

“You are being quiet,” Callum said, leading her from the grounds and into the dark estate.

“Only thinking of what our life will be like away from here.” And that much was true because she hoped, desperately, Callum would get away and without the influence of his family, would truly become a good man.

-CHAPTER-
-TWENTY EIGHT-

THAT NIGHT, FIA lay in her bed, the roaring fire painting the room in shades of orange, while outside the window the first snow fell in the Southern Kingdom —so unlike the lands she wished to be in where she knew snow already covered the ground.

She let her power move from her, snaking its way into the walls of the estate. Her magic slithered, twisting through the cracks, moving toward that awful power again.

Only a few heartbeats passed before the talisman reached for her, its oily fingers desperate in their need to feel her strange magic again. It gripped, whispering foreign words, making sweet promises until Fia wanted to give in, to let it find its way into her, wrap around the core of her, sing its saccharine song...

Elara. The Queen's face flashed in her mind and Fia snatched her magic back, pieces of it ripping as it clawed its way through the estate and back into her chest. Bile rose in her throat and she bolted out of bed, running for her wastebasket to vomit.

She sank to the floor, wiping her mouth. But the talisman had not been careful, she had felt the direction of the pull, somewhere nearby, closer than before and to the east. She crawled to her window and looked out, much of the estate grounds were to the east of her room. The grounds were dark, illuminated only by moonlight until the surrounding wall, where the city was bright, light flickering even late into the night.

There were buildings scattered across the estate grounds, the stables, several workshops, and half a dozen other buildings she didn't recognize. The talisman had to be in one of them.

She got back into bed, trying not to think of Elara, who she so desperately wanted to see. *Mate.* The word would not leave her head. She had so many questions and no one to ask them to. And anger. Why had Elara not told her?

No, she forced thoughts of the Queen away and stared into the fire, watching the flames jump. To get to Elara she needed a plan. Tomorrow, she needed to keep free from Calliope. She had no interest in spending all day pretending to wedding plan.

Queen Calliope had avoided her eye at dinner though, so avoiding her might be easy. Fia had no time to ponder why she was seeing a healer and what about it made her so guilty, but she would use her guilt if it meant Calliope would stay away and maybe, just maybe, Fia could find the talisman the next day and be gone by evening, less than a week after her return.

Callum was not yet awake when she made her way out of the spare room in his apartments. She'd brushed her hair until it shone, used the meager makeup she had found in the vanity, and put on the shortest shorts she could find. They were nowhere near as comfortable as her clothes from the Village of Frost, but they would do.

She went to the window, nearly pressing her face to the glass to try to see all of the eastern land of the estate. She wasn't sure how she would get away from Callum, but at least she could explore the buildings and look for anything unusual, anything calling out to her.

The talisman wanted her, wanted to soak up her strange magic, magic it had not felt in centuries. The talisman had gorged itself on fae magic, but its whispers still spoke of desire. She had something new—rich, human magic, and the talisman was desperate for it.

Ugh. Fia shivered. She didn't want to know the thoughts, if they could be called that, of the talisman. She doubted they were more than an echo of the desire embedded in it by the horrible kings who had controlled power. But if they wanted her magic so badly, she would let them take a bite, and make sure they choked on it.

Her magic. Her people's magic. In that way she could right her wrongs to them. There would need to be more—ways to protect the witches out there among the humans, to keep them safe when people clamored for them. But for now, giving it back would have to be enough. It was all she had to give.

She stepped back from the window, watching the snow fall lightly, just enough to dust the tops of buildings and create a white carpet across the estate grounds.

“I always love the first snow,” Callum said, nearly making her jump. She had not heard his footsteps or the door opening. “Though you must have already seen it in the Unseelie Kingdom.”

“A bit. Especially in the mountains. We don’t get much in my part of the human lands but some places do.”

“Maybe we will visit one day.” His eyes moved over her body, hungry. How much longer before he wanted more than friendship from his fiancé? How long could she keep him at arm’s length?

“I was thinking we could go on a walk today just the two of us.” She smiled her sweetest smile, but Callum shook his head.

“No, I have a bit of a surprise for you, then I have things to do with my brothers today. Come. I will show you.” He put out his hand, waiting on her.

“What kind of surprise?” She had no choice but to take his outstretched hand and let him lead her from the room, but he refused to tell her and she did not want to push and annoy him, so she followed him into the enormous dining room, the place where she had first met Elara, only now her father sat on the other side of the table.

Her nervous system came alive, adrenaline flooding through her veins.

Zachary Gray stood at his daughter's approach, spreading his arms wide as he rounded the head of the table and pulled her into an embrace. "Fia! I am so glad you are in one piece."

No. Fia put her arms around him, her throat dry, her pulse so loud she could hear it in her ears. As he pulled away and she took her seat, she was no longer the strong woman she had become in the faerie lands, she was again the cowering, groveling thing she had been in the human world.

The king must have entered while her father was embracing her, he now sat at the head of the table, his wife at his right hand. "Good morning, Fia. I heard you father was at the borderlands and I thought you might want to see him after your harrowing experience."

"Of course." Fia sat, reaching for her glass of water. "Good to see you again, Queen Calliope."

"You as well, Fia. We will return to wedding planning soon." There was a wildness to the Queen's eyes as she met Fia's gaze, but Fia did not have time to think it over.

"I was glad to hear from him. I have something to discuss with you Fia, I think it will bring you great joy," Zachary said.

There was no chance anything that made her father grin so wide would bring Fia any joy, but she nodded, as she always did, a puppet on his string.

"Are you okay?" Callum whispered as her father returned to his seat. "I thought you would be happy."

"I am okay," she assured him, unable to meet his eyes. On the other end of the tether—the mating bond, she realized with a start—Elara reached out to her. No words, there were never any words, nothing tangible, the bond was something different, not a way to track, but a way to soothe, the knowledge you were never alone.

Or maybe the bond was just a bond and what she felt was Elara, who had stolen her, threatened her, and then, somehow, become the person she cherished most. Elara who would do anything for her people, who was rough around the edges, and had promised to get revenge on the terrible man who had raised her. The piece of shit who sat across from her.

Fia straightened her shoulders. Never again. Whatever happened, however this all ended, she would never go back to who she was, even if it killed her, she would die on her feet, no longer on her knees.

Today though—today she was still acting. "What were you doing on the border?"

Before he could answer, servants brought out their dinner, an entire roast pig, turnips, potatoes, and an assortment of other vegetables. All of it smelled delicious, but they hadn't eaten so much the day before, or even her first day there. This was a show for her father.

"I heard you are planning a return to human politics," Calliope said, casting her eyes towards Fia even as she spoke to Zachary.

Strange. There was something so strange about Calliope. Something hidden. Something about the healer. She had been perfectly normal until then. And the healer had been heading towards the borderlands.

"You didn't answer why you were at the border, Daddy." Fia loaded roasted meat onto her plate, smiling sweetly, as though nothing bothered her, a skill she had perfected many years ago, sitting across from the same man.

But one look from him made her wish she hadn't asked. He wanted to let her know, wanted to cut her down, no doubt angry that she would be a princess, higher in some ways than him. That it was his doing didn't matter, reasons had never mattered when it came to his feelings about Fia, only emotions. "Well, Fia, I am hoping you will have a new brother or sister—preferably a brother—sometime soon. I am getting married again and I wanted to make sure I did not hitch myself to the same problem twice."

Everything inside Fia tightened, her pulse pounded. Beside her Callum tensed. "Surely there is better conversation to be had," he said, looking hopefully towards his father, but the King shrugged, while his two eldest sons seemed to have eyes only for the plates in front of them.

"She was interested in why I was at the border," Zachary said, stabbing a potato with his fork. "Perhaps we will have a double wedding, maybe even welcome sons together. I am sure you can understand my desire for one of those, Prince."

"I will be pleased with whatever children I have, Zachary."

He laughed. "Everyone tells themselves that, tries to love the daughter that ruined their wife, and you do love her despite yourself, still the disappointment stings, made even worse when she never quite meets your expectations."

"Zachary, please," Ellio said at the same time Fia stood up from her chair.

None of this was news to her, she had heard worse words screamed at her from above countless times, but she could not stop the sting completely. So, she let herself feel it, let the tears well in her eyes until they fell down her cheeks. She shook with her rage, for being sold, for being abused, for the countless cruelties being Zachary Gray's daughter had brought. "I hate you," she whispered, her voice cracking.

She locked eyes with Callum, letting tears flow. He stood, his napkin falling to the ground, but Fia shook her head.

"Darling," he whispered.

"No! Leave me alone!" she yelled and his face fell. He nodded.

She fled, throwing her napkin down, nearly knocking over her chair, and pushing through guards while orders to let her go were shouted, until she burst through the front doors of the estate and ran towards the eastern lawn.

Her footsteps crunched on the icy sludge and snow coated her dress before melting and soaking through the fabric. Still, she ran until the buildings she had seen earlier came into view. The lawn was quiet, with only the sound of the horses to break the silence.

Fia headed for bushes and crouched low, hoping she was beyond any sight lines and no one pursued her. She let her magic run from her, out and out and out toward that hateful, grabbing power. She touched it for only a moment, long enough for bile to rise in her throat before she snatched her magic back, curling it inside of herself. "You can do this. Just a minute longer," she whispered.

The talisman was so close, somewhere inside one of the small buildings at the edge of the estate. She considered them. Two squat, vine-covered buildings that looked to be used for storage, the stables, and then another building she hadn't been inside yet.

Rosebushes, bare except for the snow covering their branches, grew up the brick walls, clinging with thorny fingers until they reached the stained glass where they had been cut back, revealing gorgeous jewel-toned scenes.

A stone pathway led to the building, branching off at two points, seemingly leading to the gardens on the other side of the estate. It had to be the scarcely used chapel.

Once again, she let her magic creep from her. There had to be more to it than this. All their planning, all their fear, but the talisman wanted her, there was no fear, only thick desire. Red bloomed across the light dusting of snow beneath her and Fai wiped at her nose. She tugged her magic. The talisman tugged back.

Shouting came from the direction she had run from. She only had minutes before they came looking for her.

Another drop of blood stained the ground and Fia snarled, gritting her teeth and yanking. The talisman hissed, but inside the chapel bright, green-tinged magic flared for a second as she regained control and reclaimed her magic. And the talisman had given its location away.

Fia laughed to herself. She should have let Calliope bring her during wedding planning. She would have found it sooner. But she had found it now. And she would destroy it.

Reaching inside herself, Fia yanked on the bond with Elara before looking around. She had to get out of here. And she had to do it fast.

There was no gate nearby and even if there was they would never let her pass. She had only been allowed to flee the dining room because she was trapped inside these walls. But none of those golden royals knew about her powers, how strong they were in this place.

"Please," she said, running for the wall. The shouting was closer. "Please fucking work." She pressed her palm against the freezing stone wishing for gloves. Pain built inside her head but her magic erupted from her palm, a dark web that struck at the cracks in the stone, pushing and straining.

Too much. This was too much. She could not do this. At the other end of the bond, she felt Elara. Her mate was coming. Only a bit more, a little longer.

A hole appeared in the stone, so small but shimmering with magic. Blood poured from her nose, warm on her lip then frozen on her chin. The hole grew. Fia shoved her body into the dark space, the stones scratching and tearing at her clothes, her skin, she could feel it ripping. She was too big, she wouldn't make it.

She shoved the last of her magic from her with a scream, her ribs squeezing until she was sure they would break. But the hole widened--just enough for her to slip through.

She fell to the frozen ground on the other side as the hole closed behind her. Her body ached, her head pounded and her magic was nothing but a dark, empty hole inside her.

But Elara was coming.

Fia pushed herself to her feet and ran.

-CHAPTER-
-TWENTY NINE-

THERE WAS A stretch between the estate and the city proper, roads with little only them, a beautiful park with an easement of trees, but beyond it the city was alive and full of people. Fia had never moved so fast in her life as she ran for those trees, desperate to get away from the empty space, hoping every second an arrow, or worse, wouldn't hit her.

She remembered the way Elara had once thrown a fae to the ground to protect her. What would she do if someone shot her? Fia ran faster, thankful for all her training with Kalin.

She would see him again. She would see Elara. She just needed to get to those trees. Another few seconds. Behind her people were yelling, but their voices were muffled, a wall between them. A wall she had put a hole in. Had they seen or were they wondering where she had gone? Please let them be searching for her.

Callum called her name. Sweet Callum. What would his father do to him when he realized she was gone again and this time on her own? She hoped they wouldn't blame the prince, but her father. She hoped it would drive a wedge between them.

She closed the final distance. The trees engulfed her, blocking out the weak morning sun. She kept running, tripping on roots and scraping her hands on bark until she emerged into the city where a normal day surrounded her. People were going to work, carriages moved down the street. Only one man glanced twice at the woman emerging from the trees but then continued on his way.

On the other end of the bond Elara pulled. Fia pulled back with all her strength.

And her mate stood in front of her, her horns covered by a dark hood, her silver eyes blazing. "Fia."

She launched herself at Elara, breathing her scent in deeply, earthy and no longer foreign but *hers*. That was her scent being returned, changed and made whole. She wanted to kiss her, to scream at her, to demand answers or wrap her legs around her waist, to pull the hood from her and— There was no time. "We have to go."

"Yes." Elara held her tighter and they ported through darkness until they reappeared on the shore of a frozen lake.

Fia had done it. She'd found the talisman. She'd gotten away. Until that moment she hadn't realized how sure she had been that she would die. A sob escaped her, real this time, and she clutched her chest against the hollow ache inside her.

Her magic.

For the first time she truly understood what drove the faeries in their quest. She thought she had reached the bounds of her magic before, felt it dwindle from overuse but those time it had refilled, now her magic was just *gone*. What had been a deep well was shallow. There was almost nothing to refill. She had left the bulk of her magic behind with the king, and she hadn't even realized until that moment just how much it had grown in her brief time in the Southern Kingdom.

She hated Ellio for the loss.

"Fia," Elara said, drawing her back into herself, into this moment. She took Fia's face io her hands, rubbing her thumb across her cheek.

Fia quickly twisted her head and bit her thumb, hard enough to draw blood. Elara recoiled, holding her wrist in her other hand, her silver and brown eyes wide. "What the fuck?"

Without a word, Fia reached for her arm, drawing her wrist again towards her mouth, keeping her eyes on Elara.

The Queen jumped back, her heel cracking the ice on the lake. "You know."

"I know," Fia repeated. She refused to look away from Elara, though her face, *her beautiful face*, contorted with emotion. "You should have told me."

The Queen's mouth opened and closed like a fish out of water. She lurched forward, grabbing Fia's face in her hand again, less gently than before. "You were going to complete the bond, weren't you? Without even saying anything."

"End it like you started it." Fia snapped at her hoping for a reaction, but Elara only held Fia's face, so she shoved her. In all her daydreams about their reunion Fia had never imagined she would start a fight, but she couldn't stop herself. She watched Elara stumble, watch her nearly crash into the frozen lake, arms windmilling at her sides, watched as she fell into the snow at the edge of the ice.

Fia looked down on her then knelt, straddling Elara, frozen rocks biting into her knees, but this time she was not being chosen from a line-up, she was doing the choosing. "You should have told me," she repeated.

Elara gripped her thighs. Fia was still in the stupid shorts she had worn to tempt the prince. It had been too cold for them in the Southern Kingdom, now it was freezing. "You wouldn't have left. I was going to tell you, I will swear to that, and then you said you would leave and I knew, however much I hated it, that you should. So, I could not tell you."

Fia let more of her weight settle onto Elara. She was half frozen, but she would not move until they finished this. She would not go on another hour half unmated. "Would you do it again? Would you choose me?"

"Yes." Elara's fingers tightened on her skin. Tomorrow she would have bruises. She would be marked.

"And I, you." Gently, Fia wrapped her fingers around Elara's wrist. She could feel the pounding of her pulse beneath her skin. The bite had already clotted so she ran her other hand up the Queen's leg until she reached the knife strapped to her thigh. "I choose you to be my mate, Elara. With open eyes, knowing who you are, that your people will always be first, that you will be a queen before a lover, I choose you and I will continue to do so every day until my last."

She spread Elara's fingers out from her palm and pressed the blade into the soft flesh of her pointer finger until it drew blood, then brought it to her mouth.

The knife fell from her fingers as the bond swept through her, no longer a spider's thread but a chain, sturdy and unbreakable. She fell forward, barely avoiding slamming into Elara's face, but her mate stopped her, only long enough to take her face again, this time gently and kiss her.

Soft at first then insistent, her fingers moved to Fia's neck, holding her tight as her tongue swept through her mouth and the bond between them sang. This was everything. The queen was hers.

Fia shivered and Elara pulled away, her horns exposed, her hood fallen back. Fia ran her fingers over the bony surface. She trembled again.

"You are freezing," Elara said, moving from underneath her. She stood, pulling Fia with her. "Why are you wearing this?"

"I was trying something," Fia said. "Let's keep going, but we will finish this later." She wanted to finish it now, but the adrenaline of seeing Elara, of her insane desire to complete their bond, was draining from her and she actually was freezing.

Elara huffed. “We are not going anywhere. I ported here on purpose, if only you had let me get you inside, but you are, as always, impossible.”

Fia couldn’t stop the grin that spread across her face as Elara motioned to a small fishing cabin behind her. “We are not going to keep going?”

“No. Queen Seera has finally agreed to a meeting, but I think she can wait a day.”

“Perfect.” Fia grabbed Elara’s hand, twining their fingers together and pulled her towards the building.

Inside the cabin was sparsely decorated, but Elara waved her hand and the dying flame burst back to life. The single room smelled of fire and fish but even that could not cover Elara’s scent that coated every surface. “Have you been staying here?”

“Yes,” Elara said, pulling off her cloak and wrapping it around Fia. “This is as far as I could be away and still port to you and back in one go. And I’m certain Ellio knows nothing about this cabin. It belongs to Kalin’s grandfather.”

“Is he okay?” Though Fia wanted to touch Elara—every single inch—she headed for the fire and held her hands out in front of it. She was nearly frozen through, her fingers numb with cold, and she needed a minute to catch her breath, to think.

Elara's arms snaked around her waist beneath the cloak, her breath warm against Fia's neck, and thinking became impossible as she realized the body pressed against her back was naked, or nearly so.

Horns scraped against her as Elara pressed kisses to her neck, feather light but enough to make Fia ache with want, want she had pushed down for months.

"I never thought I would have a mate," Elara whispered, hands roaming across Fia's front, cupping her breasts. "Not until I saw you in the Southern Kingdom, small and scared and engaged to my enemy's son and it took every ounce of my willpower to remember my mission, to not start a war right then." Her hands moved lower, unbuttoning Fia's shorts.

"I didn't know right away. Not the way you did," Fia said. "But I knew..." What had she known? That she would not marry Callum? That she wanted the woman who had stolen her more than the man she had promised herself to? "I knew...I knew you were not my enemy."

"Of course you did not know," Elara pushed her shorts down, threading her fingers through the tuft of hair she found, before moving her hands to Fia's hips and urging her to turn.

Fia did and found her mate bared before her, small but full breasts peaked in the chill air, her hair unbound and falling around her horns. Her heart swelled inside her chest. This beautiful woman was hers, every part of her, the multitudes she contained. All of them Fia's. She grabbed Elara roughly, kissing her, trying to make up for all the moments she had wanted this and been unable to have it, for the night they did not have when Elara had crowned her.

With barely any effort, Elara lifted Fia and she wrapped her legs around the queen. She was warm and solid beneath Fia's thighs. Fia's heart pounded as Elara carried her to the bed and laid her down, pausing to stare down at her. Heat built inside Fia, so much want she thought it might rip her apart.

Elara knelt, kissing each of her knees before pushing them apart. She drew a long finger down Fia's center, smirking when she squirmed. "You were wrong about something."

Fia did not care, all she wanted was Elara to keep touching her, to not stop, never stop, until the world and all their problems fell away and it was just the two of them in the tiny cabin on the lake.

Matching the building desire inside Fia, Elara's magic rolled from her, silvery purple, like phantom hands, to run along Fia's body, making her gasp and her hips roll as every inch of her was caressed in a way she had never been touched before. *Hers. Hers. Hers,* the bond sang.

The magic ran across her lips, down her spine, cupping at her breasts, everywhere but the aching spot between her legs. "You said you knew I would always put my people before you, but you are wrong, Fia. I know I should, I have sworn myself to them, but I would forsake my kingdom for you."

Though it took effort to move at all while the sensual magic still licked at her body, Fia pushed herself onto her elbows, taking Elara's chin into her hand. "You will never need to do that. We will rule it together." She kissed her hard, wrapping her hands around Elara's horns to pull her close. "Now, shut up."

Elara smirked and stepped back before gripping Fia's thighs and pushing her legs apart. She settled between her and Fia tried to memorize the vision before her, the queen on her knees, hunger in her eyes, but she could not concentrate when Elara flicked her tongue against Fia's clit. She reached down, gripping Elara's horns, pressing her face into her center and hitching her knees around her shoulders to ride her mouth.

The Queen gripped her backside as she licked her, but it was her magic that made Fia scream out, as it plunged into her, filling her completely. Her back rose from the bed and somehow, they were on the floor, Fia once again straddling

Elara, her hips moving without thought, driving her against Elara and her wicked mouth.

This was it, everything she had been made for, the reason she had carried an ember of hope in her heart through decades. She came, screaming the queen's name. Elara stopped only long enough to move Fia to the ground, giving her only a moment to catch her breath before her magic plunged into Fia again.

She slid up Fia's body, pressed tight against her and fisted a handful of Fia's hair then licked down the column of her neck until she reached her breasts. She pulled Fia's nipple into her mouth, biting down hard enough that Fia cried out, but Elara ran her thumb over the ache, easing the pain, caressing Fia's abdomen, until her own fingers replaced the magic.

Tension built inside Fia, but she forced herself to watch the queen, watch as she fucked her, her hair falling around them like a silvery web, her muscles moving under her skin. She loved her, she realized with a start, loved her so much it hurt, loved every harsh edge and the soft corners that protected her people.

And Fia needed to taste her. She reached for Elara, pulling her lower, kissing her, running her tongue through her mouth. She moaned into her, her body tightening. Elara swiped across her clit with her thumb, once, twice, before running it in a tight circle.

Fia clawed at her back, her head falling back, but Elara slowed her movements and her free hand grasped Fia's hair at the base of her neck. "Look at me," she said in a voice that Fia had no choice but to obey. Elara's eyes were wide, pupils blown out, her mouth red and glistening. "You are mine, do you understand? My mate. My *queen.* You are mine, Fia. And I am yours."

"Yes," Fia said, twisting until she was sitting. "I am yours." She reached down until her fingers found Elara's slick core. "And you are mine." She dipped a finger into her mate and then took Elara's hand, placing it between her legs. "Can you show me again what your magic can do? Can you show me everywhere?"

Elara smiled. "Of course," she said, then Fia barely knew anything at all as sensation overtook her, magic filling her deep and wide and she screamed, sure she would come apart in the most glorious way until lips and horns were against her again and she wondered how she would ever leave this cabin, how she would ever get enough of this woman.

When they finished the sun had nearly set and every single bit of Fia ached in a way she wouldn't change for the whole world. She pulled the blanket around herself with one hand, using the other to hold a steaming cup of tea, and went out to the porch where Elara waited, looking toward the horizon.

"What you said about your people..." Fia began unsure of what exactly she was going to say, but sure she needed to say it.

"I should not have said it," Elara didn't look at her. "And I am ashamed that I meant it. I never wanted to find a mate, Fia, because I knew...They picked me to be their queen. It is shameful to dishonor that."

Fia put her head on Elara's shoulder, taking in the view and breathing in the scent of her mate. What a wonderful thing, a beautiful change and yet no change at all, as if she had been waiting for Elara her whole life. "There is nothing to be ashamed of because we will continue on as we planned. The Northern Kingdom will be my home, and your people will be my people, and we will honor them in all our choices. Together." The words came out as a question, one she desperately needed an answer to.

Elara shifted to look at her, the smile she wore an unusual sight on her face. "Yes, and I will never forget you have come from the humans, and we will work for them as well. *Together.*"

Fia pulled away, not wanting to be touching Elara when she said the next part. Snow was falling, fat white flakes that danced in the wind coming off the lake. A beautiful piece of her new world. "Promise me when it is over, we'll come back here."

"I promise."

Inside Fia something settled as the day replayed in her head. She had come so far and yet there was still so much to do, the bulk of the danger still ahead of them, ahead of so many people she had come to love. "My father was in the South. It was lucky really, he was how I escaped. I pretended to be upset by the things he said and ran away. They left me alone for the first time."

"Pretended?" Elara asked. Between them the bond was a gentle caress.

"In most ways, yes," Fia whispered, her words nearly stolen by the wind and snow. "He is getting remarried, trying to finally have a son, what he always wanted. It would have devastated me once. I worked so hard, for so long, to be enough for him. But when I was listening to him today, I realized I didn't want to please him anymore. I didn't want to be that person, I never had, I'd just never been given an opportunity to want more. Before you no one had ever looked at me and seen anything but his daughter so I'd never considered that maybe I could be more. Isn't that pathetic? As old as I am, to still clung to my father."

"No." Elara said and the wind had no chance to take her words, they were hard, cutting like a knife. "Because an adult grows from a child and he wanted you to be that way, no doubt spent your childhood teaching you that you were nothing more. And every child wants to please their parents. Mine died when I was young, at least for a faerie and the king before me was my uncle. I would not be queen except I lived my life to honor my parents." She let out a harsh laugh. "I have never admitted that before, a secret I kept close to my chest. But my father loved his brother and the Unseelie people and chose a wife who felt the same. They had no dreams of ruling, only helping. And that is how I was raised, and then they died and the softness they had worked so hard to instill in me died with them. I became hard, and the parts I could not harden I trapped away deep. It was not a choice, not something I could fix, and it didn't matter because it felt like a dishonor to try to get close to anyone when there was so much work to do. So, I did the work and closed my heart. You see, Fia, you are not the only one carrying your childhood in your heart and I am much older than you."

Never once since she had learned Elara was her mate had Fia balked or questioned it and in that moment, there was something even more than mates, something she knew for sure. "I love you, Elara."

The Queen turned, her eyes glossy and red-rimmed. "I am not sure I deserve that love, but I love you too, and I am so glad you are back."

"Will we leave soon?" Fia asked. Though she wanted to stay, to stretch this moment between them, where they were safe and together and in love as long as she could, she was also excited to see Niveren Gap for the first time, to see Kalin and, hopefully, to see Aurora and apologize for being as ass. "Did Gavin make it out?"

"Yes," Elara nodded. "He will meet us in Niveren Gap. I urged him not to go to his lands since we did not know how you would make your escape. He lives on the border. I did not want Ellio to have easy access to him."

"What if Ellio blames him anyway and no one is there to protect his people?" Fia asked. She did not want those deaths on her hands.

"I don't know," Elara sighed. "We have yet to call in troops. Trying to keep everyone safe is nearly impossible. Even if we had called them, our numbers are low, we could not protect everyone. I hate it, hate leaving so many unguarded, powerless."

Fia could feel the Queen's pain and knew she meant every word. "Not powerless for long. We should not spend much time trying to convince Seera. If she will not agree to help break the talisman, surely someone else in the Eastern Kingdom will. That is all we need right, someone from each kingdom?"

"Yes, but she is powerful."

"So is the talisman," Fia agreed. She could still feel its power, how it had gripped at her, pulling, wanting, taking. She hoped it would not sing to its master and tell him what she was or how she had been looking for it. How sentient was it? She should have learned more. She had been too eager to see Elara. She sighed. "So, maybe we do need her."

"We will have to do a good job convincing her."

"If not, we could kidnap her. It worked for me."

-CHAPTER-

-THIRTY-

THE NEXT MORNING the snow fell in large flakes, an incessant downpour that built up on the sides of the cabin. What had once been beautiful was now nothing but white and frigid.

Wrapped in a cloak, Fia watched the snow fall, waiting for Elara to finish straightening up the cabin and gathering her things. Yesterday had been amazing, a culmination of so many things, but today seemed bleaker. After they destroyed the talisman—if they destroyed the talisman—then what? Would Ellio let it lie? She could not imagine he would.

He was a cruel man from a long line of cruel kings willing to steal and imprison women for their own ends. And now Ellio had weapons, guns at the least, possibly worse, that he could use against the fae who only had magic and steel. How long had he planned this, cutting off the rest of the kingdoms from trade while he waited for a man like her father, someone with connections and no morals?

For the first time the slick, sick feeling of shame did not twist in her gut at the thought of her part in her father's wrongdoings. She had been foolish, too naive, too desperate, but she would stand against him now. He had never seen anything more than a pawn in her and it would be his undoing. He should have known better than to send her to Daonith. Fia had been raised without love, but with the world at her feet, spoiled and brazen to everyone but Zachary. Not the kind of girl that should be given to a prince, a bomb of a woman just waiting to be set off.

"Are you ready?" Elara asked, pulling the door shut behind her as a gust of wind lifted their hoods.

"Yes." Fia put out her gloved hand and together they moved through wind and darkness to emerge in a snowy forest.

The wind was calmer here. No snow fell, but grey clouds blocked the sun and scurrying animals in the trees sent drifts of snow down to the forest floor.

"I am nervous to go to Niveren Gap," Fia admitted as they made their way over shrubs and fallen trees while Elara's magic refilled. Fia's had refilled as well, but she could still feel what she was missing, like a puzzle without the edges, rattling inside of her.

"If you can stand the cold, you will love it," Elara assured her. "And the people will love you. The Unseelie will not care that you are human, we are not like the Seelie, all of us are different, you no more than the rest."

"Is it warm in summer?" Fia asked. She didn't think she could stand to be frozen all year long.

"Yes, rarely hot but in the spring the snow melts and runs down from the mountains and by summer everything is luscious, green, and beautiful. The city will be even more beautiful once magic is restored and we can all bolster it. Before magic was taken our people were never hungry, despite the harsh conditions we grew crops and caught fish, and I made sure everyone ate."

Fia could imagine it easily; Elara before she was queen, still working to take care of her people. "When did you move there from the Village of Frost?"

The smile dropped from her face, her expression dark. "When I was ten, and then two years later my parents died...were murdered, so I had little chance to return to the Village until I was older. They never found out who killed them, but I know it was Ellio. My mother had been powerful like me. It was hard for her when her power was stolen and she had to watch, helpless, as crops withered and people starved. She went to Soleil again and again to try to understand the cause. This was before we truly understood what was going on. And Ellio was scared of her. Come on." She grabbed Fia, almost too roughly and they ported.

Once again it was snowing. They were in the mountains, the snow halfway to Fia's knees and she marveled at the faerie craftmanship that kept her legs warm and dry.

The world spread out below them, little towns and villages nestled in the valleys between mountains. So much life, so many faeries who only wanted to live in their small corner of Daonith. What a responsibility she had taken on, freeing their magic would help them, but she would bring war to their doorsteps, to their children.

There were more questions she wanted to ask, so many things to know about her new people and her mate, but the darkness still clouded Elara's face, so instead Fia pressed close to her, their shoulders rubbing together, warming her as they trudged through the snow.

Even scowling, the Queen was beautiful, her pale hair glimmering in the snow, her body graceful with each move, and despite her growing apprehension, being near Elara filled Fia with want. Their day together had done nothing to ease the need for her, instead with each touch it grew.

She wished they had longer to just be, to learn each other, and build a life before the rest of the world came crashing in. Balancing so much responsibility with new, exciting love was a balancing act she worried she would not be able to pull off. Even Elara, who cared for her people more deeply than anyone Fia knew, found it hard. How could she manage what Elara could not? What would she do if she had to choose between Elara and helping the Unseelie?

Memories of the night of the party when Aurora had come between them filled her mind. If Elara had touched her, if her magic had even begun to roam and fill Fia the way it had yesterday she would never have left. Even without the completed bond, it would have been like ripping off her own arm.

And now with the bond—Gods help her, even half frozen, nearly up to her ass in snow, Fia wanted her desperately, wanted the weight of Elara on top of her once more, wanted her horns digging into her thighs.

Elara cut a glance at her, her eyes brighter than before. "What on earth are you thinking about?"

Fia felt a blush spread across her cheeks. "Horns," she smirked, picking up the pace, not that it mattered how far they got, they were only biding time for Elara's magic to refill, but Elara was taller and kept up with her easily, even as the freezing wind pulled at their cloaks.

"Anything else?" Elara's voice was velvet.

But she did have a question, and as they weren't going to disrobe anytime soon, she thought it best to change the subject so they didn't end up with frostbite in peculiar places. "Your magic—when you touched me..." She cleared her throat, pushing the memories from her mind. "It reminded me of my own. Is it like that?" Gods, there was still so much she needed to learn if she was going to stay in Daonith.

"In some ways, but not exactly. Mine is more literal, like hands, yours is a connection to you from what I understand, an extension of your mind whereas mine is more tactile."

"How tactile?" Could she feel Fia, like really *feel* her, when she touched her with her magic?

"*Very.* When I want it to be. I am not sure if it is the same for all fae. Each of us wields our magic in our own ways, unique to us. I just have a lot of it."

And she would have more. Fia swallowed, imagining the destruction Elara could cause at her full strength. When they freed Elara would the Southern King tremble? But some deep part of her, tucked away in darkness, wanted not just the king to suffer, but her father. Wanted to see him fall before the storm of a woman the universe had given to Fia.

Not for the reasons she should, either. Not because he had hurt and killed so many. Not because he used his power to steal weapons and sell them to foreign kings, but because he had never appreciated her, never wanted a daughter, never given her a chance. Now she would destroy him, destroy both the men who had tried to use her like a pawn.

"I want to train again when we have a chance," Fia said. "And learn. I want to learn everything I can. If I'm going to be with you while you lead your people, I want to know what I'm doing. I want to be helpful."

A grin spread across Elara's face and Fia thought soon she might grow accustomed to seeing it there, but it was only visible for a second before Elara pulled her close and kissed her. Her tongue swept across the seam of Fia's mouth, and she opened for her mate, letting her explore as they traveled again, porting away from the snow.

They broke apart as they landed and though the sky was clear and the sun was bright, the temperature was still low. They were in a valley, hills and small mountains behind them, while ahead loomed jagged peaks that seemed to reach into the sky, stretching out towards the horizon in both directions.

"You wanted to see Niveren Gap," Elara said, brushing snow off Fia's cloak then her own.

"This is it?" There was nothing but mountains, no sounds of people, no clatter of carriages.

"This is as close as we can port," Elara said, her silver and brown eyes on something in the distance. Fia followed her gaze to a small gap between two of the tallest mountains barely wide enough for them to walk abreast.

Together they moved forward until the mountains swallowed them like a great beast. This was as far from the talisman and Ellio's magic as the faeries could get. Even the humans knew of this place, though they didn't call it Niveren's Gap, didn't have a name or a location for it at all. But history remembered the frozen port where once, long ago, it was rumored the toughest, fiercest sailors had ventured into glacial waters to trade with the faeries.

Now the waters were too treacherous to pass, even for the mightiest of human ships, because they would have to sail them without any of the technology they had come to rely on.

Besides, it was illegal to try. Faeries only wanted to trade at the borderlands, or at least that was what they had been told. What everyone believed. How Ellio and his ancestors must have worked to spread their lies and keep the humans from interfering as they built their stronghold while the other lands starved and died around them.

And she had almost been part of it. Fia reached for Elara's hand, squeezing it as they walked on, the pass widening just enough for sunlight to make it through the trees above, warming them.

Elara pushed off her hood. But the widened path lasted only a few minutes before it grew impossibly narrow and Fia was forced to fall into step behind the Queen.

What a stronghold. If any army wanted to come to the city they would either have to walk one at a time, bringing no supplies, or climb across the enormous, jagged mountains.

"How do you get supplies to the people who live here?" Fia asked, her voice echoing off the sheer stone that surrounded them.

"We grow a lot. Everyone is encouraged to keep a garden, and we help with seeds and other supplies when we can. It's much easier to supplement diets than provide them entirety. There are also a few farmers who grow the necessities and raise livestock, but the majority of our meat comes from the ocean. There are a lot of people in Niveren Gap who make their living on boats."

Boats in frozen waters full of icebergs. Fia shuddered to think about it. "That's a hard life."

Elara nodded. "Yes but having never relied on supplemented crops helped the city when magic was stolen. However, many of the Unseelie knew that so when the magic was taken they moved here, more than they could take at first."

They. "You were among them...the people who moved here. That's why your family left the Village of Frost." And she was hundreds of years old. There were so many faeries who had never had the bulk of their magic, faeries who had lived and died under Ellio's thumb.

"Yes, though I shouldn't complain much. My uncle Mithos was the king then and he let us stay with him in the castle." She sighed, trailing her fingers along the stone and Fia wished she could walk next to her, see her face. "He never quite got his footing after the magic was lost, but he was a good king. He cared for his people. Once the magic fell there were no feasts in his great hall for many years, we ate fish and seaweed like everyone else. I foraged in the warm months with the other children. My uncle tore out half the beautiful flower gardens and replaced them with fruit trees and vegetable gardens. He took care of his people. And they didn't hate him, not really... they just had to blame someone and..."

"They should have blamed Ellio," Fia said, reaching out to squeeze Elara's shoulders. The Queen's words were clipped, her voice too low to echo and Fia wondered if she'd ever spoken any of this out loud before. If so, not often.

"Yes, but my uncle's true failing was that he was not as powerful as me and was afraid to fight. When rumors started that magic hadn't fallen and instead had been stolen he never went to the Southern Kingdom, but my mother wouldn't let it rest and my father wouldn't let her go without him. And then they never returned. That's when I started going."

"I'm surprised Ellio let you into his estate like he did," Fia said. His lack of concern had always stunned her, how easily she had been given access.

"Well, he occasionally needs an Unseelie in his lands to keep the talisman active, or so I suspect since I am sure he needs a human. For a while I did not go, thinking I could free our magic that way, but it only led to him kidnapping my people. So I go, and neither of us say why, but I frighten him enough that he treats me like a Queen, I will give him that. He never tried to hold me."

The path widened enough for Fia to walk beside Elara again and she did, wrapping the Queen's fingers in her own. For as long as her now extended life might be, she knew she would never understand how this beautiful, complicated woman had come to be her mate, never know exactly when her fear of her had shifted into love. Elara was not a soft lover, she was hard and guarded, quick to anger, quicker to fight, but she believed in good things—in change— in a way Fia had never had the courage to even hope for. Not until now.

Voices came down the pass. Elara stopped walking and dropped Fia's hand to rummage in the bag on her shoulder.

From its depths she pulled out something wrapped in cloth. Her long, nimble fingers unwrapped two silver diadems. One was larger than the other, inlaid with amethyst and green fluorite. That one Elara placed upon her own head, nestled between her horns.

The second was the delicate, single stoned tiara she had given Fia for the party. Her breath stuck in her chest as Elara placed it upon her head. "We can have a nicer one made soon, but I want you to come to Niveren Gap as a queen."

"No," Fia said, her voice choked with emotion. "I love this one." The one Elara had given her when she could not admit they were mates. The one she had given her before they had even kissed. A symbol when it was all they had, when the world could not yet know what they were to each other, when *they* could not know. A token of Elara's love before it was spoken aloud.

Elara leaned forward, placing a gentle kiss on Fia's mouth, then her forehead. Her eyes blazed, but her mouth was soft, her body warm despite the cold. She placed her hand out and Fia took it once more. "Are you ready?"

Was she? Was she ready for this responsibility? For she was not just Elara's mate, she would be the Unseelie's Queen, an appellation she did not take lightly. Pushing back her shoulders, Fia lifted her chin. None of this would be simple, she was not fool enough to think they would easily win this war, but she would love these people as fiercely as she loved this woman. For all the things she had done wrong in her life before, she would make up for them now. She would be better, stronger. She would, for the first time, be someone she could be proud of.

-CHAPTER-
-THIRTY ONE-

THE GAP CURVED slightly, the mountains pressing in so close the rock brushed Fia's shoulders as she walked, then ended at a towering stone gate that seemed to be carved out of the mountain itself.

There was a portcullis just big enough for two people to fit through then smooth rock. Rounded portions jutted out slightly, inlaid with small windows, covered with crisscrossed steel high above their heads. Guard towers, it had to be.

From above there was a rustle and Fia looked toward the overhanging mountains. She saw nothing, but her magic pushed at her insides, desperate to fling out, to find what was lurking, because someone was up there. She could sense their magic.

Easy. She breathed deeply. There must be archers above, or magic wielders to the same effect. Elara's hand tightened around her own, but the Queen didn't seem concerned, calming Fia.

The portcullis began to rise, the thick wooden doors on the other side swung open. Fia's knees almost gave out at the sight of Kalin, grinning widely, waiting for them. "My favorite ladies!"

Guards behind him smiled, though not nearly as widely at Kalin, nodding towards their queen, a few giving apprehensive looks towards Fia.

Fia launched herself at Kalin and he grabbed her around the waist, lifting her into the air and spinning her around before setting her down, putting his hands on her shoulders and looking her over. "You're well?"

She nodded and stood on tiptoes to kiss his cheek. "Yes. I'm very good."

"I can see." He touched her tiara. "I am happy for you both. Very happy." He nodded at Elara. "Would you like me to walk you home?"

She shook her head. "No. I'd like to be the one to show Fia the city, but will you join us for dinner later?"

"Of course." He gave a slight bow and turned, heading down one of the narrow lanes and disappearing into Niveren Gap. Fia watched his large form until she could no longer see it, beyond thankful he was unharmed.

The city spread before them, teeming with life, children ran by with sleds and horses pulling carts moved through the muddy roads carrying goods behind them. Great mountains surrounded the city and Fia craned her neck to look up.

"People live in them," she whispered.

"Yes. We have limited space and many citizens," Elara said.

Switchback roads were carved into the mountain, running up from the city before disappearing into the mountain. Peeking out from the ridges, carved into the grey stone were windows, bright with fae light. Behind some she could even see movement, people going about their lives, tucked into the mountains themselves. Others had more than windows, huge open balconies, including one where a couple drinking coffee waved down at Elara and she waved back.

"Come on," Elara inclined her head down a road leading into the heart of the city and Fia followed, trying to take in everything. Chickens hurried by, leaving prints in the mud, enormous greenhouses, nearly as big as the houses themselves, filled the yards, growing vegetables even in the cold winter air, and people, so many people.

Unseelie made their way through the streets, some like Vinessa, Kalin, and Elara, others even more foreign to her—with wings and fangs and skin like snakes. Some rushed past and some meandered on. A group of children laughed as they ran by, books tucked under their arms, one stopping to stick his tongue out at Elara who stuck hers out in return. Nothing Fia had seen shocked her more.

"You know him."

"Yes. His mother is Kalin's sister." Elara continued to walk, as though this was all normal to her. And it was. Fia had seen her in her birthplace but never in her *home*. Here she was beloved, not the intimidating horned Unseelie Queen but Elara, their friend, the woman who worked for them, who had gone again and again into enemy territory, risking herself to save their magic, create a future for their children, to bring food back to their lands, and let those that wished move out of Niveren Gap and return to their homelands, or wherever they might go.

Elara smiled at her, the sun glinting off her crown, and she wrapped her arm around Fia's waist. "This is what's worth fighting for. This is why I stole you away."

"It's incredible," Fia whispered, watching a man push a cart full of fish toward a busy market, reminding her of the Village of Frost and the blanket she had loved, needed to buy to prove to herself that despite her hardship there was still beauty in the world. So much beauty, so much more than she had ever realized.

A tear slipped from Fia's cheek and she pushed it away, hating how much of her life she had wasted, the decades spent wishing for her father's approval. How much beauty had she missed in the human lands? The friends she might have had, the connections she never made because she was too worried about a man who would never love her. All the nights spent worried he would get caught, arrested for crimes he deserved to be punished for. And he had sold her like cattle, not even waiting a month before trying for a new heir.

"Fia?" The smile was gone from Elara's face and her hand drifted towards the knife sheathed at her waist before changing course toward Fia. She palmed her cheek, concern etched on her face.

"Sorry," Fia covered Elara's hand in her own. What a spectacle they were making in the middle of the street.

"Nothing to be sorry for."

"You don't even know why I'm crying," Fia forced out a laugh. "I'm just feeling sorry for myself, which is ridiculous because all my problems were self-inflicted. Look at what you've been through."

"Don't compare." Elara shook her head, moving her hand to cup Fia's neck. "I have endured for many years, but you were sold to a foreign nation against your will and stolen by another. You can cry if you need to cry."

"No, I want to see more." Fia steadied her breathing. Zachary Gray did not belong in this city, and she wouldn't allow him to be there, not even in her thoughts.

"Do you want to go to my home, or would you like to see the ocean?"

"The ocean?" She knew they were close, of course. Niveren Gap had once been a trading city and she'd seen the carts of fish, but it was hard to imagine how they would get to the sea, surrounded by mountains as they were. "Let's go there."

"Good choice."

Fia followed Elara through the city, trying to take everything in, the people outside despite the chill, the markets and storefronts, the rumbling sound as wagons went by until they stopped by a row of open-topped carriages and Elara motioned to one. "It's a bit of a walk. Come on." She helped Fia inside and they both settled into the soft seat.

The carriage came alive, the air filling with warmth, the wheels beginning to move and faint instrumental music played. The carriage was some kind of public transportation, and it took them across the city before coming to a stop on the side of a main road. There was a line waiting and Elara held the door open as they exited to let a family climb inside.

The mountains seemed even larger than the ones they had entered through, but there was a larger pass between those at this side, and before she could see it Fia smelled the salty tang of the ocean.

Elara took her hand, trying to lead her forward but Fia planted her feet in the soft, lichen covered ground. An hour in Niveren Gap had made one thing abundantly clear.

Her fingers moved of their own accord to the tiara on her head, running over the stones. "I can't wear this. I'm not these people's ruler—I can't be. I don't know them. This city..." She swallowed against the lump in her throat, not wanting to say any of this, but knowing she had to. "This city is incredible, these people...but I'm just a human and I just arrived from the human lands. I can't show up without warning and *rule* them, Elara. They picked you, not me. I can't do this."

Some unnamed emotion crossed Elara's face, and she put her hand to Fia's cheek once again. The touch was so soft, yet it still filled Fia's body with heat. "I did not crown you to rule these people, I crowned you because despite how much I love this city, despite the safety I feel here, no matter where we go there is danger for you. There are those who will see you and dream of what they could gain from Ellio if you were returned to him, and you are human, easily recognizable. I want everyone we pass to know you are *mine*, and that whatever riches they dream of will pale in comparison to the pain I will bring down on them if they lay a finger on you."

The air seemed to leave Fia's lungs. "The same as at the party." She should have known. She probably should care, it was a branding after all, but all she really felt was safe.

"Yes." Elara lowered her hand. "But one day you *will* rule them, make no mistake, because we will win this war, we will bring the magic back and return here to live, and you will have decades upon decades to learn all you need to know. Now, can I please show you the sea?"

Fia laughed. "Yes, of course."

"What you said though...that you care more for what is good for my people than the power..." Elara's eyes softened. "I am glad you are here, that the pact brought you to me."

"So am I." And she meant it, so deeply in her soul. Never had she imagined her life would end up here. Up until the moment Callum had picked her, she'd never imagined a life in Daonith at all, much less one surrounded by the Unseelie, so unlike her, yet now that she was here, she couldn't imagine anything else, any other way she might live.

Together they passed through the gap in the mountains, much shorter than the last and under another portcullis to a large glacial bay. Despite the chunks of ice floating in the water, fishing boats bobbed, and people walked on the rocky shore. Across the water was the other side of the bay, ragged and rocky and beyond that the sparkling sea, a brilliant blue reflecting the sun.

A shiver went down Fia's spine that had nothing to do with the cold. The faerie bay of legends was real. Long ago humans had traded here. They could do it again. She could be the Unseelie's queen but also a human, she could be that bridge, bringing the people together again without Ellio, without the need of the narrow borderlands he controlled with an iron fist.

Elara had fallen behind, letting Fia walk on her own to the shore, where waves crashed into rocks and children made little towers of smooth pebbles. She turned when she heard Elara's voice to find her talking to Saskia. She hadn't even noticed her approach, but she was as bone-chilling as ever, even as she gave a closed lipped smile to Fia.

"You survived. Good job. I had little hope for you, but I should have trusted Elara."

"Uh, thanks." Fia tried not to look at her claws. "I'm glad you're well, also."

Saskia let out a grunt. "Shall I prepare rooms in the castle or send them to one of the inns?"

"The castle. We are trying to win Seera's favor. We have to woo her a bit."

"There are other ways, Elara," Saskia said with a voice that made Fia's shiver.

"I am aware," Elara said and her tone left no room for argument. "But that is not our way, despite what lies have been told about us."

A muscle in Saskia's jaw twitched and she flexed her fingers, making Fia think whatever she wanted to do was exactly her way and if Fia had to guess that way was violence. The woman looked built for it.

When Fia had first seen Elara, she had thought she was terrifying, the hard lines of her face promising brutality. She still did think so, but it was nothing compared to Saskia. Side by side the two of them looked frightening enough to turn the tide of any war. Nothing like the golden power Ellio clutched in his fist, daring the world to defy him. They did not need anything extra to show their power, they simply were powerful.

"The rooms will be prepared," Saskia ground out and turned sharply, disappearing under the portcullis and down the gap in the mountains.

"She didn't seem pleased," Fia said.

Elara shrugged. "She is often not pleased. She would not be suited to leadership unless people were hoping for an abundance of bloodshed."

"Not you?"

The Queen's eyes narrowed. "I only provide the necessary amount of bloodshed, Fia."

A flash of the guard, his neck an open wound, played in Fia's mind and she pushed it away. Her own father had done worse, and she had ignored it time and time again. She would slit a thousand throats if Elara was taken from her. She could not fault her for the freedom she had granted her. "Niveren Gap is beautiful," she said, looking out at the bay once more as a fisherman pulled in a net full of wriggling pink fish.

"I thought you would like it. I come out here when I need to think. I didn't see the ocean until we moved here but it has never lost its beauty."

"There are many beaches in the human lands, ones with white sand and hot water, perfect for swimming, but I think this may soon become my favorite."

A horned child ran by, net over his shoulder, screaming to his friends to keep up. Children everywhere, all of them playing. She hadn't seen a single child in Soleil.

"Ezriel's beaches get warm enough to swim in during the summer if you ever miss it. It will be hard for us to visit the human lands again, Fia. They do not know about the Unseelie."

"I know. That will be okay." There wasn't much for Fia to miss. Television probably. Definitely her phone, her fingers still itched for it sometime. But she had never made real friends, not like she had here. Her only family was her father and that meant nothing. "But we can change that eventually, you and me. After we free magic, we could fix more than that."

Elara closed the gap between them in one long stride, capturing Fia's lips with her own, sweeping her tongue through her mouth, claiming her. Her hands moved beneath Fia's cloak, fingers grasping at the fabric of her shirt as she bit down on her bottom lip.

Want, hot and fierce, coursed through Fia's body, the need for Elara tangible, for her to touch more, taste more deeply. The bond between them went taut, as Fia's desire surged, pooling thick in her core.

A fisherman made a loud whistle and the two of them pulled apart, cold air taking up the space Elara had filled, but the heat inside Fia remained.

"Welcome back, Highness," the man said, winking as he tied his boat to the wooden dock. "This is the human woman we've heard about, I take it." The hair peeking out from under his cap reminded her of Vinessa, thick green strands, though his skin was a much deeper pink than hers. The thick beard on his chin was green as well, and incredibly bushy. He looked Fia over and nodded his head once. "I heard you went back to that lifeless kingdom. Brave of you. I like that in a woman."

"And I like a man who can work with his hands," Fia said, and he laughed.

"I like her, Elara."

"So do I."

-CHAPTER-
-THIRTY TWO-

THOUGH ELARA'S HOME had been described as a castle, Fia had not really believed it. None of the royalty she had met so far had lived in a proper castle. Elara's home wasn't as huge as the word might suggest but it was a castle, complete with a surrounding wall, several towers manned by guards, and a courtyard where an honest to god blacksmith worked, though he was making horseshoes not weapons when they showed up.

Fia was looking forward to a hot bath, scrubbing every frozen inch of her skin, then pulling Elara into bed to get dirty again. Screw a tour of the castle, they could do that later, possibly after dinner which she also desperately wanted.

After they arrived and Fia managed to stop gawking, they headed through the courtyard and towards the main doors, flanked by two enormous bushes carved into the shape of dragons.

"Seriously, this place is amazing. I love it so much."

Elara's face was the brightest she'd ever seen it. She touched her hand to her heart. "I am so glad."

"Fia?"

She spun towards the voice. Aurora stood under a covered hallway, a furred hat pulled over her golden hair, her blue eyes wide. All the horrible things Fia had said to her, the nasty accusations, came rushing back. *I know you would slit my throat to advance your cause because for all your pretty reasons you are not helping your people as Elara is, you are freeing yourself.*

She ran to Aurora, dodging people and greenery. She reached out, ready to pull the princess into a hug before stopping short, unsure if Aurora would accept the gesture. "Aurora, I am so sorry. You've only ever tried to be my friend."

A grin stretched across Aurora's beautiful face. "The mating bond really makes you wacky, huh?"

"You knew?"

"I suspected. I've never seen Elara sweet before, so I knew something was different about you, and I mean you're cute and all, but..."

Fia didn't wait for her to finish, cutting off her words as she dragged her into an embrace, squeezing her tight. "Bastard Father Club can't fall apart so quickly."

Aurora laughed. "No, we must persevere, I want to see the look on his face when he realizes he brought the human who would ruin him into his home. Plus, eventually the Southern Kingdom *will* need a leader."

Of course. Fia hadn't thought through to the next logical step, but once Ellio was dealt with Helio couldn't be allowed to rule. "Queen Aurora has a nice ring to it." It sure would make Fia's swirling, hazy plans for human fae relations easier. For a brief moment she let herself imagine it, the borderlands controlled by Aurora, human boats coming into the bay to bring supplies to the Unseelie, all the people she cared about thriving.

"We're good," Aurora said, winking. "The way I figure it, since I technically kidnapped you, you get to yell at me a little bit before I hold a grudge."

"Well, when you put it that way..." Fia laughed, some of the tension she'd been holding since she left the Southern Kingdom releasing.

Elara's arm was draped over Fia's abdomen, gentle breath stirring Fia's hair. When Fia had come out of the bathroom the night before Elara had already fallen asleep on the bed, half propped up in a way that suggested she hadn't meant to sleep at all.

Fia had eased her down onto the bed and tucked her in before crawling in beside her, only feeling disappointment for a moment before sleep overtook her as well.

Now, the sun streamed in through the curtains neither of them had closed, and beyond the glass snow fell in large flakes, creating a mound on the windowsill.

Would she really have thousands more mornings like this? After everything that had happened it seemed too good to be true. She had escaped the Southern Kingdom too easily, surprise working in her favor, but again? The thought of succeeding, of spending her life waking up in Elara's arms was a fairy tale unlikely to come true in a world that had proven itself, time and again to be cruel.

So she decided to cherish every moment, dedicating to memory the feel of Elara's arm against her, the brush of her breath along Fia's neck, the sweet, earthy smell enveloping the whole room, and the precious bond between them, languid and happy like a cat in the sun now that they were together.

Elara stirred, making a small, sleepy noise, her fingers trailing across Fia's skin until she cupped her breast. "Morning," she whispered, kissing the skin her breath had previously caressed.

Fia turned molten, her toes curling beneath the blanket as Elara's other arm wrapped around her, holding her tight. The Queen's fingers brushed against her nipple, then she pinched, making Fia inhale sharply.

But there was no time to catch her breath as her other hand moved lower, and her leg pressed in between Fia's separating her thighs. Horns pushed against Fia as Elara continued to kiss her, the back of her neck, her shoulders. Her fingers found the wet space at Fia's center, and she moaned into her skin, her body undulating against Fia.

The bond was tight, pulling them together, frantic and delighted. Her mate. Her Queen. Each horrible moment of her life leading to this moment, this woman, this kingdom.

Elara worked Fia's clit, slowly, so devastatingly slowly, Fia ground into her and the Queen chuckled. A moment later her magic joined, its warm tendrils brushing over her body, up her thighs, her collarbone, her throat.

"You are so fucking beautiful," Elara whispered, her pressure and pace increasing but still not enough. Not enough pressure, enough friction. Never enough.

Her magic slid down, across Fia's stomach as the Queen increased her speed, prodding at her entrance as Elara's leg moved further between her thighs, holding her open as her arm held her steady on her side, unable to move. "Yes?"

"Yes," Fia bit out, still unused to the sensation of the magic but desperate for it, for the way the Queen fucked her, so unlike anything else. The magic plunged into her and her eyes rolled back in her head as the queen's thumb made a tight circle on her clit.

She moved her mouth to the shell of Fia's ear as she drove her closer to the edge with magic and hands. "There are so many ways I'm going to fuck you. So many places." She licked the column of Fia's neck.

"Elara," Fia gasped as the magic receded, but the queen's fingers never stopped moving, never stopped their hard, unrelenting circles, until Fia thought she might explode. No, she would explode. She could feel the orgasm building within her and the Queen's name slipped over her lips again just as magic plunged into her, driving her fully over the edge.

She screamed out, back arching, her body shaking but unable to move as Elara held her tight, her movements slowing, pressure lessening. When Fia's body stopped trembling, Elara loosened her grip, letting Fia lie on her back. She took a deep breath, but it did nothing to slow the pounding of her heart because she could see Elara fully for the first time that morning, hair tangled around her horns, cheeks flushed with desire.

Fia reached for her, pulling her down into a crushing kiss, all tongue and teeth. She rose to her knees, a fistful of the queen's hair in her hand, refusing to let her pull away until she was ready.

Elara wore only a nightgown, and she made quick work of taking it off before pushing the queen down to the mattress. She was so beautiful, a work of art, her purple hair a riot of color against the white sheets, her full breasts rising with each intake of breath. Perfect breasts that Fia lowered her mouth to, nipping at the dark nipples, pulling the skin between her teeth before running her tongue over the stiffened peak.

"I have things I want to do to you too," she said, locking eyes with the Queen. *Her* Queen. And she would worship every inch of her.

The day passed quickly, a blur of exploring the city and meeting countless people, all who seemed to love Elara. She was different in Niveren Gap, softer, smiling. Yet, despite the love, everyone respected her and understood the sacrifices she had made to keep the city secure.

The faeries were all so ancient. It was easy to forget the youthful faces held hundreds of years in them until they mentioned old towns, places that no longer existed because they had fallen apart after the magic was lost, old lives, the past human princesses, so many things that were all history to Fia.

And then one woman, with a light smattering of fur across her skin and big, almond eyes asked how it had been for the humans. If they missed the magic too and Fia's stomach dropped. Living in Daonith it was so easy to forget what was taken because her magic felt like a gift, like something that had only come from faerie magic, when in truth it had been stolen. The human lands had been drained so completely that witches had been forgotten, thought of as something more like a myth, an old story, something so rare it had barely been real at all. What else had been lost? What else did the humans not even know should belong to them, taken by faeries to make them reliant, to make them flock and trade at the border, begging for scraps of magic to heal their sick, to fix their blights?

"I don't know," Fia admitted. "I didn't know anything. I don't know if it was hidden on purpose or just forgotten because we don't live as long as you, but no one talks about it."

"People know," Elara scoffed and then stiffened when Fia turned to her. "Your leaders, the people in charge, they know."

No. That couldn't be right. "How would you know?" The words came out more accusatory than she meant them to. Even though she had just alluded to the same thing, it didn't mean she wanted to accept it as truth.

"Because they have to know. I've spent enough time in Ellio's godforsaken house, watched him wine and dine leaders. They knew about me, that much is for sure, and yet you didn't about the Unseelie. Power makes people lie, makes them hoard what they have, unwilling to lose it. You of all people know that."

The woman who had been speaking to them backed up slightly, having stepped into something she didn't mean to and wanting no part of it.

"You have power," Fia said. "You're a Queen."

"And you're a powerful criminal's daughter, so we both know I'm telling the truth. I've worked hard to stay uncorrupted—not having the bulk of my power, fighting for it every day really helps. Believe me, every time I go to Soleil so my people don't have to, I'm reminded of just how powerless I am. But yes, your leaders know, your father knew, maybe not the exact details, I don't think Ellio gives those out to anyone, a secret passed from father to eldest son, but he knows there are ways to steal power. He wants it. You know that."

She did, and the hatred for her father hardened in her. She had never been anything more than something to trade for more, and now he worked on his next heir. Part of her hoped he had another daughter, that he never got the son he craved, but she wasn't cruel enough to truly wish that on a sister. "I know you're right. I've known for months. It just sucks to hear it."

Before Elara could respond Kalin appeared, Saskia not far behind, their faces grave. “She is here.”

“She’s early,” Elara said before turning to Fia. “Come on, it’s time to meet the Eastern Queen.”

-CHAPTER- -THIRTY THREE-

THE SUN SET over the mountains, coloring the peaks in pinks and purples as the Western convoy made its way down the pass toward the gates of Daonith. Fia scanned the crowd before them, there were at least two dozen people, more than she had expected.

They split in half, and a woman with a halo of bright, fire red hair made her way down the space between them. No human had hair that color, nor skin that held such a gold-flecked hue. Before seeing Seera, Fia had thought of Ellio and his children as golden fae, and perhaps they were, but if so, Seera was flame come to life.

Steps behind her came another woman with the same flame-red hair, though hers was pulled back in a tight braid behind her head. "Will you not open the gates, Elara?" Seera yelled up. "I know you wanted me here."

"I don't know, Seera. I was hoping Ezriel would get here first," Elara yelled back, a hint of humor in her voice.

"I live to disappoint," Seera replied. "I hear you've finally fallen in love. Mina wept for days," Seera was clearly joking but Elara stiffened and even at the distance, Fia could see the look of irritation on the woman behind the queen.

Had Elara...? Of course, she was six hundred years old, Fia hadn't thought she'd been the first. But still, it struck something inside of her. Part of Fia filled with rage, even as Elara yelled something back Fia couldn't hear over the pounding of blood in her ears.

Beside her, Kalin leaned down, his voice breaking through the rising tide of emotions. "It's the mating bond heating your blood. You don't actually want to murder any Eastern princesses because you *know* she is yours."

"I don't?" Fia asked, though of course she didn't. That would be insane. Yet the anger...

"I don't know. I think I like her like this. She looks like she might actually do some damage for the first time," Saskia said as the gates started to open.

"It was a long time ago," Kalin said. "She only wanted to upset Elara. She wouldn't have said it if she'd known you were freshly mated."

"Yes, she would have," Elara said. "She's a raging bitch. But you, Fia, have nothing to worry about at all." She cut a look at the people on the tower around them and they moved back, affording them the illusion of privacy. Elara's fingers trailed down Elara's arm, falling to grip her by the hip and pull her close, until her lips were at Fia's ear. "I will prove it to you later if you need, though I thought I did a thorough job this morning."

The heat inside Fia turned from rage to desire and she exhaled, tendrils of her power twisting back into her. "Is she going to keep doing that because I don't usually...Well, I'm not particularly jealous but I just wanted to kill a woman I've never met."

Elara moved her mouth in fluttering kisses along Fia's jaw. "She very well may, but I'd really appreciate it if you didn't murder her sister. Or anyone really. But I love you, and I will respect whatever you feel the need to do."

Fia laughed, the sudden bark of it burning her throat. "The whole mates thing is kind of intense."

"Yes, not telling you was awful. Now, I really must go meet her. The whole thing is important, though I'm forgetting why at the moment." She fisted a handful of Fia's hair.

"Important..."

Kalin cleared his throat. "I'm going to dump a bucket of cold water on you in about five seconds."

"You wouldn't dare," Elara hissed, but she moved back from Fia. "I'll murder *you* if I have to meet Seera for the first time in decades looking like a wet cat."

"You'd miss me too much." Kalin grinned, brightening his face, tree-bark skin crinkling around his eyes. "Besides, Fia likes me and she'd be really mad."

"Ugh," Saskia frowned, clicking her nails against the stone wall. "Can we please go?"

Two hours later Seera and her contingency were settled into the castle. She'd brought quite a few people with her, and the quiet halls were fuller. Workers—Elara had looked downright horrified when Fia had referred to them as servants—rushed by with arms full of bedding while Eastern fae explored the space, laughing and touching artwork in a way that, despite how new Fia was to the city, made her want to bite them.

The two royal Eastern women were even more beautiful up close, with full lips as bright red as their hair and shimmering skin, glittering as though gold had been dusted across it, but Princess Mina's eyes had a brightness that her sister's didn't. Though the Queen smiled and joked there was a shrewdness to her, like a jungle cat lying in wait, taking in her surroundings, sizing them up at every opportunity.

After they'd been given time to relax, Elara brought them all together. They gathered in one of the vast sitting rooms, the large space had been stuffed with enough comfortable emerald and cobalt colored chairs and plush rugs that the space felt cozy, especially with flames roaring in the giant fireplace and several bottles of wine left in various corners.

"So, Ezriel will be joining us as well?" Seera asked, pulling the cork out of a bottle of wine with a pop and pouring herself a hearty glass. Her sister stood feet away while others talked in small groups around the room.

"Should be here soon," Saskia said, her black leather ensemble outfitted with even more knives than usual. Fia had found herself becoming increasingly fond of the angry faerie.

"Good. I'd like to have a drink. I hate travelling," Seera said, making her way for the far side of the room.

"Sorry," Elara whispered. "I need to go woo her a bit."

Fia nodded and headed to get a glass of wine of her own before busying herself at a table piled with tiny, delicious smelling pastries. She smoothed the sides of her dress and readjusted her tiara. The dress was simple, made of a soft, thick fabric, with wide, floral embroidered sleeves and a heavy skirt that brushed the floor. Unseelie clothing— simple, well-constructed, beautiful, and practical.

She smiled to herself, grabbing a flaky pastry. Somewhere in the last few months she'd come to love the Unseelie, not just their Queen, but all of them, from the small Village of Frost to this gorgeous city and its resilient inhabitants.

"You are—" someone said beside Fia and she turned to find Princess Mina, her mouth slightly agape. "Shit."

"Unusual greeting," Fia said, taking a sip of her wine.

Mina laughed. "Oh, it's all the rage in Western Kingdom."

"I'll try to remember that if I ever come for a visit," Fia took a bite of the pasty and nearly moaned; it was possibly the best thing she'd ever eaten. "I might need a moment alone with this."

Mina laughed again and maybe, despite the irritation prickling along her mating bond, Fia liked her. "You're not just her lover, you're her mate. Aren't you?" Fia nodded in confirmation and Mina winced. "Then I am so sorry about my sister's initial words. Well, I was already sorry for them, but now doubly so. You must have wanted to strangle me. Or so I hear. I haven't found my mate."

There was no point in denying it. “Yes. The feelings are intense. But you didn’t say it, so there is no point in holding it against you.”

A shadow fell over them and Kalin selected a chocolate croissant. “Mina. You look very well.”

“So do you.” She grinned up at him. “Still wider than a man has any right to be, I see.”

He gave a low chuckle. “I appreciate you being here. I assume you are the reason behind her coming.”

“Not completely, actually,” Mina said. “I’d supported it, of course, but she recently had a change of heart.” Mina glanced towards her sister who was still talking to Elara across the room. Neither Queen seemed completely at ease, but neither was reaching for weapons either. “So, what is this meeting about?”

Fia cut a look at Kalin. Mina was nice, but not nice enough that either of them was about to answer her question before Elara got a chance. “That is for the Queen to answer.”

“Of course. Well, I won’t bother you any longer.” Mina left, heading for her sister.

Neither of them spoke until she was well out of earshot then Fia turned to Kalin. His eyes were wide but there was a touch of mischief in them along with the alarm. “Yes, she’s up to something but she's always up to something. I liked her well enough long ago but never enough, not really."

Fia glanced across the room, at the mixture of Seelie and Unseelie, though with their gold-tinged skin the Eastern Kingdom seemed something in between. She lowered her voice. "Can we trust them?"

Kalin shook his head. "Probably not, but what choice do we have? Everything we've found indicates it will take a fae from each Kingdom and a human to render the talisman powerless."

"There's so much we can't control. It's awful." Fia put the pastry down half finished, no longer hungry. Something in her subconscious tugged and she found Elara looking at her. Their gaze met for a moment and oh, how she longed for her, wanted to touch her, to feel horns between her thighs, fingers tangled in hair, lips swollen. She shook her head and Elara dipped her chin, the barest movement but still summoning Fia, like a rope stretched tight between them. "Excuse me."

The moment she was near Elara something righted deep within her, like the pressure in the room had been a touch too high and now had normalized. Her mate's arm snaked around her waist, pulling her close, their bodies flush. "Seera, I'd like to formally introduce you to the Princess Consort of the Unseelie Kingdom, Fia Gray."

Princess. The word clanged through her, blood heating, and she knew her cheeks flushed pink. Should they shake hands? She had no idea what to do with herself, so she went with a classic. "It's lovely to meet you."

Seera only raised an eyebrow. "Princess of two kingdoms in a few months. Most impressive."

A hiss issued from Elara. "You will watch your words with my mate."

"Mate?" Seera looked to her sister for confirmation. "Interesting. To mate the first human you met. I did not even know they were capable of such a thing."

"I would imagine there is much you don't know, Seera," Elara hissed.

This was going terribly. Fia needed to do something quickly, or she suspected the two women would come to blows. "You think you're surprised? Imagine my shock. I thought not having my cellphone would be the hardest part." She plastered on a grin.

And was rewarded with the barest hint of a smile on both the Eastern women's faces. "What is a cellphone?" Seera asked.

"Like a communication device." No reason to get into the rest. "Pretty much every human has one and we can talk to each other on it or send messages."

"Sounds convenient. From my understanding electricity has served you well in the past few centuries. Have you noticed a difference?"

"Um..."

"I think you have forgotten the average human lifespan," Mina said. "Fia is probably only fifty or sixty years old."

So close. "I'm twenty-nine."

"Oh!" Seera's hand shot up to her mouth. "Goodness. That must be so strange. But you'll live longer here, correct? Such a short life is so tragic."

"I hope so," Fia said. If she didn't die in the next few weeks, which was a definite possibility. "I've really learned to love Daonith." She squeezed Elara's hand, still on her waist.

Like a switch had been flipped, the arrogance returned to Seera's face. "Have you seen much of it?"

The temperature dropped, the shadows seemed to darken, and Saskia was at Fia's side. "I believe they have spotted Ezriel's party coming up the pass. Perhaps you want to come greet them?"

"Take Fia," Elara said. "I will stay here."

"Don't worry," another voice said and Aurora was finally there, her blonde curls perfectly set, her eyes dark with makeup and wearing a rose colored dress similar to Fia's. "I will keep Seera company while you greet my favorite king."

"There you are," Seera smiled in a way that just might be genuine, or something close to it. It was easy to forget Aurora was a princess and spent most of her life traveling the faerie lands. She knew the art of small talk and making people feel seen. Maybe she would be the key to relations between the Unseelie and Eastern Kingdom, or maybe she could teach Fia a thing or two about charming humans, when the time came.

A look passed between Elara and Aurora then Elara gave one tight nod. "Very well. We will return for dinner. Highness, make sure to bring your sister as well as any advisors. We have much to discuss now that we are all together."

"Not all," Seera said, her voice low. Dangerous.

"No," Elara said, her voice just as dangerous, though the gravel of it sent a shiver down Fia's spine that Seera's voice had not. Not fear, never fear with Elara, not anymore, though she was still the weapon she had always been. "Though it is my sincerest hope that soon the leaders of all of the courts can come together."

Seera opened her mouth to respond but Elara turned to Fia. "Come, darling. Ezriel will be glad to see you again."

-CHAPTER-
-THIRTY FOUR-

BEFORE THEY MADE it halfway across the city to the gate tower at the pass, Ezriel and Vinessa were before them. Vinessa's beautiful pale pink face split into a wide grin and she pulled Fia into a hug, her wings spreading out to surround them.

"I worried I would never see you again." She pulled back and inspected Fia. "I hope you have found all you want and you will forgive some of my earlier outbursts. I did not...I did not know."

Fia returned her warm smile. She had no desire to have Vinessa as an enemy. "All is forgiven."

"Unfortunately," Ezriel said, giving Fia a tight-lipped smile before directing his attention back to Elara. "We come with bad news. Beatrix has died."

A muscle in Elara's jaw tensed and she flexed her fingers like she might reach for Fia, but Fia had no idea who the heck Beatrix was and voiced as much, moving towards Elara because she could not stomach seeing discomfort on her face.

"The other human Queen," Elara clarified, snaking her arm around Fia's waist. "Which means you are, as far as I know, the only human in Daonith."

Fia shook her head. "My father was there when I left. Could he keep the magic going?"

"Yes," Elara said. "And the King would not want him to leave." She glanced up and down the street.

Some fae were glancing at them, their eyes snagging on Fia and she realized she was still wearing the tiara.

"We should go inside. My chambers, Ezriel."

The king nodded, taking his wife's hand. Fia didn't realize what was about to happen before they ported, wind and darkness overtaking her for only a moment before they reappeared in the living space outside their bedroom. "Shit. Warning next time, please."

“Sorry,” Elara said, not sounding the least bit sorry as Ezriel and Vinessa appeared in front of them.

“I thought you couldn’t port in Niveren Gap,” Fia said.

“You can’t port into or out of it, nor the gap that leads to the gate, but you can once inside. Few have the magic though so it’s not common. That doesn’t matter.” Elara pulled her crown from her head, tossing it onto a table before sinking into one of the stuffed armchairs. She looked exhausted; there were pale purple circles under her eyes, and the silver rim of her iris’s had turned a stormy grey. “What will it mean if Fia’s father returns to the human lands?”

Ezriel sat as well, pressing his elbows into his thighs and leaning forward. “If our research is correct, the magic of the talisman will immediately begin to fracture”

“And we have no idea if anything we have learned is correct. What if it’s all wrong, Ez?”

Fia planted herself on the bench in front of the bay window overlooking the city and watched the two of them. She’d never heard Elara use a nickname for Ezriel before, never seen her quite so unsure of herself and she hated that she had nothing to add, no words to help.

“Don’t think like that,” Ezriel said. “We know his grandfather was married to a Western woman when the magic started to disappear, a woman who was good friends with the human queen at the time. The only thing that makes sense is that he used Western spell magic. And you can trust my knowledge of spell magic."

"There were human queens before the talisman?" Fia blurted out.

"Yes," Ezriel said, looking over to her. "I will try to find some history books for you. I should have done so sooner. But even before magic was involved humans were married to fae to foster healthy relations between our people."

"But why would a Western fae help them steal magic from her own people?"

Elara laughed. "People do things against their own interest all the time if they think it will bring them more power, bring their children or husbands more power. Power ruins people."

Indeed, it did. Fia had seen it many times, again and again; men desperate for her father's good grace doing things they swore they never would. She'd watched them lose wives, lose friends, while gaining power, gaining higher office, or money or whatever drove them. She'd never seen it make them happy, only desperate for more.

“So, that’s good right? If they don’t have a human?” Fia said, shoving down the nervous magic that rose in her, wishing she already had Ezriel’s books and understood more.

“Maybe.” Elara sighed, the sound coming from deep within her. “It might weaken the talisman, but it will also make Ellio desperate, and we don’t know what he knows. And the effect won’t be immediate. He doesn’t keep Unseelie’s in his kingdom at all times, as far as I know. I can’t be certain, but I believe it takes days.”

“But that may be different,” Ezriel interjected. “Even before the talisman the human lands were separated from us by the mist and by the land itself. There are many more Unseelie near his kingdom than humans, plenty live on the border whereas few humans live near your border and even if they did it is so narrow, there is little land to occupy.”

“So, we don’t know what will happen,” Fia said.

“We don’t know,” Ezriel repeated. “Maybe if we keep you here the talisman will drain itself and we won’t have to act.”

Vinessa let out a hollow laugh. “If only we were so lucky, but luck always seems to go to Ellio, doesn’t it?”

“Do we wait then?” Fia asked, possibilities swirling in her brain, a world where she did not have to go back, where Elara didn’t have to fight, where war was averted. She could see from the faces around her their minds were conjuring dreams as well.

"Maybe," Elara said. "We were not going to act immediately even before Beatrix died. We need to convince Seera to join our side then decide on a plan. A day or two will not matter much after hundreds of years."

Could it be that easy? The tension that gripped every inch of her body said no. And how much would it change? How much would any of this change? Ellio had not been stealing weapons from the human military for no reason. He meant war. Destroying the talisman was dangerous, but, Fia feared, it would be nothing compared to what would come after.

"How are things with Seera?" Vinessa asked, pulling at the sleeves of her jacket like she didn't know what to do with her hands.

Elara shrugged, her face tight. "She is as she always is. Seera's main concern has always been Seera, even when she was a child. We are of a similar age, and her parents brought her with them when they visited. My uncle would drag me to the castle to keep her occupied before her sister was born. She was an awful child, I would try to play with her like I played with children in my village, but she seemed to see me as an enemy, as someone to defeat."

“Her sister seems more reasonable,” Fia said, the words slimy in her throat. In her more rational brain she liked Mina, but the bond said otherwise. But there was no time for the pettiness of new mates. She was a princess now, diplomacy was more important than her desire to drag Elara into the bedroom just behind them, to strip her down and—

Elara cleared her throat, sending a pointed look at Fia. “Yes,” she said stiffly. “Mina should have been the first born. The Eastern Kingdom would be better for it, or even for allowing some common sense in their line of succession. But not all believe in democracy.”

Ezriel huffed and Fia saw the delicate balance he had struck with Elara fading. “And electing the niece of the current king is democracy, not nepotism?”

“It does not matter,” Vinessa said before Fia could interject. “Are we really going to squabble over forms of government right now? Is that how *our* kingdoms are best served.” Elara and Ezriel both looked properly chastised and Fia caught Vinessa’s eye and smiled.

“We told Seera we would speak to her at dinner,” Fia said before anyone else could continue the conversation. If she and Vinessa had to serve as peace keepers it was a role she would gladly take, and knowing Elara’s temper, probably one she should get used to. "We should all get ready for that and present a united front. She's not going to join us if she thinks the two of you can't even get along."

"You are correct, darling," Elara said, inclining her head at Ezriel.

Outside the window the sun was setting, but the last of its rays caught in Ezriel's hair as he nodded back, making him glow. "Indeed. We are both blessed in our partners, Elara. That much is clear."

Elara didn't quite smile until she looked at Fia, then the corners of her lips pulled up and her eyes sparkled. "Worth the wait."

The room where the meeting would be held was more like a dining room than the formal great hall of Ellio's estate, a warm, inviting space with a shining wooden table flanked by a dozen matching chairs, all of them holding a purple velvet cushion. Yet the room seemed cold, the warmth drained from everyone including Elara, who sat at the head of the table, Seera on the other end.

It seemed almost silly to have them so far away, they looked like they would have to shout, and maybe Fia would have suggested closer quarters if it wasn't for the look in both women's eyes. A look that made her nervous, all the excitement the queen's arrival had promised slowly draining from the castle as she listened to Elara explain what they were up against, the stolen magic that had killed crops and starved whole towns, the talisman they had finally found, the way they had everyone they needed except an Eastern faerie and how they hoped it could be Seera. The only thing unmentioned was Fia's magic.

Underneath the table, Fia gripped Elara's knee, her nails biting into the thick leather fabric of her pants. Beside Seera, Mina's eyes were wide and when she saw Fia looking at her she nodded so slightly Fia wasn't sure if she had seen the movement at all.

Seera's fingers templed together, her lips a thin line across her beautiful, golden face. "Little magic was stolen from my kingdom." Her voice was disinterested.

Aurora made a disbelieving noise. "That is not true! Your numbers are just small, you have less magic to take, less people to feed. But it is not the point. Did you not hear about the weapons he has accumulated? We are down on power and he intends war."

"With all of us?"

Now it was Mina's turn to make an incredulous noise. "Sister, you—"

Seera held up a hand. "I am not saying no. I am saying that..." She considered her words. "My numbers *are* small. Smaller even than the Unseelie and I do not have an impenetrable fortress. Neither do you, Ezriel. And it seems that no matter what actions we take, war will be upon us. If I act with you, then you will be in a great position, Elara. You are strong, you have Niveren Gap. My people live on plains. They will be slaughtered."

"They will be slaughtered either way," Saskia hissed from beside Kalin, who had barely moved since the meeting had started. "Do you not wish to give them a chance?"

"Again, I wish to think. Are you demanding an answer now?"

A moment passed. Another.

"No," Elara said. "I am not demanding an answer now, but I will need one soon. And I will help defend your people, Seera. I will not leave them to be slaughtered. None of us will. If we form an alliance it will last through the war. We will all fight together. And Fia can go to the humans, ask for their help."

Seera laughed. "The humans? When have they ever intervened on our behalf? And did they not supply the weapons you are so worried about?"

"One human did," Fia said, trying not to let her voice shake, to keep her shoulders raised. "My father. He is...He does not represent all the humans. There are good people. People who would help." Or she hoped there were. The truth was she had no idea who she would ask. Her father had been the politician, the businessman. She had not been invited to his meetings. She had seen his more criminal associates occasionally, was taken to fundraisers a few times a year to look like a doting daughter, but she had never been treated like his equal.

But there were people, *good* people. She knew they were out there, that the entire human world was not full of monsters. How she would find them though? A problem for another day.

Seera let out a low laugh. "Again, I will need time to think." She stood and the several armed men she had brought to dinner stood as well. "I will eat in my room and give you an answer by the end of the week." She was nearly to the door before she turned. "Mina?"

The princess cleared her throat, a battle clearly raging inside her. "I will stay for dinner."

"Oh," Seera said, her voice low. "I see."

"Yes." Mina nodded and turned back to the table, swallowing hard. She did not seem to breathe until her sister's footsteps faded down the hallway. When the soup was served her knuckles were white against the spoon.

"It is hard to stand up to family members," Fia said quietly. "Though maybe it is easier when you are not raised to be quiet, though now I am making assumptions your childhood was like mine."

Mina put down her spoon, her shoulders lowering. "You assume correctly. I have met your father, and you have my condolences."

Fia laughed. "There is joy in knowing how disappointed he must be while unable to lay a hand on me."

"He will *never* lay a hand on you again," Elara growled, turning in her seat. "Never."

The mating bond tightened and so much love poured through it Fia's knees might have buckled if she were not sitting, and though they were in a crowded room all she could see was Elara, the silver lined eyes that saw right into her soul and did not balk, had never balked, had seen the best in her before she had seen it in herself.

"I know," she whispered, stroking her thumb along Elara's knee until Kalin cleared his throat and she laughed.

"The recently mated are..." Saskia grimaced, clearly unable to find a word to express her disgust. Darkness swirled around her like she might cover herself in shadows rather than endure the two of them in love.

"One day it will be you," Kalin said, laughter lacing his words, his shoulders shaking with the effort of suppression. "I so look forward to hearing desperate longing in your voice."

"I do not long," Saskia said.

"Have you never been in love?" Ezriel asked between sips of his soup.

"Who are you to ask about my love life?" she snarled, and the King held his hands up in surrender.

Mina's spoon clattered as she put it down and the table silenced, bodies turning toward her. "I will speak to her," she said, raising her napkin to wipe at her mouth. "I do not think I realized until now that we could all be one. The divide between us has grown in recent years but I can see your alliance is true. We should be in it."

Vinessa smiled and reached down the table to briefly squeeze her shoulder. "Change is hard. Your sister will come around."

The legs of Elara's chair squeaked against the floor as she pushed back her seat and stood, making her way to Mina. What was she doing? Fia tensed when Elara sat in the seat

Seera had vacated. "You have always been the better of the two of you."

Fia's heart jolted in protest, anger and magic rising within her, but she pushed it down. This was not a betrayal, this was hope. For a moment she hated the overactive new bond between them screaming Elara was hers, because what she was doing did not make Fia angry, it made her proud.

Her mate continued, "We do not need the Queen of your people with us. I went to Ezriel and Seera because I believed it was the right thing to do, but all I need is a powerful Eastern fae. You are powerful, Mina. You can stand with us whatever your sister's choice."

Mina's face paled, but there was resolution in her eyes. "There is..." Her words halted and she stood abruptly, dropping her napkin to the table. "I will talk to her." She left, following the same path as her sister.

"Shit," Ezriel said, rubbing his hand over his face, voicing exactly what Fia was feeling.

What were they going to do? Fia nearly said the words aloud, but what would they help? If Mina and Seera both refused there were other faeries in the Eastern Kingdom. They could find some of them. Elara must have spent time there when she had a relationship with Mina. Maybe she knew someone. The thought wasn't exactly pleasant, but it was better than nothing.

"We'll start plans for fortifying your defenses," Elara said. "I'd offer to take in your people but if my own are here I worry we would not be able to feed them."

"I know," Ezriel said, leaning back in his chair.

"Do not despair so soon," Vinessa said, an unnatural brightness to her voice. "Neither of them has said no yet. You were not immediately agreeable to Elara's vision either. We were all mad when the magic was lost, but so much time has passed, it is hard to imagine a better world. Let them dream of it for the night. They'll come around."

The words were beautiful. If only Fia could believe them.

-CHAPTER-
-THIRTY FIVE-

BUT SEERA DID not come around the next day. She came down for breakfast, said she was still contemplating, then went into the city and they did not seen her again except for the moment it took her to walk back into the castle and into her room.

"Kick her out," Saskia said, sharpening a knife while sprawled across one of the couches in Elara and Fia's sitting room. "She cannot treat the castle like a bed and breakfast."

"That's not going to help," Fia said, pacing back and forth in front of the window, watching the snow glimmer in the setting sun. There was a blanket of white across the city and all the puddles in the streets had turned to slick ice, still people made their way from building to building and children screamed in the streets throwing snowballs at each other.

"Do you have a better idea?" Saskia asked, not taking her eyes from her knife.

"Give her more than a day. She is taking her people into war," Fia said, without much conviction. She hoped for the best, but in truth was not sure Seera had ever intended to hear what they had to say.

"You are going to wear a hole in the rug, and it is a very old rug," Kalin said, his eyes tracking her. His already pale skin was paler than usual and there were dark circles under his eyes.

"If she does not answer by tomorrow, I will make her leave," Elara said. She had not moved in almost an hour, sitting by the fireplace as the room sank deeper and deeper into darkness. "There is always the possibility that she—"

Her words cut off at a sharp knock on the door followed by one of the workers yelling for them all to come, her voice too high. Fia froze. Kalin was across the room before Elara had fully stood, yanking the door open.

A red-haired Unseelie with antlers like a deer stood wide-eyed on the other side of the door, her chest rising and falling as if she had run up the stairs at a sprint. "Oh, Kalin! You need to come. You all need to come right now."

"What happened?"

There were more voices shouting through the castle and Fia could make out Ezriel yelling something, his voice growing closer. He came to a stop behind the antlered woman. "Elara." His voice was stiff and Fia's heart fell and continued to fall when his eyes stopped on her and softened into something like... guilt? Pity?

She clutched the fabric over her heart, which was suddenly too heavy in her chest. She'd seen that look on men before, there was always a body behind it. "Ez..."

He shook his head softly. "You should stay. You don't need..."

"I will not stay!" She pushed past him and into the hallway, down the staircase, the others on her heels, until she came to Vinessa who stood beside one of the tables near the castle doors, her wings limp at her back. She put up an arm in a feeble attempt to keep Fia away, but she pushed past her and towards the box they were all gathered around.

Vomit rose in her throat. "Where did it come from?" she screamed, looking around wildly at the gathered crowd. "Who brought this?"

"A...A Southern Emissary. I did not know him," a man answered softly, swallowing hard.

Beside Fia, Elara trembled, though if it was sadness or rage Fia did not know, as they both stared down at Gavin's severed head, congealed blood on the hay beneath his neck. Gavin who offered to train her, who was kind from the first moment they had met. Gavin who helped her sneak back into the Southern Kingdom when he had only wanted to return to his land. Gavin who would never meet his mate.

There was a note beside his head, reflected in his unseeing eyes. Eyes that seemed to still look at Fia, to hate her, to blame her. Elara reached for the letter, but Fia moved faster because it was her name scrawled across the blood stained parchment, because she was the one who had asked him to take her back, because she was the reason Gavin was dead.

The castle was silent as she opened the envelope and when she pulled out the paper ash fell with it, fluttering in the air like dust motes in the sun's setting rays before settling at her feet.

Fia,

I hope this letter finds you well, or at least better than Gavin. My youngest son still believes in your innocence, and while I may not know your reasons for returning, I know they were a lie as I knew from the beginning.

You are such a clever girl, running like you did. How did you get away? Far too clever for Callum. Far cleverer than your father told me or I would not have tried to marry you to him. He is a kind boy, and I wished for him to have an obedient wife who would give him babies and a happy life.

I have strayed off topic, I am told I am too sentimental with my children. Is my daughter with you? I miss her dearly, as do her brothers. But the point, Fia, is that you are needed here. Lord Gavin's lands will still be burning as you read this, his people shrieking inside their homes. Can you hear them?

Return to me, Fia. Come back, tell me your secrets. Come back and things will stop. Come back and the next head will not be your fathers.

Sincerely, your future father-in-law,

Ellio

Her fingers shook so violently she worried she would rip the paper, so she let it fall. Elara grabbed it before it reached the ground.

"No," she said, repeating the word again and again with a desperation in her voice Fia had not heard before.

Soft fingers touched her back. Vinessa. She gently led Fia away. One step. Then another. Everyone she knew was around her. What did they think? How harshly did they blame her? All day she had thought of nothing but Seera agreeing to help them, but what was she moving toward? War?

This was war. Awful, bloody death. And she had been running toward it, pretending she knew what it would hold, that she was strong and prepared. She was nothing but a girl playing games. A stupid, lovestruck idiot who thought herself a hero of people she barely knew. She had barely known Gavin and now he was dead and she would never know him. Never hear him belly laugh or learn his favorite foods.

Now he was a head in a box and what was she supposed to do?

At the end of the hall, between sobbing people Fia did not know, Seera appeared and all her self-pity was instantly replaced with white hot rage. This was what led people to murder, how they killed on a battlefield without mercy. Hating herself was too hard but hating Seera was easy.

"Will you join us now?" she screamed, wrenching free from Vinessa's gentle grasp.

"Fia, what happened?" Mina asked, stepping from around Seera who had stopped walking and stood staring at the scene in front of her.

"Look for yourself," Elara hissed, holding the box. There was blood on her hands, dark and turning brown. The whole room reeked of it. "Answer my mate, Seera. Does Gavin's head in a box hasten your response?"

Seera's eyes widened for a moment, nostrils flaring before she straightened her shoulders. "Do you think this means I should join you? Do you think I wish my own head to be in a box?"

Mina spun on her heel, turning to face her sister, her golden face an awful, sickly color. "Seera, you cannot be serious!"

“Of course she is” Fia said, her voice strange even to her ears. “You never intended to join us, did you?” There was a blade strapped to her side, but she did not need it because her magic lashed at her skin, hot, demanding.

Seera pulled her gaze from her sister. “You are not the only alliance I have been offered.”

“That’s where you were?” Mina said, taking another step toward her sister. Around them workers scurried away, disappearing into doorways, and Fia did not blame them because something was boiling in the room, about to roll over the edges.

Gavin was dead. They would all be dead. And she was a foolish, foolish woman for not realizing how enormous this task was sooner, how dangerous, but none of that mattered now because she loved the people around her in a way she had never loved anyone before.

They were her family. A real family, so unlike the one who had raised her. And yes, she was an idiot for thinking she would be some savior, that the tiara Elara put on her head had made her something she was not. But she did have power, and she did have love, and the stupid, hopeless belief that somehow things could be better.

"You would ally yourself with Ellio before us? You would give him your power? Your people's power?" Elara said, magic glinting like claws at her knuckles.

"If I refused, he would kill me, you stupid lovestruck idiot. He will kill all of us. I will give up power if it saves my own neck." She turned her vitriol to Fia. "You brought this on us. Did you think he was stupid? That he wouldn't know what you were doing? When these people are ash around you, remember that it was your—"

Seera stopped talking when Mina stepped in front of her and something had changed in the princess, something impossible to name but fundamentally different. "You *never* deserved the crown."

Seera's eyes went wide for a moment before narrowing. "Do you think you did? I gave you everything. You have spent centuries tasting the best of Daonith while I did what needed to be done for our people."

"You have never acted for our people. You have acted only for yourself since the moment you were born. What did he promise you when you met with him?" Her hand slipped into the folds of her dress.

"I will be Queen of an empire. I will marry Helio and he will finish what his father started."

There was such a deep sadness and anger in Mina that Fia did not dare move, some part of her knowing she had to let whatever happened happen, that Mina was the only one who could change things. The others must have felt the same way because no one moved. The air was so thick it felt hard to breathe and when she did the scent of blood filled her nose.

"Abdicate," Mina said, chest heaving.

Seera laughed, a horrible sound made more horrible when her sister's dagger sliced across her throat and laughter turned to wet gasps. More blood. Fresh splatters of it across the floor and the golden queen fell, her red hair splayed around her.

Elara stepped toward Fia, half-heartedly pushing her behind her back but Fia moved beside her, watching as Seera took her final breath and Mina fell to her knees, the dagger clattering into the growing pool of blood. "I had to," she said. "I had to." She kept repeating the phrase, staring at her sister, not moving even as the blood washed over her fingers, clutching at the floor.

A clang of metal sounded as Saskia sheathed her own blades and knelt beside Mina, her clawed hands gentle on Mina's back. "Yes, you did. You did right for your people." Her gentle circles on Mina's back turned to tugs beneath her arms and she helped her stand, pulling her into her arms and looking beyond her to Kalin.

He nodded at Saskia and looked toward Elara then Ezriel. "I will send a missive."

"A missive?" Mina sniffed

"You are Queen now, yes?" Ezriel said. He had pushed Vinessa behind him just as Elara had. There was blood on her shoes, splattered up her leg, dark red splotches against her pale pink skin.

"Oh, I cannot. I did not mean..." Mina pushed away from Saskia and looked down at her sister. "She was never...She was never what I wanted but she was my sister. I loved her."

"Of course you did," Fia said. "Why don't we go get you cleaned up?" She glanced at Elara and she nodded.

"I would like a moment to myself," Mina said, her voice quivering. She would likely sob the second she was alone. "But you have your alliance."

"Thank you," Elara said. "This will never be forgotten. The alliance between our people will be long lasting."

"And ours," Ezriel said. "We will weather this storm as one. A new age is beginning. The unification of Daonith."

Swallowing hard, Mina nodded and then, with a final glance at her sister's body, she disappeared up the stairs.

-CHAPTER-
-THIRTY SIX-

THE FOLLOWING HOURS were some of the worst of Fia's life, made worse by the knowledge she was only at the beginning of things that would horrify her. Who else would die if they started a war?

The next day they buried Gavin in a grove of aspens, just outside the pass to Niveren Gap, in the same cemetery as Elara's parents. Fia wanted to take him back to his own lands, but it was too dangerous and she knew Elara's protestations were right. Besides, if the letter was true those lands were on fire.

That fact remained with her later as she watched Seera's body burn, dark smoke rising towards the cloudy white sky,

Elara's hand steady and warm in her own even as a dusting of snow fell, making her horns glitter.

"We do not have to watch," Elara said.

"I know," Fia said but did not move. She had barely known Seera, had spent less than two days with her but she knew her, had met others like her, desperate for power, devoid of all the important things that should fill a person. She could have been her. She might have been if Ellio had been the one to offer her power instead of Elara. She'd wanted it so badly, wanted some control over her life.

She did not want to think about who she could have been, the thoughts made something awful roil in her stomach. But she did, offering the truth minutes of her life, promising herself it would never be her, she had changed. She let herself mourn the life she could have had, mourn the life she had never been given, the love her father could have offered but never did, the mother who had killed herself rather than stay, the mother she had daydreamed would take her away but never could have, not really, and now was gone.

The friends who never cared for her, who liked her for money and the power they hoped she would give them, but never loved her. Perhaps, before this place, no one had ever loved Fia. Maybe that was what had saved her, the thought of marrying

Callum, of one more person forced to be around her, another person who was supposed to care about her but only saw her as a thing to have, had been too much, had stopped her from hating Elara and Aurora who for all their sins had seen Fia, not only for what she offered but for who she was. Who had needed her but still given her a choice.

A single tear fell down her cheek and she wiped it away. "How bad is it going to be for Mina?"

The guards who had come with the sisters now seemed unsure of what to do, torn between the dead queen and the new queen, between the woman they had sworn to protect and the one they wanted to follow. But Fia knew, however few there had been so far, there would be consequences.

Elara sighed, a weary sound. "Honestly, I don't know. It has been a long time since I have spent any significant time in her kingdom. Seera was not beloved, but she was the Queen."

"And now Mina is?"

"I suppose so. Their crown passes through the heir and Seera had no children. By law it is Mina's, but I do not know if their laws account for murder."

"Is it hard...to kill someone?" The flames danced on the funeral pyre, Seera's body now fully consumed.

"Yes," Elara said. "As it should be. I never want it to be easy. I hope you never have to feel everything that comes with it, because it is not just the moment, not just the death. It follows you. Changes you."

How badly Fia wished her mate could have lived a soft life but wishing changed nothing. Instead, they stood surrounded by the smell of burning flesh, death stretching before them, and she knew she would learn the feeling, a baptism in blood she had managed to avoid for so long.

"I love you," she whispered because it seemed important for Elara to know. However dark things got her love would not change, there was nothing that could drive Fia away, no depth of despair.

"I am glad I found you, but I am sorry that you must go through this." Her fingers tangled in Fia's, and she pulled her away, back toward the castle and their room, warm and cozy, but that night, as Fia watched the fire, unable to sleep, she could not help but imagine bodies turning to ash in the flames. Here, Mina burned, and beyond the wall, others, far more innocent, burned as well and those souls weighed on Fia.

She did not yet know what it felt like to kill but she knew what it was to carry the weight of the dead. The weight of those who might die plagued her as well. It was too late to turn back, no way to change the path they had chosen. More would die and carrying them for a few hours was exhausting, what would years of it do to her?

"Could you modify our appearance?" Fia asked, thinking of her time in the Western Kingdom.

A spread of dried meat, cheese, fruits, and pastries lay before them, but they had hardly touched it. Three days. That was all they were giving themselves to plan, all they needed really. Break in, destroy the talisman, steal it if they couldn't, and get out. Still, there were so many tiny details, getting everyone there, who did what, how they would do it. If they let themselves they could have planned for months, but nothing would be different in the end.

Ezriel shook his head. "No, that is too much magic. Just changing you was draining. The flowers in our rooms died."

Oh. Fia's stomach sank. "You should have said something."

“I did not want you harmed,” Ezriel said simply. “And it was all I had to offer.”

Mina’s eyes were red and puffy, her skin sallow, but she had worked steadily on a plan to get them into and out of the city with Aurora, the two of them bent over a map. “I should have known,” she said, and the others fell silent. “She was gone so often, but I didn’t think she would lie to me.”

“You did the right thing when you had the chance,” Aurora said and Fia placed a hand on her shoulder, giving it a quick squeeze. *You did too,* she hoped the squeeze said.

While she watched them plan, Fia grappled with her own guilt, unable to offer much help. She should have trained harder, worked on her own magic. She should have gone inside the damn chapel before she fled. All she’d wanted was to get back to her mate and it had cost them knowledge.

She had told Aurora her suspicions and Aurora had confirmed there was something strange inside the chapel. She’d sighed and muttered she should have known, but she hadn’t been inside the chapel since she was barely more than a child. She had simply forgotten anything worthwhile was inside the moldering building at all, sure her father would keep something valuable even closer. She’d sworn she’d searched his room, spent nights inside the tunnels, then admitted the truth was she didn't know what she was looking for. They were faeries, there were magical items. She'd simply thought whatever was in the chapel belonged there, had always been.

They all could have done more. But the magic had been gone so long that none of it had seemed urgent and Aurora had lived easily. Nothing had bothered her until her father started bringing in weapons and they realized he was planning for a war. She had done nothing until it was almost too late, only sat around, watching, feeling guilty. Fia understood more than she wanted to.

They had all been too slow, even Fia. She'd had no idea what was happening in Daonith, but she'd known plenty about the blood on her father's hands. All it would have taken was one anonymous letter to a reporter, a tell-all book, a thousand things she could have done as her criminal father legitimized himself and rose and rose and she smiled in pictures and did nothing. It was so easy to do nothing.

"How do we break it?" she asked, trying not to pick at her fingernails or chew at her lips. "The talisman. How does it break?"

Elara looked up at her. Her silvery purple hair did not shine as it usually did and she'd pulled it into a sad bun at the back of her horns, but still she was beautiful. "I'm not sure exactly. I've never done it. It will probably have defenses. Runic magic—like the king used to ward this city against porting—has been lost, so it shouldn't have that, but there will be protection and we will just have to do our best to destroy the talisman or take it. It may be easier to destroy here where we won't need to rush."

She nodded. "And what if it does have runic protection?"

"Then we're fucked," Mina said flatly. "Runes can only be undone by the witch who created them."

"Witch?" Fia's mouth went dry.

"Do not look so horrified," Saskia said. She had also contributed little. She had never been to the Southern Kingdom, never met the king. She would be there for protection. "No one expects to you to learn runes. That was magic held by your people and lost many generations ago."

"Oh," she said, a thousand possibilities springing to life in her mind before dying quickly. She wouldn't know where to begin to look for information on runes, and even if she did, she would not master them in time to be helpful at all.

Anger flared, as it often did, at how the King had stolen the human's magic so completely she had not even known she was a witch—had hardly believed there had ever been witches.

She settled back into watching and listening, trying to take in everything she could, praying to whichever god, human or fae who might be listening, for just a few things to go right, for her to find a way for her magic to matter, and for the freed magic to stand a chance against weapons.

Dead bodies already piled up. The guard with the slit throat, Seera, and Gavin. Sweet Gavin. She had thought she would have decades with him, that he would become a friend, someone she would visit and who would visit her, whose lands she would learn and explore. Instead, he was dead, those lands on fire.

In the deep recesses of her heart, she burned him into the beating flesh, a deep, painful memory like a bruise, one she would come to again and again, prodding it so often it would never heal and she would never forget.

She would add to the pile of bodies her own enemies, stack them higher until she could add Ellio, her crowning achievement.

-CHAPTER- -THIRTY SEVEN-

DESPITE THE HATRED she nursed like a babe, when the day arrived, terror dug its nails into her, her body shivering with rushes of adrenaline.

Everyone she loved seemed to be gathered and everything in her, down to her atoms, screamed to stop them, imagined their decapitated heads in boxes, dripping blood onto her shoes. She forced those thoughts away and inhaled a steadying breath, taking Elara's outstretched hand. There were so many people, Elara, Kalin, Vinessa, Ezriel, two of their guards, Mina, and a single Eastern woman. The rest of her guard waited inside the castle. Mina had refused to let them come, saying she'd done enough damage to her kingdom and if she died she would not leave them with nothing.

Perhaps she would be a better ruler than her sister if she got the chance. Did Ezriel worry about the same thing? He had barely spoken all morning. Did Elara?

But Elara would return. There was no other possibility. Because if she did not...Fia swallowed. She simply had to survive. So many leaders stood on the precipice of ruin. Should they have sent others?

Her breath quickened along with her heartbeat. In a single day Ellio could take out every other leader in Daonith. This was foolish. Beyond foolish.

"We cannot do this," Fia said, voice high.

"What?" Elara pulled her away from the others.

"What if you all die? What will happen? Others should go."

Elara's eyes widened. "I am the most powerful Unseelie, and you want me to send my people into danger? Fia..." Disappointment. That was disappointment in her eyes.

"I am afraid."

Slowly, softly, as though they had days only for themselves Elara kissed her. Her fingers trailed along Fia's cheeks, across her jaw, featherlight. "We are the best chance our people have. They chose me and it has been the highest honor. I will not dishonor them by not seeing this through. You would not want me to."

"I know." Fia swiped at the tear running down her cheek. The Unseelie had chosen well in Elara. No one would fight harder for them. She was a good leader, the kind most people only dreamed of. But Fia loved her. Elara, her mate, the beautiful horned woman who equally terrified and captivated her, not the Queen, not the fighter.

Again, Elara kissed her, but this time it was fiercer. Fia's stomach fell and twisted as they moved through space and reappeared somewhere even colder, wind whipping at her, pulling at her clothes.

"Forgive me," Fia said, her vision obscured by the hair blowing into her face, though she could still make out the bright-white, snow-covered terrain before it fell away off the side of the mountain they were standing on. "I know we have to do this, but I only just found you."

"I know," Elara said, her voice as gentle as Fia had ever heard it and she wished she could forget the look that had passed across Elara's face, wanted her to know she would fight for these people, even if she occasionally balked. "I have waited even longer for you. But we cannot stop this war, even if we hid, he would come for us, burn our lands like he burned Gavin's. We have to weaken him before this is a true war."

"I know," Fia repeated her words back to her. "I am with you. I am just not as brave."

"You are plenty brave," Ezriel said and Fia nearly jumped. The sound of the wind had covered his arrival. "You have to be afraid to be brave, otherwise you are just a fool."

"I am not sure that's how the saying goes, dearest," Vinessa said. She wrapped her delicate arms around herself. Her wings seemed fragile in this place, thin and bare. "Oh, I hate it here. No offense, Elara."

"The Sawteeth are not my favorites either."

"We have been here before," Fia said, remembering her first journey with Elara. The mountains had been harsh then, but now it was fully winter. "Are we staying in a cave again?"

"Yes, but this one is nicer. I did not show it to you before. I didn't know if I could trust you with all of my secrets." The wind roared and snow began to fall in enormous, biting flakes.

"Come with me while they get the others," Vinessa said, her eyes catching on Ezriel and Fia could read the emotion there, the mirror of her own, the fear and longing and knowledge it would never be enough time, if they died today or a hundred years from now it would not have been long enough. She dragged her gaze away and pressed close to Fia, one hand on the small of her back, leading her through the assault of snow until they were in a cave.

Deeper and deeper they went, until the wind was a faint whisper and the cave grew warmer, golden light flickering. A few more feet around a bend they found Saskia, the dancing flames turning her into some sharp toothed beast.

"Finally," she barked. "There are cots in the back and blankets if you need them. I know the Teeth can be alarming at first. It will do us no good if you freeze to death."

"Her people are from here," Vinessa whispered to Fia. "Near the bottom of the mountains there are bands of faeries like her. I think it explains some things, or so I tell myself."

Yes, it certainly did. Fia could not imagine what a childhood in this place would look like, how harsh it must have been. Why didn't they leave? She didn't dare ask Saskia any of those questions. "Are we spending the night here."

"That is my guess. Has Elara been as secretive with the plans as Ezriel?"

Fia shrugged as she poked at the fire with a large stick until it perked up. She'd been with them for the start of the planning, but then Ezriel and Elara had disappeared together to work out the final details. When Elara had come to bed, demanding answers had been the furthest thing from Fia's mind. For all of her nerves, she trusted Elara, would follow her into hell and back if she must. What did the details matter?

"I doubt I'll sleep tonight," Vinessa said, disappearing for a moment and reappearing with a cot.

Neither would Fia. With every passing moment their day of reckoning drew closer, and every moment she doubted herself, grew fearful, only for it to fade, for her to remember why she was fighting, to think of Elara and have certainty fill her heart, to think of Ellio and become enraged. A maelstrom of emotions whirled and tugged inside of her.

"Here," Saskia said, shoving a beautiful dagger at her handle first. Strange swirling symbols were carved into the gleaming wood. "My great grandmother was a witch, and this was her dagger. I don't know what the runes mean but I know I am not a witch, and you are. Perhaps it will bring you luck."

Every emotion inside of her quieted as she wrapped her fingers around the handle. This. This was why she would fight. These people, this place, thousands of years of history and hard-working people and rugged mountains, all of it deserving freedom, for magic to cover the land as it was meant to. For herself, for the things that had been stolen from her. Tears welled in her eyes, but she blinked them away, knowing Saskia would not approve. “Thank you.” She sheathed it at her side. “Thank you so much.”

“You honor your people. My Gran would have approved of that.” She nodded. “Come on. Help me get things set up, Princess.”

Lying beside Elara, the gentle—and some not so gentle—sounds of the others snoring surrounding them, Fia could not sleep. She let her magic twine out of her, only the fine sparks of gold visible in the darkness.

Elara shifted. “You should rest.”

“So should you.” Fia let her magic drift towards the ceiling, feeling the history, the people who had sheltered in the cave, and far away, distant yet still insistent, the pull of the talisman, growing desperate for her magic, but not yet breaking.

All it would take was another human, someone taken from the border, or more likely, someone willing, someone beautiful, young, and happy to follow a faerie into Daonith, unaware of everything their arrival would cause, only wanting the beautiful life the faeries promised. She could see Helio, his blonde hair, his playful eyes devoid of all the cruelty they usually held, smiling at some woman, dragging her into his war.

Or Callum. Would it be him? It would be so easy to call on any of the women who had knelt beside Fia in that borderland room, tell her he had made a mistake. That he wanted her. And she would come.

Her magic faded, leaving the room in darkness. “I’m ready for it to be over,” she said, childish but true.

“It will only be beginning, I’m afraid,” Elara whispered. She pulled Fia closer and pressed a kiss to the back of her neck as her arms wrapped around her. “Now sleep, Sweetness. You will need your strength tomorrow.”

And too soon she was right, the sun rose outside the cave, and as though even the mountains themselves wished them well, the storms quelled, the mountain eerily silent, bright and white in the morning light.

None of them spoke as they ate their breakfast of eggs and dried meats, barely looking at each other.

Fia did not want to do this, wished she could stay inside the cave forever, and yet she was as ready as she thought she would ever be. She let her magic swirl around her, more golden than ever before, brushing across the tops of the mountains and down the sides, following rivers and waterfalls, through towns and villages, all while making promises to the talisman.

Soon. Soon. Soon.

-CHAPTER-
-THIRTY EIGHT-

THE CITY OF SOLEIL sprawled before them. There was no wall around the city and roads spread like veins from arteries. Around them Fia heard the soft pop of faeries porting from place to place.

Soleil was nearly indefensible. How had she never noticed before? Even if they had guards on every main road leading into the city there was nothing to keep them from porting. None of the runic magic or tall walls that guarded Niveren Gap. The only real defense was how the other side of the city led only to the great plain between the faerie lands and the misty border of the human lands, all of it tightening in toward the narrow piece of land neither race owned, surrounded by the calm sea where Soleil and the Southern Kingdom traded with the humans.

"Why hasn't he built up his defenses?" she asked Kalin, who was so close to her side she could feel the heat from his body.

"His castle is well guarded and unless one has your powers, very hard to get into undetected. But I don't believe he thought he would be attacked. He holds the power, he has the largest standing army and the highest population except the Unseelie, and we have nearly no army at all."

"The fae were a peaceful people once," Aurora said, glancing at Elara who gave her a sharp look. "Well, we were. Many of our cities are as open as this one. That is part of why nothing was done when some realized that the power wasn't leaving, it was being drained. Not only would they need to raise an army, they would put their people, their starving people, in great danger."

"What a bastard," Fia said, glancing around. "We should go." Her magic was slowly returning, pressure building in her core.

The talisman was already reaching for her, she had felt it since she first arrived in the city, its magic lapping at her magic, drinking her in, yet...different. Something had changed, something she could not quite understand and did not yet dare to prod at.

“Let’s head towards the wall, wait for our cue,” Vinessa said, her wings hidden under a thick cloak, though their points were still visible if someone looked closely. She was also pink and Kalin was huge and birch patterned, so they were not exactly inconspicuous. Luckily it was early and the streets were nearly deserted.

Kalin nodded towards the others then slipped down a side street, pulling his cloak further over his head, hunching his shoulders and wrapping his arms around himself, concealing his size and making himself less threatening. Fia watched him until he was out of view.

“Stay near me,” Elara hissed as they made their way through the back streets, doing their best to avoid detection. They were only a few blocks from the vast estate of the King, and it took only a few steps before the tall, vine-covered walls came into view.

Her heart beat faster, fear, oily and dark, coating her insides at the same moment her magic began to vibrate inside her. She had escaped from this place, she had been brave and powerful and opened up a fucking hole in an ancient stone wall before putting it back together, all under the King’s nose, all without him knowing. How long had they searched for her before they had known she was gone? She had done it. She had walked into this estate, more afraid than she'd ever been in her life, and she'd done exactly what she'd meant to do.

She'd do it again.

She let her magic build inside of her while they pressed themselves into the shadows. This was where she had escaped and yet the wall was still hardly guarded here. They still did not know how she had done it, did not suspect her of being a witch, or they'd be watching more than the entrances.

A single man walked across the top of the wall, something hanging from his side. A gun. A fucking *gun*. All because of her father, because he was a liar and a cheat and a monster. But still, she did not let fear rise. She had seen the powerful magic Elara had done even without her full strength. She would make a shield the bullet could not penetrate. She had to. What they would do in the future, against hundreds of guns, Fia could not think about. Not yet.

"Just another moment," Vinessa said, barely loud enough to be audible. Her pink skin was bathed in shadow from her cloak, her eyes wide, darting around.

Ezriel put a lazy arm around her shoulder, turning towards the others with a smile like they might be chatting, like nothing at all in the world could bother them. Just friends on a visit to the city, looking up at the wall.

Far away an explosion sounded, followed by screams, and the man on the wall moved quickly in the direction of the sound. Fia bit into her lip so hard she drew blood.

A moment passed, another.

Then Kalin was there, "Done," he said, still smelling of smoke.

"Go," Elara said. "We don't have long."

Forcing her body to move, Fia went to the wall, stretching out until her fingers touched the vines growing up the side of the stone. "Please," she whispered to it, but all that replied was the talisman, its greedy magic lapping at her, searing up her skin.

Her own magic rushed in return, prying into the cracks in the stone like fingers, feeling through every inch of it, dark and gold and beautiful, pushing, prodding, heating her from within.

Elara's hand closed around her own. A small hole appeared.

Behind her someone hissed.

The hole grew slowly, each inch of progress weighing on her. She dug deep into her magic, gritting her teeth against a scream, forcing out more and more until the hole was big enough for even Kalin to get through. "Go!" she called, motioning everyone forward, her worry growing as each person slipped into the estate grounds, until finally it was her turn.

The hole closed behind her with a strange, grinding sound that reverberated inside her. She wobbled, hot blood running down her nose and fell forward, grabbing onto the first person she could reach for support. Saskia let her, wrapping a clawed hand around her shoulder.

"You did very well, mortal."

"No time," Mina said, her eyes darting just as Vinessa's had. "Where do we go, Fia?"

For a brief second she gave into the magic, making sure the talisman had not moved. Her magic skittered along its pull, following the power that pawed at her to its home until she could feel its resting spot. Ellio had not moved it. Foolish. Foolish or a trap. "Still the chapel," she said.

"Hurry," Aurora motioned towards the others before running at a sprint towards the small, wooden building.

Fia rallied her strength and followed, crashing through the gardens, her feet beating along the stone path. Compared to everything else on the estate grounds, the chapel was nearly dilapidated, the wood old and swollen, the paint peeling away. A king who no longer worshipped. Or one did not want anyone to know what he truly bowed to.

Yanking the door open, Aurora ushered the others inside then shut it swiftly behind them. Maybe no one had seen them. Maybe this would be easy.

Fia paused for a moment, taking in the rows of wooden pews, marked where they had once held cushions, the worn floor from decades of feet walking upon it, now covered with dust, the thick layer marred by a single set of footprints, moving towards the front and then back.

Her eyes followed the footprints to the talisman, a glowing, shimmering jewel, floating in an encasement. Her heart skittered. Whatever encased it was magic, gold and silver twisted together, streaking like lightning around the edges, and she knew, instinctively, that the spell holding it was powerful.

Ellio had not moved it because he did not believe they could breach its defenses. The behemoth spell was why they had needed the strongest fae from each kingdom.

Magic slithered up her spine, the caress gentle yet deadly like a capricious lover who might strike at any moment. The talisman was desperate for her, pulling at her magic, dragging her power into itself. She tried to shield against it, but it was like fighting the sea and the more she kicked the quicker she drowned.

Until Elara's palm slid into her own, smooth and warm. The talisman balked, hissing. "Come on," she tugged her up the aisle.

Every cell in Fia protested, demanding she dig her heels into the ancient wood, not move any closer to the glowing crystal, brighter with each step. Defiantly, she moved, Ezriel, Mina, and Aurora at her heels.

"You can do this," Ezriel said, his breath on her neck. "You are a witch, more than we hoped for."

Fia wanted to reply but her mouth was dry. The magic around the talisman buzzed like electricity as they stood around it. Ezriel's hand slid into her other palm, then Mina joined him, then Aurora. They circled the crystal until Fia was facing the door, where the others still stood, ready to defend. Bile rose in her throat at the sight of them, at Vinessa with her cloak thrown off, a dagger in her hands. She looked so delicate, her vine-like hair pulled into a thick clump that ran down her back, her skin nearly translucent. Her wings fluttered, taking her an inch off the ground.

"Ready?" Aurora asked, standing across from Fia. Her voice was a note too high but steady. The others agreed and Elara squeezed her hand. She turned towards her and brown and silver eyes locked onto her.

Her beautiful mate. She loved her. Loved her so fiercely and desperately. She would follow Elara into the most dire of circumstances, but she did not want her here. Though Elara was more powerful than her by far, she did not know how she could concentrate if danger came, how she could protect herself when Elara could be injured, could die.

Her momentary distraction cost her. The talisman tightened its grip, snatching her magic. Beside her Ezriel straightened, his magic fighting back, warming her hand. "We cannot wait any longer," he said, casting a lingering, love filled look towards his wife then tearing his eyes back.

Beside him Mina began a countdown from five and the magic around the talisman grew to a gilded cage, sparking so brightly Fia struggled not to look away.

"One."

They threw their magic toward the talisman and the cage rattled, sparks flying. The talisman hissed, the sound growing louder, the magic boring deeper until it was shrieking, so loud she wanted to cover her ears, and her magic thrashed inside her chest. Mina's yell mirrored the talisman's screech, then Fia joined her when a spark of smoldering magic landing on her, igniting her cloak. She jerked away from the others, throwing her cloak to the floor.

Only Elara was steady, a purple haze growing around her, strong magic that moved in dark lines towards the talisman. It screamed louder as her magic engulfed the cage wrenching the webbing apart. Smoke issued from it, stinging Fia's eyes.

For a moment she was entranced, pausing in the stomping of her smoldering cloak to gaze upon the beauty of the talisman, the sparkling green jewel calling to her, but the pain of the burn marring her arm brought her back to the present. She shoved a wave of her magic toward Elara's where her tendrils wound around her mate's, dark purple and brilliant gold.

Somewhere outside the chapel people were shouting, their running footsteps coming closer. Ezriel stiffened but made no move to stop Vinessa as all the guardians ran outside. *Do not be distracted. This is for them.* Mina was clinging to Aurora whose magic had found its way into a small hole made by Elara and Fia. Her sky blue magic moved toward the talisman, slowly. Too slowly.

Ezriel looked pained, clearly struggling not to follow his wife. He took a step back.

"It is for nothing if we do not destroy this," Fia bit out at him, reaching out for his hand again. His magic was warm, muted iridescent. He nodded and it shot forward like a sword, cutting into the cage.

The bond between Elara and Fia grew as desperation built and the sounds of fighting outside rang through the chapel. The chain that bound Fia and her mate became a gaping hole, Elara's mind wide open, and Fia let herself sink into it until she was barely aware of her surroundings, putting her all into supporting Elara, holding her up, making her steady.

The cage around the talisman fell and the shrieking of the enchanted crystal grew louder until Fia was sure her eardrums would rupture. It sparked again and though none landed on her, the burn on her arm split open, blood pouring out, and she was thrown from the bond and to the floor.

Elara moved towards the crystal, reaching out for it, her face fierce, harsh, all the humanity gone as her palm made contact. Black flames erupted around her. Fia screamed and Mina rushed forward, throwing herself and her own golden magic at Elara, until they were both engulfed in her protection. But for how long would it hold against the burning talisman?

Fia scrambled up, but as she did movement caught her eye. Helio was in the doorway, his handsome face contorted in rage as the talisman's scream began to fade, it's relentless pounding growing slightly dimmer.

He raised his arm, pointing a silver gun right at his sister. Fia's tried to move, tried to put herself between them, screaming until her throat was raw, but she was not fast enough, could not make it around the talisman quick enough to grab Aurora, could only catch her as she fell, blood pouring from her chest, soaking them both, the floor beneath them a crimson river.

-CHAPTER-
-THIRTY NINE-

NO.

No.

Magic exploded out of Fia, pouring from her hands, her mouth, wrapping around her, around the corpse in her arms, shrouding them. No. That wasn't enough. It would not do. Aurora could not die. This could not happen. And Elara would not be next.

She shot her magic toward the talisman, every bit of rage she had bottled up her whole life moving like the bullet had, dousing the unburning flames surrounding Elara and Mina who still grappled with the talisman, shattering the last of the cage around it before wrapping around the jewel at the center, tighter and tighter.

Somewhere someone else was yelling, a voice she recognized. Elara tugged at the bond. But Fia was nothing but rage and desperation. Aurora was slack in her arms, the ground beneath them growing slick. Hot blood, cooling quickly, seeped into her clothes and she gripped Aurora tighter.

Magic poured from her, filled her. She *was* magic. She was power. Anger and power and everything that had been taken from her, her magic, her mother, happiness from the moment she had been born, all of it in service of her father then the king.

More magic. She would find him. She would rip his flesh from his bones.

Another shot rang out. Enough. She stood, laying Aurora gently down. Her magic moved with her, surrounding her like a shield, and she rushed toward the talisman, the stupid crystal. Nothing but a rock.

She reached for it. Felt the runes etched on the clear surface. A witch had done this. A witch would end it. She held her palm flat, turned to Helio to find only chaos, a battle raging inside the chapel. The door had been blasted off, one pew was smoldering.

All for the stupid, small crystal in her palm. She closed her fingers around it. Felt Elara at her shoulder. Still magic poured, only from her hand now, magic gold and silver and purple and black.

When she opened her fingers again the crystal was dust.

She looked up, her body suddenly sore. Her knees went weak, but Elara caught her. "Stand. We have to leave. We aren't done yet."

Then the worst sound she had ever heard. A guttural cry and Helio flew back into the chapel, the gun falling from his hand as he crashed into a pew, cracking the wood.

Callum came in through what had once been the doorway. "Tell me she lives," he said, his eyes on his sister, his foot on his brother.

"No," Fia said, taking a step towards him. "Callum I am so sorry. Helio killed her. They have lied to you. Our fathers have worked together to steal magic, to bring weapons into your land. This is why they wanted us married. I am sorry I tricked you and even sorrier Aurora is dead. She believed in this."

Callum shook his head, looking down at his brother. "Say it is a lie." Magic crackled around him, soft blue like electricity.

"You know it is not," Helio growled, shoving Callum's foot aside and pushing himself to his feet. "You have always known, but you were too gentle and stupid to admit it. But pulling the wool over your own eyes does not change what has happened. Our sister was a traitor. She deserved to die."

"No," Callum said, rage and sadness making his voice quiver. Magic shot from him and his brother once again flew, this time into one of the wooden beams holding up the chapel, his head cracking when it hit.

Vinessa ran into the room, blood dripping from a rip in her wing and a cut under her eye. "The king is coming. We need to go."

Fia looked at Elara, sent all her love down the bond. "Trust me," she said, before running towards Callum, stepping over the limp but breathing body of Helio and standing in front of her former fiancé. "Callum, come with us. Help us get out and come with us."

Magic swelled around them, no longer held back. Maybe they could do this.

"No. This is—"

"Don't be the fool he thinks you are!" Fia said, grasping him by the chin, forcing his gaze toward this dead sister. "Helio *killed* her. All of us were in this room but he aimed for his own sister and pulled the trigger."

“Forget him and move!” Saskia yelled from beside Vinessa. “We do not need him but from the looks of it we need you. We need to move. They have more guns and I am not practiced against them. We have only moments.”

“How do we get out?” Fia said, her fingers digging into Callum’s skin.

“You got in. You know better than me. I *am* the idiot he thinks I am.”

“Distract your father, do what you can, then run. Can you port?” She barely knew this man. She should leave him. But there was such grief in his beautiful blue eyes, and he had never harmed her. Maybe, just maybe he could be a good man.

“Yes,” he said.

“Then hold onto me when we move,” Elara said. “Take Saskia. We will port to just outside of Niveren Gap. I think I have enough magic.”

Saskia pulled him from Fia’s grasp, spinning Callum towards her. “If you’re doing this Princeling move your ass and quit wasting our time.” She pushed him toward what had been the door.

Fia followed, looking back once at Aurora. They should take her. They shouldn’t leave her. She made a move, but Elara grabbed her. “No. She is dead and her soul is gone.” She pulled

Fia. "She will have peace. That is only her body and—" Her words stopped at the scene in front of them, at Kalin whose wooden skin was charred. He ran toward them, limping heavily.

And the King followed a dozen guards at his back.

"Father!" Callum said, stepping out in front of them, spreading his arms wide.

"Toward the fence," Fia whispered and he took a sidestep. But how would she do it before they shot again and this time, they would aim at her. There was no way they could make it through.

"Where is your brother?" King Ellio asked and for the first time since Fia had known him there was fear in his voice.

"He lives," Callum yelled then added in a whisper, "The runes that prohibit porting inside the walls are on the guard tower."

Fia did not hesitate. She let her magic move as it had when it had searched this place before, only now there was so much more of it, nothing stealing from her, holding her back. An advantage because she did not think Ellio had yet realized the talisman was destroyed, nor did he know she was a witch.

She glanced at Elara, then Ezriel, catching their eyes and giving them a small nod as her magic found the mark on the ancient stone. A mark and another and another.

Which one? Vaguely she was aware of Callum and his father arguing, that his fear for his eldest son was the only thing keeping them all alive. Which mark? Which mark?

A witch had done this. Perhaps a previous wife. *Tell me.* She knew this. It was in her blood, her heritage. She could not read runes, but magic emanated from them, magic so similar to her own. She closed her eyes as Callum's voice rose. She had only moments before the King's impatience won.

Magic for...Magic for...

Magic for protection. She knew it in her gut. No.

Magic for...sight. Her own slid into the ruin and she could see into the shadows of the city. She pulled herself from it.

And the next was the answer. She could feel the hardness of it, the way the wind didn't move near it, solid and unyielding. She dug her magic into the symbol, burning just as the talisman had burned her until there was nothing but a scorch on the stone.

She prayed she was right. For a moment she contemplated destroying the others, but then she glanced at the King just as he made a quick motion to one of the soldiers behind him and Elara grabbed Fia, pushing her behind her back.

"Port!" Fia screamed as magic swirled in the soldier's fingers, her eyes darting around to watch the others reach for each other, hope flooding her as Callum reached for Saskia and she reached for him. She felt the tug of porting and relief filled her as they moved through the air, leaving behind shouts. She clung to Callum as tightly as Elara clung to her, pulling her through the wind until they appeared at the beginning of the pass and the others appeared around them.

One of Mina's guards was clutching at a bleeding gut, one of Ezriel's hadn't made it and Fia hated that she hadn't learned her name, but the rest of them were there. Shaken and pale, everyone who had ported bleeding from the nose, but alive. All except Aurora. Would they bury her? Burn her?

Saskia pulled herself free of Callum. "You told him to take me? What if he had not?"

"I would have brought you, don't worry," Kalin said, grinning despite his wounds.

Fia did not feel like grinning. In a rush, Callum pushed past her and up the path, making it only a few steps before he lurched forward and vomited all over the rocks.

-CHAPTER-
-FORTY -

STRAIGHTENING, CALLUM WIPED at his mouth, face still pale. "She planned this with you? She wanted to be there?"

"Yes," Fia said gently, taking a step toward him, trying not to think of Aurora, how they had left her body behind. How they had abandoned her. How she was dead.

"There is no time. We need to get in the city gates," Elara said, rousing everyone from the haze that had overtaken them now that the adrenaline had left their bodies.

"I will get him there," Fia whispered, locking eyes with Elara. "Give him a moment."

A muscle twitched in Elara's jaw and several seconds passed silently between the two of them as the others made their way to the city, Mina bringing up the rear, pausing for a moment near Callum to whisper something.

"Please," Fia said. "He is grieving." They all were.

"Move quickly," Elara said. "Bringing him here was an enormous risk. I won't have the two of you sitting unprotected outside the city." The bond went tight, emotion surging down it and Elara pulled Fia into her arms, kissing her fiercely, roughly. Her ragged breaths brushed Fia's skin as the kiss ended. "We are at war, Fia. Do not linger."

Fia nodded, wanting more, wanting to stretch this moment, knowing all too well that the future rushed at them, more war and death and bodies. But the moment could not last, there was no magic for that, no power in the world that could freeze time, even among the immortal fae.

As Elara headed toward the gate, toward Kalin and Saskia who waited for her, the jagged rocks of the pass casting them in shadow, words left Fia. What was there to say to Callum? What solace did she have to offer?

But he had to move. She had lied to him, played him for a fool. She could not leave him surrounded by his own sick, mourning his sister alone. "I am sorry," she said, because it was true.

His eyes were red-rimmed. "You lied to me again and again."

Fia nodded. "I did."

"But first you were honest. I knew you did not want to be there. I knew what was happening to you. But my father...Helio...They knew what they were doing. He had a *gun*, Fia. A gun. He shot her."

"Callum, I am so sorry. I loved Aurora, not as much as you, but I thought we would have lifetimes together. I thought she would grow to be my best friend. She deserved so much better." Gently, her fingers trembling, the day's events finally catching up to her, making her knees weak and her eyes heavy, she took Callum's face in her hand, holding his chin gently. "But right now, I need you to move. I need you to come inside the gates. *Please.*"

Ahead Elara called her name, and Saskia started to return to them. Even she looked haggard, her clothes torn, her shoulders slouched. "Princeling, you must come. *Now.* Walk or I will drag you."

Fia cut her a look. "Not helping."

"No?" She motioned to him, where he had moved a few paces. "Some men need more direction than others."

He glared at her. "Sorry my dead sister slowed me down."

"You are forgi—"

Fia yanked her arm, then recoiled when Saskia bared her teeth. "You don't need to act like that."

She leaned closer to Fia as they walked behind Callum, lowering her voice to barely a whisper. "He needs an emotion other than sadness, or we will have to carry him into the castle. Let him be mad. I'm not scared of him."

"I can hear you," he snarled, anger twisting his soft features. Then the gates of Niveren Gap were visible, guards shouting from above, the portcullis already opening with a great groan. Callum stopped, neck craning to look toward the shouting voices. "I had heard, but I did not believe..."

"Welcome to the Gap," Elara said.

Everyone moved faster, running into the city and Callum followed. Fia watched as the gate lowered behind them, looking for a sign of movement, heart pounding with fear they had been followed, that their own wards would fail and these people would die.

Elara's hand closed around her upper arm. "We are safe for now."

But Fia did not think she would ever feel safe again.

-CHAPTER-
-FORTY ONE-

ALL SHE WANTED was a moment alone. A moment to breathe. But the castle was full, people seemed to multiply everywhere she turned, surrounding her, asking questions, looking and leering with wide eyes.

She forced her way through the gathering crowd, murmuring apologies and hurried to the rooms she shared with Elara. The second the door closed and the noise faded, Fia fell to her knees and sobbed until she could barely breathe. She wiped her nose, trying to gather herself and with each exhale magic flickered around her. So much magic.

Without the distraction, she could appreciate just how much magic she had, so much her body felt full, magic stretching her insides, twining around her organs and veins, bursting free.

Not enough magic to save Aurora. Not from a bullet. She had possessed enough magic to get her friends home, to destroy an ancient rune with barely a thought, but her magic had not stopped a human weapon. What would she do when more were upon them? What if the bullet came for Elara? They had just found each other.

The door creaked open and Elara entered. "Fia..." She knelt beside her and then she was upon her, kissing her fiercely, their breath mixing together, nails scraping. Then tears, Elara's tears on Fia's face, mixing with her own until they pulled apart, chests rising and falling rapidly, both of them on the floor.

"What if he comes here?" Fia asked because it was all she could think of. Other thoughts pushed in, again and again, so many different thoughts but the fear of Ellio coming into Niveren Gap was unending, lurking beneath everything else.

"The runes will keep him out. He cannot port in and the gate is nearly unbreachable."

Nearly. "The runes did not stop us," Fia said

Something unreadable moved across Elara's face. "What you did..." She stood and Fia did the same, watching her as she threw open a window and paced across the sitting room.

"Elara..."

She stopped. "I have only met one other witch who could break another's runes and it was not so quickly. I don't know what possessed Callum to even say it except he is young and has never met a witch, knows only that you work in runes. Anyone who has met a witch would not have even suggested it because it is impossible. You are powerful, Fia."

The magic inside her suddenly felt cold, foreign. "No." Of course she wasn't powerful, she'd never been powerful, always powerless. If she'd been powerful her mother might be alive, she would have freed herself. If she was so full of power, why had she been so weak?

Crossing the room in two strides, Elara took her hands in her own. "Do you think Ellio knew? Do you think that is why he brought you here?" Those silver and brown eyes searched her for answers she did not have.

She thought of her past, of her family, the little she knew. She'd never seen a spark of magic even once in the human world, if she came from a line of witches their magic had been completely stolen. "If Ellio had known he wouldn't have let me out of his sight. He would have known how I got away."

Elara's sighed. There were bags under her eyes, and blood on her clothes. She pulled Fia down onto the couch. "A war is coming, my love."

"I know," She ran her fingers across Elara's cheekbones, moved them to her horns. "What do I need to do?" The words scratched at her throat. She wanted to hide, to be the scared, small woman she had always been. But she was mated to a queen, her body full of power. Her days of running were gone, gone the moment she had let Elara place a tiara upon her head. She would not flee while her people died.

"You need to learn everything you can. There are books, and people who knew witches better than I did. I know it is a lot to ask but—"

"It is not too much to ask. If you fight, I fight."

The fierceness in the Queen's face turned soft, gentle, as a small smile pulled at the corner of her lips. "Together."

"Together."

A whole war lay ahead, more death, more loss, but she was not alone. Never alone again. There were answers to find, plans to be made, a kingdom to free and lead back to prosperity. And all of it done side by side with her friends, hand in hand with her mate.

www.ingramcontent.com/pod-product-compliance
Lightning Source LLC
LaVergne TN
LVHW100502110826
845146LV00002B/483

* 9 7 9 8 9 8 6 2 0 2 9 2 1 *